The Girls

N.J. Mackay is Niki Mackay in flimsy disguise writing standalones. Niki Mackay studied Performing Arts at the BRIT School, and it turned out that she wasn't very good at acting but quite liked writing scripts. She holds a BA (Hons) in English Literature and Drama and won a full scholarship for her MA in Journalism. She has three published novels, *I Witness, The Lies We Tell* and *Loaded* – both featuring PI Madison Attallee – and one other standalone thriller, *Found Her.* She is also the co-host of the podcast #CrimeGirlGang

ALSO BY N.J. MACKAY

Found Her
I, Witness
The Lies We Tell
Loaded

The Girls Inside

NJ Mackay

This edition first published in Great Britain in 2021 by Orion Dash,
an imprint of The Orion Publishing Group Ltd.,
Carmelite House, 50 Victoria Embankment
London EC4Y 0DZ

An Hachette UK Company

1 3 5 7 9 10 8 6 4 2

A CIP catalogue record for this book is
available from the British Library.

ISBN (Paperback) 978 1 3987 0812 9
ISBN (eBook) 978 1 4091 9693 8

www.orionbooks.co.uk

In memoriam Sue Duncan and John Marshall

PROLOGUE

She takes one last, hungry look at her daughter. There is something almost unnervingly perfect about a sleeping child. Watching her lying there – her breath soft and even, eyelashes fanned across her plump cheeks – spikes a pain through her heart that is so terrible, so vivid and real that it is physical. It is heartache beyond anything. A long, excruciating chasm that leaves her surprised she is still standing. It is the type of pain that fells you.

She goes closer to the bed, allowing herself these last precious moments. She bends, kneeling next to the girl, and inhales. The sweet smell of her strawberry shampoo and lavender bubble bath. The slightly musty odour of the soft toys, piled high, which likely need washing. She presses her lips to her daughter's forehead, almost wishing she would wake and demand that her mother stay as she had so many times before. But not tonight. Tonight, she doesn't even stir.

The woman moves downstairs and pops cash in an envelope for the sitter. She writes the girl's name on it – 'Jennifer' – in shaky scrawl and yells goodbye to her.

Then she steps out into the night. She ignores her car, walking briskly down the road, forcing her feet to move one in front of the other. She knows too well that if she stops, even for a second, she might not be able to keep going.

Half a mile on, she reaches the postbox at the end of Picket Lane. She takes the envelopes from her bag, sliding one inside the other, reading the name printed in her own neat lettering and she knows – just knows – that the recipient won't let her down.

A panicked thought rises in her mind just for a moment – will she ever see her child again? – but she pushes it away. Too late for that now. Too late to change her mind. She walks on and on. She gets to the little shed on the sprawling allotment. A place familiar to her. She has knelt there many times, hands in the earth, mud and leaves prickling her bare knees, telling her child which seeds to plant and where. A little slice of the outdoors in the city. She goes into the shed, which she's spent the week emptying, moving their things to the garage at the house.

Everything she left earlier is still here now. Everything she needs to do this. To carry out her plan to its bitter end. She takes the can of petrol and pours it liberally over every surface of the shed, every wooden panel. Then she gets the box of long matches, strikes one, and the flames fly.

Her last thought before the angry fire consumes the building and everything in it is of her daughter. Her precious girl.

CHAPTER ONE

The offices are hidden down back streets and housed in a tall, shiny building. Parsons and Rice occupies the entire first floor.

I head up the stairs and sit awkwardly, feeling out of place, in the reception area, which is just a cordoned-off part of a large open-plan space. There are rows of people, heads down, huddled over their keyboards. The receptionist who saw me in with a 'Can I get you a drink . . .?' is sitting clacking away, fingers flying over the keys. She is the only person I can see with a desk of her own, separate from the other banks housing many occupants.

A tall, fair-haired man comes over after what seems like ages – though can really only have been seconds – and looks at me with a slight head tilt. It is an expression I've seen before, one of sympathy.

'Blue Sillitoe?'

'Yes,' I say, standing.

He grins, broad and disingenuous. 'What an unusual name.'

I smile thinly. 'It's the one I was given.'

He nods as though he understands entirely, which obviously he doesn't. I get this all the time, of course. Who the hell names their daughter Blue, after all? My mother was a hippy, I suppose. My memories of my very young years are of the sweet smell of dope smoke and patchouli, and whimsical music played on scratched records. A woman like that would think nothing of calling a child after a favourite album. She told me it was either Blue or Ocean. I'm not sure Ocean would have been any better.

'Follow me.'

And I do.

Through the warren of people, out into a set of rooms that still offers little privacy because of the glass doors. But he ushers me into one of them and sits behind a large desk, gesturing for me to take the chair opposite.

He frowns and asks, 'Were you offered a drink?'

'I'm not thirsty.'

I'm starting to feel annoyed now. I glance at my wrist-watch pointedly. For all he knows I could have a myriad of places to be.

He says, 'Firstly, thank you so much for coming in. I do appreciate your time.'

I blink. Don't say anything. Wondering if he will ever get to the bloody point.

'I could have discussed matters over the phone, but I really felt it would be better to meet in person and when I spoke to the police, they thought . . . well.'

The *police*? All I'd had was his secretary calling to summon me to his office for a 'delicate matter' that needed to be dealt with in person. It's not every day a solicitor's office calls. I thought about not turning up at all, but curiosity got the better of me.

But now, the mention of law enforcement makes my palms dampen. I press them against my thighs.

'I have no idea what you're talking about,' I say.

He sighs. 'Perhaps it ought to have been them.'

I snap, 'Can you just tell me what's going on?'

'Natasha Dryden.'

4

My eyes drop down to the floor. No carpet, just floor-boards. Or perhaps some sort of linoleum made to look like wood. I scrape the end of my steel-toe-capped boot across it, looking for a groove or an edge. Definitely linoleum. Awful stuff. Real floorboards are lovely. The first thing I did when I bought my flat was rip up the carpets in the rooms that still had them, by that point musty and dense. The master bedroom had been bare when I looked around and I'd seen the original beautiful floor. I knew it was under there. I sanded the entire flat myself. A labour of love. Now every time I walk through my place barefoot I feel immense satisfaction. My flat comprises the top two floors of a converted Victorian house, which would have been grand and sprawling in its heyday. Hidden away inside its walls were lots of original features that others had tried to cover up, but which I dug out diligently like buried treasure.

He says, 'Ms Sillitoe.'

'Blue is fine.'

'Blue, then. And please call me Matthew.'

I look up and meet his eyes. 'She's dead?'

He nods, suitably sombre.

A rushing sound starts up in my ears. A sort of explosive whoosh, then a faint crackling. Fire has its own sounds that once heard can never be forgotten. It is a vast and engulfing, physical thing with a soundtrack. Fizzing and popping. You can describe it in actions too. Flames *lick*. Smoke *rises*. Embedding itself wherever it can. Getting into things like lungs.

I suddenly feel very faint and lean forward, resting my head in my hands. Pushing the wheeled chair backwards, my feet rubbing along the awful, not-tiled, pretend floors.

He murmurs, 'This must be a terrible shock.'

I tell him, 'I haven't spoken to her in twenty years.'

He nods but nothing about him denotes empathy. Each move practised and, to my mind, insincere. I'm probably being unfair, of course. This can't be an easy task.

I look up at him. 'How did she . . .?' I pause. 'You mentioned police.'

The nod again, grave this time. 'In very sad circumstances. I'm sorry to tell you that Natasha Dryden took her own life.'

That sound. A fizz, a crackle. Like some demented version of that cereal advert. *Snap, crackle and pop.* I almost laugh, feel my mouth misbehaving. I clamp my hand to my lips.

'Can I have some water, actually?'

'Of course.' He seems glad for the excuse to leave.

Natasha.

Brave.

Fierce.

Bold.

Suicidal? It had been many years, of course. My memory was unreliable in the best of circumstances. But the thought of her . . . letting go of anything, especially her own life, seemed far-fetched to me.

But what did I know about her now? Nothing, really. By choice.

I use the brief seconds Matthew is gone to slip my socked feet out of my boots and push them against the awful linoleum as reality shifts and rearranges itself around me.

He comes back with a tall, thin glass filled with ice, a slice of lime and water. I take it gratefully, sliding my feet back into my boots. Trying to sip water through too many cubes is a difficult and unwieldy task, and I struggle for a second. But finally, the cool liquid gets through, soothing my mouth and my throat.

He tells me, 'The police would like to talk to you.'

I frown. 'As I said, I haven't seen her for many years.' And then: 'Why are they involved?'

'They have to investigate all deaths when the case isn't cut and dried.'

Not cut and dried.

'But what does it have to do with me?'

I realise as soon as the words are out how awful that must sound.

'Well here's the thing. Natasha left a will.'

I shrug.

He smiles. 'You're asked to be at the reading.'

'Now?'

He shakes his head. 'No, no, tomorrow.'

I frown again.

'Because of the delicate nature of . . . well, Natasha being a client, I was forced to reveal the contents to the police, in light of her death.' He adds, 'She left instructions. For them to contact me.'

And I do smile at that. Natasha bossing people around. Even now she's dead.

Will reading. I can't get my head around it, and so for probably too long, I don't respond. Nor do I respond when he asks if I'll make it. Instead I ask questions, which get scant answers. I realise he doesn't know much at all. But he does know where it happened, and I am able to get the details of the location from him, even though he is reluctant to give them. I leave feeling fuzzy, clutching an address in my hand. I'd forced him to go into what little detail he had. About what she'd done. How and where. I wasn't surprised by his answers, though I was gently horrified nonetheless.

Possible overdose.

Burning.

Herself.

A small dwelling, which she sat down in before she lit the match.

I wonder if she was dead before the flames rose to their full glory. Or at least not conscious. I hope one or the other.

Investigation ongoing. No foul play suspected.

I suppose they must have investigated Lisa's death then, too. I wouldn't know. I'd read about it on the internet and been rocketed back to the uneasy days of my childhood. She'd killed herself. Drug overdose. I didn't go to her funeral. The past is just that, isn't it?

A lot of people who grow up the way we did don't make it. That's a fact. We are often eaten alive years later. By addiction, depression. At our own hands.

Survivors who – once liberated – can't handle it. The delicious, terrifying freedom.

It's a hard thing to come to terms with. A strange place to find yourself. With a shaky, unstable past, detached from the reality everyone else knows.

I walk and walk. The city is a maze, but I know its streets and I know them well.

When we were girls, we used to study maps of the capital. We weren't allowed television or many books but for some reason amongst the limited possessions in our dormitory there was an A to Z of the city of London. Natasha claimed she had lived there as a child and remembered it, though I was never certain that was true. To me it sounded far enough away from where we were and different enough that I might find – if not happiness – then at least not nothing.

I don't have many memories from before Mum and I arrived at the Black House and details of how we got there were vague and unforthcoming. I learned about my childhood years later, mostly via newspaper and magazine articles. One lurid book with bold red writing plastered across its cover. But back then, before we were gone, us children pieced things together via each other's experiences. Eventually those dialogues merged and became real in my head. But I know better than to trust my own mind. Warped as it was when I was so young and so impressionable.

I eventually get to the address Matthew Parsons had scrawled in his twirly, looping hand.

It's an allotment. I walk into the small, cordoned-off green areas. Gardens in a city for those who want a patch of the outdoors. Little lines run between each plot and they are filled with plants and long tall stalks with things climbing up them. Even this I don't like. I much prefer the steady, man-made reality of concrete and walls and roads. I know nature can be a brutal prison as only those who have lived in deepest countryside can. Some like it. I often hear my fellow city dwellers talking dreamily of retiring somewhere green and idyllic. Not understanding that it can get so dark out there where nature rules that you can't see what's right in front of your face. There is always light in London. From streetlamps and buildings. People work around the clock here.

I see it then. A shed on one of the larger patches. Or what was a shed and now is just a skeletal structure. Iron railings forming a frame that had once held wood. And a body. That burned to death.

There is yellow tape everywhere. Crime scene tape. Though Matthew Parsons assured me there was no crime. No suspected foul play, as he put it.

Play seems an odd word to encompass such awful things.

Foul. Play. I assume in this instance he meant murder. Hardly a game. Unless it is, of course. My knees feel soft and I pause, resting a hand on a bench. I have come far enough. I can smell the leftovers of what went on here and it's more than I want. More than I can manage. *Fizzing. Popping. Crackling.* The smell of smoke, stinging my eyes, seeping into my hair. The taste of it thick in the air. I press a hand to my mouth. Push my feet into the ground. I am safe. This is now.

I turn slowly. And walk. Out of the awful expanse of greenery. Away from the terrible smell of freshly dug earth and burning. Back to the solid footing of pavement. The moving cars, rushing past. The people everywhere who don't give me a second glance. I feel more at ease as I walk back to my flat. Up the stairs. Closing the door behind me. Pressing my back to it and sinking down. The tears come as I curl my arms and body around my legs. They fall in silent, shoulder-shuddering waves.

CHAPTER TWO

I don't eat at home, which had been my intention. I drink a large mug of green tea and then I head into Planet Pop, suddenly desperate to see Isaac. He is there behind the counter. A thin man, naturally so. Built with the sort of metabolism that means he can eat cream cakes all day long and look exactly the same. He was once beautiful and still has his good looks now, though they are worn and fading.

He looks up at me as I come in and grins. When I don't smile back, he narrows his eyes. 'Blue?'

I tell him, in garbled words, hearing myself laugh at one point: 'I haven't seen her for twenty years.' Then: 'I can't think what the hell she'd have left me.'

He says, 'I'll come along.'

'What?'

'To the reading.'

I say, 'I don't know if I'm going to go, actually.' I am toying with the idea of forgetting the whole thing ever happened. I can easily block Parsons and Rice's number from my phone. Tell the police, quite honestly, that I have nothing to say about a ghost from the past.

Isaac says, 'Don't be stupid.'

And now it's my turn to scowl at him. He grins back and I sigh. 'OK.'

He says, 'I'll call Oren and tell him he'll be on his own for the afternoon.'

'You think he's ready?'

Oren was a mess when he first started here, almost six months ago now. He'd just done a long term in prison, not his first sentence, but while he was there his mother had passed away. He'd been unable to attend her funeral. Though he'd continued to drink and use behind bars initially, after his mum passed, he started attending NA meetings. Isaac ran that meeting – something he'd been doing for as long as I'd known him, which felt like forever. He had told Oren that if he kept clean One Day at a Time, there'd be a job waiting for him. He'd done well in the six months since he'd been out, but we hadn't left him alone yet.

Isaac shrugs. 'I think so, but we'll find out tomorrow, I guess.'

I nod. This is his way and I know that even if Oren ransacked the place, which wasn't far outside the boundaries of belief, Isaac would accept it.

He says, 'We'll cash up and bank what's there though, eh,' with a wink at me. 'A morning's takings won't be as tempting as a week's.'

I nod, not pointing out that we have some rare records worth thousands of pounds. Isaac knows this. But it's his shop. He likes to give people chances, sometimes more than one. I can't argue with that, since I've benefited from it myself over the years. We empty the till and I count everything, putting it all in the right bags – a task that is second nature now. When I'm done, I hand it to Isaac, who opens the bottom drawer of the till and gets out a thick paying-in book. He doesn't 'do the internet' and no matter my encouragement and nagging, he absolutely refuses to do online banking.

He packs it all in his bag and hands it to me. 'So call the solicitor and we'll see him tomorrow?'

I nod. 'I will.'

I switch places with Isaac and settle in behind the counter, lowering the seat for my size, feeling the warmth from where he just sat below me and the familiar grooves of the rickety floor beneath my feet.

He gets to the door and pauses, head cocked to one side. 'You all right kiddo?'

I swallow thickly and nod. He keeps looking and I shrug.

He smiles. 'I'll be out for the rest of the day, so you lock up?'

I nod again.

'Tomorrow then. If you need me before, just call.'

'I will.'

He leaves with a wave at the door.

CHAPTER THREE

I have no idea if I'm supposed to dress up for something like this. And nothing in my wardrobe would class as particularly smart even if I am. I live in army boots, band T-shirts and various black jeans in differing stages of frayed decomposition and faded thinness.

In the end, I go for the newest pair, a plain black T-shirt and a black blazer with dark sequins around the lapels. One of the best things about working at the shop has been that I've never needed to worry about any kind of dress code. I can come as I like.

Isaac turns up outside my flat and parks his rickety VW on my drive. I climb into the passenger side. The day is crisp and bright and I wind down the window. He parks and pays an eye-watering number of coins into a meter. It would have been quicker and definitely cheaper if we'd caught the train, but Isaac abhors public transport with a passion.

We walk until, eventually, the glass building stands before us. A shiny, obnoxious reminder of what's to come. Sunlight glinting off its sharp angles. It is with a sigh that I step in, waiting for the lift. At the last minute a stressed-looking woman hanging on to wobbling spectacles and yelling, 'Hold it, hold it!' runs towards us, but the doors close, despite my manic pressing of the open button.

As we step out of the lift onto the first floor she is there, out of breath and leaning forward, resting her hands on her thighs. She murmurs, 'Must give up smoking.'

Isaac laughs. 'One of life's great pleasures.'

She looks at him, her expression startled, and he gives her his most charming grin. A lot of people recognise Isaac but can't pinpoint where from. He was in a band who were big in the 70s and 80s. The band split in 1987 after the drummer choked to death on his own vomit. Isaac had a breakdown of sorts which led to him giving up his long love affair with heroin and getting sober. He'd bought Planet Pop outright and people still come from far and wide to see him in the shop. He 'suffers' this with relatively false modesty. I can well imagine him on stage lapping up the adoration.

Isaac is still in a recovery program, which he thinks he'll be in for the rest of his life, and a lot of recovering addicts do stints working at Planet Pop. I'm the only long-term member of staff though. Isaac has two children and an ex-wife who doesn't speak to him. And he has me.

He grins at the woman, who doesn't smile back. Unperturbed, he turns to the front desk, walking up to it with his usual confidence. I trot along behind him, the out-of-breath woman with the red hair huffing along, too.

I realise, feeling increasingly horrified as she pulls a gleaming police badge from her grey, slightly crumpled suit jacket, that she is probably here for the same reading.

The receptionist signs her in then turns her glassy smile to me and Isaac. Before I can stop her, or turn and run away, she says, 'Oh, Ms Sillitoe, what good timing.'

My heart sinks as the policewoman turns her bright eyes on me.

'Blue Sillitoe?'

I stare at her – a deer caught in headlights. She's older than me by maybe twenty years, closer to Isaac's age than mine. And despite the ruffled introduction I got to her and the fact that she's still panting slightly, she looks capable and clever. This shouldn't make me nervous. I've done nothing wrong. But I am intrinsically scared of police. And of teachers, and any form of authority. Nobody could blame me for that. I was bred to believe these people wanted only to harm and hurt me. Logically, I know that's not true. When rescue had eventually come, after bleak hours spent stumbling round the dark woods of North Wales, ashes in our hair and not enough clothes to keep out the freezing night, it had been people in uniforms who had found us. Taken us in. To safety and food.

The woman puts a hand out, her fingers long and slim. Nice hands with slightly chipped pink nail polish that seems out of keeping with her suit.

She smiles. 'DI Grafton.'

I take her hand, shake it.

She pulls mine up, looking at the stars imprinted on the back of it and says, 'Cool tat.'

I nod, pulling it back and tugging down the sleeve of my blazer.

It is cool, though. I love the colours that run up and down my right arm. Covering a multitude of scars so thickly layered they give my skin a texture all of its own. The artist I'd seen to do the long sleeve for me had gasped when he saw the state of that arm. I didn't say anything, offered nothing in the way of explanation, just asked if he could help. And he had. It's a triumph. Taking something ugly and giving it its own ferocious beauty. I've been back to see him many times since then and my body is now a collage of beautiful little surprises.

I feel a shudder of annoyance in my bowels. There are so many ways I've moved on. I had a counsellor who'd pushed and pushed at me once until I almost broke. I couldn't handle the pain needed to heal in any real way. But I have survived. I manage. I have some kind of life. I am free.

And here I am today dredging up a past I try hard never to think about.

I'm about to turn around and tell Isaac that I want to go when Matthew appears, grinning from me to DI Grafton. Now it's too bloody late.

I point to Isaac. 'My friend's come along.'

He says, 'For support.'

He grins at Matthew, who forces a smile back and says, 'Good idea.'

I follow them all back through the open-plan into the little glass boxes. Trailing behind like a naughty child.

Matthew smiles at us again once we are all seated. I frown back and glance at DI Grafton, whose face is impassive, and Isaac who looks perfectly at ease. The spectacles the DI had been holding clasped to her nose in the foyer are now sweeping back her thick red hair like an Alice band. Matthew Parsons – evidently not used to his charms being ignored – clears his throat, adopting a more serious face now.

He says, 'We are all here today for the reading of the will and testament of Natasha Lydia Dryden.'

Lydia.

Had I known that?

We never knew surnames, or we weren't supposed to anyway. All of us were known by our Christian names only. Of course we told each other. But she'd never mentioned being Lydia. The sound of those letters together makes me think of fluttering butterfly wings. Something delicate and urgent. The name, I decide, doesn't suit her at all. *Natasha* is much better, with its clear syllables and sharp pronunciation. Much more her.

Lydia.

'Ms Sillitoe?'

'Sorry?'

Grafton leans into me with a smile that makes her hard face look gentle. 'Mr Parsons was just telling us that you are one of two beneficiaries. In Natasha's will.'

I swallow and it is a thick gloppy feeling. Then I say, 'Oh.' Rather pointlessly.

The solicitor clears his throat again. I am reminded of an actor preparing for a performance. Getting into character before wowing audiences with beautiful soliloquies.

'First, there's the matter of money, of which there's rather a lot. There is a large amount due to you.' He looks pointedly at me and slides a piece of paper across the table, as though to say the number aloud is somehow tasteless. I look at the amount. It is big and I'm not really sure what the hell I'd do with it. I have everything I need. I blink once, twice, unsure what to say.

He smiles at me, a benign expression, and seems to assume I'm gleefully overwhelmed.

'She was rather savvy with properties and sold several in the year before her, ah . . .'

DI Grafton says, 'You oversaw the sales?'

He nods. 'I did. More what I do, if I'm honest.'

'Property law?'

He nods again.

The beautiful glass offices. The insane amount it costs to live anywhere in London. Money to be made for sure. Less so in this sort of thing, I suppose.

'When she asked me to oversee her will and testament . . . well. I could hardly say no.' He looks at us both sombrely. 'Though I had no idea it would be needed in the near future.'

DI Grafton smiles. 'And she remunerated you well, of course. For stepping out of your comfort zone. Work wise.'

His skin flushes at that and I suppress a smile. Isaac lets out a little laugh, though, openly enjoying the solicitor's moment of discomfort. So she had paid him to deliver her death messages. And Grafton knew and wasn't about to let him claim dibs on a charitable act.

He says, 'Naturally. Ours was a business relationship.' No longer smiling.

'Of course.'

I say, 'So all of this money? It's mine, just like that?'

'Not quite just like that, no. There are certain conditions. One, in particular.'

I'm aching with impatience now and almost entirely certain that I'll just say no and be done with the whole affair.

DI Grafton breaks in then, 'We also can't release funds to you or make any of her requests entirely permanent until we have a definitive ID. Due to the nature of her remains . . . identification isn't proving a simple thing.'

Nature of her remains.

I think of blackened crisp skin and bones burned to a cindery dust. I think of my mother and feel sick.

I say, 'I don't even want the money.' I can add Natasha's grave to my visits to Lisa's and regret it all in my own bloody time.

Matthew pipes up again, 'As I said, it's not just about the money.'

I snap, 'Well?'

'Natasha has . . . *had* . . . a child.'

19

There is a silence then. A pregnant pause with a weight and feel all of its own.

A child.

Natasha is a mother. Like the Aunts. I push that thought away. A wave of nausea washing over me. No. Not like the Aunts. Hopefully not like them. But then again . . . burned. Alive. In a shed. By her own hand.

'A . . . a girl?' I ask, stammering over the words as though they are stuck in my mouth. But I already know with a strong certainty before he says:

'Yes.' Adding, 'Penelope. Pen for short.'

Penelope. Pen.

I draw. It is the only thing I find soothing. It is my talent. I scribble things from my mind onto paper. When I go to visit Lisa's grave I draw pictures of her, Natasha and I, and leave them there where presumably the weather, or maybe somebody else, takes them. They are my small offerings in lieu of anything better.

Pen. The word brings a nice sort of comfort to me.

The maker of images and words. Filler of blank pages. A good name for a little girl.

'She wants me to have her?'

He nods. 'Said you would hesitate, but expected you'd say yes. Ultimately.'

Then he gets out an envelope. Pale pink with my name written in a flouncy flourish. In handwriting unchanged in twenty years. There is a kiss trailing off the e. X. As though this is a casual note passed during lessons.

That nausea again. I feel a wave start in my head, dropping down the length of me into my feet.

Isaac asks, 'Are you all right?'

Then Grafton snaps at Matthew Parsons, 'Water.' And then: 'Bring a mug of sweet tea, too.'

When he is gone, they both turn to me. The detective kneels in front of me. Her eyes are green, which is rare in real life. I focus on them now. She says, 'This must be a terrible shock.'

'It is.'

'I know about Pen. I thought and had been hoping the will may shed some light on our next moves with her. I didn't know you were specifically named as Natasha's choice of guardian, though I suspected it may be the case, especially when Mr Parsons stressed that Natasha had asked for early meetings to be in person.'

'Where . . .' I swallow. 'Where is she now?'

'She's being looked after.'

'Social services?'

She nods.

'How old is she?'

'Ten.'

I see Grafton exchange a look with Isaac and when I look at Isaac's face he smiles, but it comes out as a grimace. He mutters, 'You OK, Blue?'

I shake my head. He takes my hand and squeezes it. I grip his back. My palm pressing into the array of heavy rings, mine clinking against his; a mishmash of decorative hardware.

Ten years old. Just like me when everything changed. Alone and afraid. Not knowing where she'll spend tonight or the one after. I hate Natasha in this moment. I hate her deeply.

Parsons comes back, with the receptionist following awkwardly behind, carrying a tray with a wobbling glass of water and a china cup of tea. A man who cannot carry refreshments. Who has left such things far behind. Or maybe that's unfair. I don't know.

I drink the tea. Parsons starts addressing Isaac and DI Grafton instead, when it becomes clear that I am beyond taking anything else in.

The meeting concludes. There's an awful lot of 'take your time' and 'discuss it with someone you trust', with pointed looks at Isaac. Punctuated with the contradictory 'decisions need to be made'. Squeezing the idea that I have time far away.

We get outside and I am stunned by the brilliant sunshine. Inside I feel dark and stirred up. Isaac is close by and when DI Grafton holds a card out to me, I stare at it dumbly. Eventually he takes it.

She turns to me, waiting for me to meet her eye. 'Blue, I know this must be very surreal for you.'

I look at her blankly.

She says, 'You don't need to decide straight away.'

Which is, of course, a lie.

CHAPTER FOUR

Annie Grafton walks away from them, her heart pounding and her palms slightly damp. What the hell had *he* been doing there, of all people? 'Friend' Blue Sillitoe had said. He surely wasn't her lover? He was old enough to be her dad, by a long mile. Then again . . . ageing rock star, you never know. He talked a good talk, and Annie had even admired him, from a distance, of course. But people could say all kind of things, couldn't they? Who knew what was true and what wasn't? If people were honest all the time, she'd have no job.

He hadn't acknowledged her though, and for that she was grateful. She'd seen he recognised her. Everyone always did because of her bloody hair.

Shit.

Her phone rings and she almost drops it, pulling it from her bag. She picks up with a sharp 'What?'

Ian's pitiful voice breaks in, 'Happy to hear from me as ever then.'

She stifles a sigh. 'Not at all – I didn't see who was calling.'

'Are you busy?'

'I'm always busy,' There is a silence that stretches out, immediately filled by her guilt. 'Sorry, I didn't mean to snap. Are you OK?'

'Not really.'

She's at her car, and another has parked so close to hers that she struggles to get in. In the end she presses her car door against theirs, not caring one bit if she scrapes their paintwork. What an idiotic place to park.

Finally, she manages to squeeze herself in and winds down the window. Her air con has died and she's had not a second to get the bloody thing in for repair.

'Annie.'

'Sorry, yes, I was getting into my car.'

'You're working?'

She rolls her eyes, the question making her feel more annoyed than it probably should. 'I am, yes.'

'Oh. I won't keep you then.'

This is it – her chance to say, 'OK cool.' And hang up.

Instead she hears her own voice betraying her. 'It's OK, Ian. What's up?'

For ten minutes she listens to her soon-to-be ex-husband moan about nothing and everything, gearing himself up to the grand finale – he received the divorce papers and isn't it so sad?

Not for her. Freedom looms, just out of reach but very nearly there. She murmurs something non-committal and finally manages to hang up the call.

Driving back to the station, Annie thinks about Blue Sillitoe, Natasha Dryden and the child sitting now at social services offices while her future is determined. Her connection to Isaac doesn't matter, she decides. It's tenuous at best and will have no impact on her ability to handle the case. She wonders whether she has time to stop and grab a coffee and heads towards the drive-thru Costa, praying that there isn't a long queue. Hopefully by tomorrow, Blue will decide what to do about Penelope Dryden and if the kid needs to stay in care, Annie will sort it out then. Not much more she can do today.

She beeps at an idiot in a large Audi who is clearly trying to kill her. He gives her the finger, which she sends straight back. She considers pulling him over, flashing her badge, but it's between that and the Costa, time-wise, and the coffee wins.

CHAPTER FIVE

We make our way back to Isaac's car and get in. He doesn't speak, fiddling instead with the CD player until crooning country music fills the space. His unlikely love of soulful hillbilly ballads has always amused me and it calms me a bit. He doesn't push me, and I'm grateful because I have no idea what I feel, let alone trying to formulate it into words just yet. I sit quietly, looking out of the window.

Time is a funny thing.

At the Black House we were woken every single day at five on the dot by an alarm that sounded for three whole minutes. It was loud and blaring enough that you couldn't go back to sleep even if you wanted to. Our days were odd. They were either overly structured or we were simply left to our own devices. There was no in between. No balance. What later became apparent was that Joseph Carillo suffered from severe mania and the periods of overstuffed activity coincided with his 'up' cycles.

All children of the Black House were housed in dorms. I shared with Natasha, Amy and Lisa. They were the closest thing I had to family and I loved them fiercely. My mother and I had come to the Black House shortly after my fifth birthday. It was to be the last one I celebrated, until a well-meaning foster family tentatively tried to spoil me on my eleventh. It didn't turn out brilliantly. I don't think I'd ever felt as acutely embarrassed as I had sitting at their kitchen table, surrounded by their actual children, while they bought out a cake and sang.

We pull up outside of my flat and Isaac turns to me. He doesn't speak but he does turn the CD off, kill the engine and looks at me with his intense eyes.

I say, 'I'm terrible with kids.'

He shrugs. 'How do you know?'

'What the hell, Isaac?' My voice is high and incredulous. 'You can't possibly think this is a good idea.'

He says, 'It only really matters what you think.'

I glance down at the envelope in my hand, which I've been clasping so tightly my knuckles look almost black underneath my pale white skin. Like lychee stones pushing at the pulp.

I half whisper, 'I can barely look after myself.' Still looking at my hands.

He takes my chin between his thumb and forefinger, turning my head to look at him. 'You, Blue, can indeed look after yourself. You've done it beautifully so far. You can in fact do anything you put your mind to.'

Tears prick my eyes.

He says, 'Do you remember when you started coming into Planet Pop?'

I nod.

'You were so fragile and so . . . cross.'

I say, 'You can see why.'

He holds a hand up. 'Come on now. No need to be defensive. This is me.'

He's right. I love Isaac. Something I'd believed myself to be incapable in the brief years between leaving the Black House and meeting him.

He says, 'You've got less cross.'

I laugh, but he doesn't.

'Anger isn't your natural disposition, Blue, and neither is shirking away from things that are challenging. You are a survivor, not a victim.'

I nod. He has said this to me so many times before and it's a mantra that I repeat to myself when I need strength. Carillo stole from the people he 'recruited' but I have vowed not to let him steal the rest of my life. Though I am sore with the past still, there are little bits within me that if pressed will bleed out all that pain, all that anger. Justified, hot and doing me no good. I think about my mother and how much I loved her. How much I hated her. How strongly I felt she had betrayed the trust of a child. I think about the frightened little girl left waiting, not knowing where she'll sleep tonight. I think about flames and fire and Natasha. Goddamn her.

He says, 'Think on this. Give yourself a few hours, go into your beautiful flat that you made so all by yourself, read the letter.'

I sigh, but nod.

I don't go into my beautiful flat, though. Instead I watch him drive away, a small swell of dust spurting up behind the spinning wheels of his car, then I turn and walk. I propel myself forwards without really being aware of my surroundings. I hear the dull background noise of cars. My eyes flit to an empty billboard covered each day in new graffiti. Some good, some awful, the latest an explicit word in red dripping paint.

Eventually I arrive at the gates of the cemetery and head in. It's not cold today, but it's not bright either. I find that I am sweating and I wipe a hand across my face, pressing my fingers to my eyes, forming floating black spots when I release the pressure. There are a few other people here, quietly going about their business, and the gardener is doing his usual rounds. He nods at me and I nod back as I worm my way through headstones. Eventually I come to hers. I sit down amongst the cluster where she is buried. Hers is one of the newer additions and it stands steadfast, straight up and proud, not like others, which are old and worn and stick out of the ground at wonky angles, crooked with age. Like separated adolescent teeth in need of a good scrub and a brace. The scetch I drew on my last visit is still here, held down by a large grey rock. A pencil rendition of her face peeking out from beneath.

I have it in my mind that I can no longer remember what she looked like. It's probably not true, but I don't want to forget either way. The only time I really let myself think about then is when I'm here. Next to Lisa. I think of that place. The people in it.

I think of my mother.

Most people have pictures, don't they? Of their child-hoods. Proud documentation shoved dutifully into bursting albums, or framed and placed on available surfaces. Ready to be paraded out to strangers and visitors. Big events marked. I suppose those would include, but not be limited to, things like first birthdays, first days at school, gradua-tions, marriages. I have a couple of Polaroids and a random photo of my mother holding me as a new-born. You can hardly see my face for all the blankets and she is young in the image. Too young. Her smile uneven and unsure, hair stretching towards her waist, bangles sinking up to the crook of her arm where I'm nestled. I don't know who took that photo, though I've pondered it a lot over the years. Wished that before she'd died, we'd had the kind of relationship where I could have asked. I don't suppose it matters. She gave me that picture before everything went to shit. I'd spent months with it always in the pocket of whatever I was wearing at the time, or it would have gone up in flames with everything else. Now it is tucked away in a box in my flat.

Some days I talk to Lisa. Down there under the mud, in a box, likely little more than dust by now. Today I should have loads to fill her in on and yet my mind is peculiarly blank but for the envelope clutched in my hand. That is why I am here. To share the burden of this moment with another. I don't like to offload on her though. I always think she had enough of that in her life. I should have spoken to her while she was still here. This is the same pointless thought I have at every visit. She found me online and reached out more than once. And I ignored her every time.

I slide my finger into a corner of the envelope and pull out a single sheet of paper and three photographs.

Dear Blue,

If you're reading this, I'm gone and my smarmy solicitor will have outlined what I am asking of you.

It's a biggie and if there was any other way, I'd have found it. But this is how it has to be and I'm sorry. I know you've built a life for yourself and I'm proud of you. Lisa and Amy would have been, too. Three of us made it to London, which is better than none eh?

I found out you were sent here straight after. I went to Cardiff. Lisa went to Bristol. Maybe you already knew that. Maybe not. Lisa told me she wrote and wrote and we talked a few times about just showing up, surprising you. I thought you wouldn't have wanted that. Any more than you probably want this, so again – I'm sorry. If there was any other way, I'd have found it.

Brodie and drippy Nenny are still in Wales – did you know that? They don't know about Pen. No one does. I've made it clear in the documents Parsons has that they are unsuitable, though I doubt I needed to. They're unlikely to even be a consideration. You may want to contact them, though I don't know what good it will do.

I know you visit Lisa often. I've seen the pictures you leave there. I'm pleased about that. I hate the thought of her being left alone.

I knew you, Blue. We knew each other more than most people ever do, or maybe more than people ever should. But you were little then. I hope I still understand you a bit. If you're who I think you are, you won't let her down. I've enclosed some pictures. She doesn't look like me really. I see Nenny in her sometimes, but luckily she has a stronger way about her. She's a tough little cookie. Just like you – the last one standing.

N xx

CHAPTER SIX

Five a.m. My eyes snap open, my whole body coming to with a long gasp. I push out a hand, scrabbling for the letter that says so little and still too much. Picking up the photographs that came along with it. I can imagine Natasha carefully selecting them, putting them into an envelope. Knowing how I would react.

Because she did still know me.

The pictures show a smiling, toothy little girl. She does look a bit like Natasha's mother, Sienna, known by us as 'Aunt' because that's how all adult females were to be addressed, or 'drippy Nenny' behind her back, so nick-named by her own daughter. But the little girl has a spark even in a still image, the kind that I never saw in Sienna.

None of the Aunts were exactly vibrant by the end, though I suspect they once were. Certainly my mother had been. It wasn't just the passage of time that had dulled them. Most were very young women still, even by the end. My memories of my mother at the Black House were of an old woman, but she hadn't even turned thirty when she burned alive.

I had a sort of understanding that we were eventually expected to somehow morph into them, the Aunts, with their dour expressions, faces drawn and serious, their long white dresses, a parody of that worn by happy brides everywhere, and their sandaled feet. In all weather they had bare legs and open-toed shoes, and out there it often turned freezing. I couldn't understand how that could be . . . that we would one day be them.

The women at the Black House weren't women, they were ghosts. Faint whispers of things that used to be.

I had memories of my mother laughing, singing, cooking, beautiful in her long floor-length colourful skirts and jingly-jangly bracelets. Admittedly I saw less and less of her during my five years there. But what I did see when she stood at the front of the classroom or ladled out food to the long queue of always-hungry children, was a robot.

We hadn't been like that as girls. Maybe Amy had been heading in that direction by the end. But not me or Lisa. And Natasha was so brimming with life that it could be overwhelming.

Natasha.

Suicide?

I couldn't get it out of my head. *Why?*

The little girl in the picture looks like she has inherited her mother's spark, grinning broadly directly at the camera, reassuring me that I'm not making it up. Not fabricating it

How many nights will it take in foster homes for that shine to wear off?

Would nights with me be any better?

My life is little in some ways, but I like it. It is safe and has love in it – something I could have only dreamed of way back when. I have Isaac, and lately I'd say I also have Oren. I enjoy my friendships with them, Isaac especially, who I would be lost without. I like my interactions with customers – surface mostly, but built on a shared interest, which makes conversation easy enough.

Which is your favourite Pistols song? When was grunge at its finest? Why are all the great music movements so brief?

These are discussions I can have and manage. Friendships are hard when you have a past like mine and romantic relationships are more hassle than I can bear. I dated very briefly in my early twenties but having to constantly skirt questions about my family, my childhood, where I grew up, is exhausting. There is the boy I think of often and wonder how he has done. If he is OK. My last memory of him, of us, walking, me wounded, through the dark wood. We'd stood at the edge of it. Bedraggled and disorientated. Natasha had stepped away from me and he'd let go of his mother, just for a moment. Come to me and held my good hand in his, his voice telling me that it would all be all right. It wouldn't, of course. How could it be?

I've never reached out, always stayed away. From what I've witnessed of romantic interactions myself, the cost hardly seems worth it. My mother and all the women at the Black House other than Sienna Dryden paid for their romantic notions with their lives. They lie in unvisited graves six feet under. They were buried with crispy skin and clawed hands, with no worldly possessions to leave behind. Because they loved Joseph Carillo and believed he loved them back.

It was hard for me when I read the reports and books about them – and there have been a plethora – to reconcile those nothing women who fed, taught and reprimanded us, with the young women they must have been. The young girls who threw away everything they had for love. That sacrifice spoke of a passion they never demonstrated to the rest of us. They refused to look at us properly, refused to see what had happened to their dreams. Refused to do the right thing, even though none of them were necessarily bad people.

Perhaps I am more like the Aunts than I think, sitting here wanting desperately for this little girl with no one to call her own to be someone else's problem. More like them than I ever wanted to be.

We vowed never to be like that. Never ever. We'd stand up for those who couldn't defend themselves. We'd look out for each other. Natasha was the one who made us swear it. She'd pricked our fingers and had us press the bubbles of blood together. Sisters. We'd be different; we'd be tough. I am. I know that whatever else I am, I have a hard core that has kept me safe. Lisa could have gone either way and Amy . . . well.

But Natasha. She was fierce even when it cost her dearly.

So how has she ended up doing this? I just can't reconcile the image of the girl I knew with this way out.

I pick up the phone and impulsively dial DI Grafton, who says she'll speak to Matthew and come and collect me later that day. I tell her I'll come with Isaac. The thought of sitting in a car with her, trying to find words, is too much. She sounds relieved, but she also warns me that a story about the fire and Natasha's body will appear in the papers today. Adding, not many. Maybe even just local. My heart quakes at that. The barrage of information and dragging up skeletons this 'little story' will entail because those who are interested in such things tend to be almost as fanatical as the communities they're obsessed with.

CHAPTER SEVEN

Isaac comes to collect me and we drive across London for the second time in two days. Seemingly Oren hadn't looted Planet Pop, was very glad to have been trusted and is covering again today.

We park up outside the red-brick building – a care home for children, an orphanage – and go inside.

I hate places like this. Every single government-run institution I've been in – which is way too many – has the same cloying smell. Of bleach and desperation.

Cleaning in places like this is outsourced – sought-after contracts that companies bid on. But the government offices have a blanket rule on these things. They go with the cheapest. I only discovered once I'd left these places behind that you can get all sorts of sprays and wipes that smell of things like vanilla or fresh washing. I've since developed a sort of fetish for these products. My favourite is a room spray meant to smell like 'summer breeze'. It doesn't, but it is fresh and has none of the nose-burning qualities of the cheap bleach forever embedded in my memory banks.

This place has that smell. The walls are all painted uniform white and are mostly bare aside from notice-boards with too many things stuck to them, clamouring for space. I see snippets of the information contained as we walk past. 'Revision groups', 'study sessions', 'coun-selling for trauma'.

Voluntary, of course. Encouraged by the grown-ups who run these places with the best of intentions. But who could be happy here, in a land where you are either unwanted or had the misfortune of being born to people incapable of loving you?

I have no good memories of being in the care system. My memories were happier within the confines of the Black House; at least there I had Amy, Lisa, and Natasha. I'd hated being fostered, too.

As we walk, my heart beats quickly and I can feel my palms growing damp. I should have taken a beta blocker before I left the house. But now it is too late. Instead I focus on breathing and placing one foot in front of the other. Pressing them firmly onto the floor as I go. Isaac rests a hand on my shoulder for a moment and I pause to smile at him. Placing my own hand on top of his. I am not alone. I am not unwanted. I am not staying here.

Eventually we get to a cosy-looking office and a youth worker in appropriate 'casual attire' comes out and greets us.

DI Grafton is there and I hand her the letter from Natasha. She stays standing, looking at it as we all settle down. When she eventually takes her own seat, she holds out one of the photographs and says, 'Cute kid.' To which I have no reply. She asks if she can keep the letter for now.

I say, 'As evidence?'

She shrugs. 'There's been no crime as such but yes I'd like to log it.'

I nod. Half glad, half distraught to see the envelope with that familiar scrawl on it leave my possession.

The youth worker, Dee, is a big woman with a wide face and plaited hair with beads on the ends that jingle-jangle as she moves her head. She has a booming laugh and a lot of nice things to say about Pen. Almost like a sales pitch which, I suppose to some degree, it is. I wonder if someone had done this for me once and how the hell they'd have gone about it.

She finally stops speaking, eyes trained on me, with a smile that looks kind.

DI Grafton says, 'Obviously this is a big decision for Blue.'

Dee nods. 'I understand.'

It's not, though. A big decision. It's no kind of decision at all. Natasha did still know me – the real me – and talking things over with Isaac had only confirmed the truth in my own heart, as it always did.

I say to them both, 'I'll have her.' And there is a silence. Isaac reaches for my hand under the table and squeezes it. DI Grafton's eyes catch it and she looks away.

Then she says, 'It's a big thing taking on a child. And one who's grieving for her mother.'

I nod. It is and I get that.

DI Grafton adds, 'The terms of the will state that you also own Natasha's property, Penelope's family home.'

I shake my head at that. 'I want to stay in my flat.'

DI Grafton looks at Dee who says, 'We feel it might be better for Pen to have that continuity. Even if it were just a temporary thing.'

I shake my head again. 'I don't want to move.' And I can hear a high pitch to my voice now. I wipe my hands on my jeans, dropping Isaac's momentarily, and take a deep breath. 'Please.'

Dee asks, 'You've got a support network?' looking pointedly at Isaac.

He says, 'Whatever help Blue needs, I'll be there.' Adding, 'I'm not as scary as I look.' To which Dee roars with laughter and some of the tension leaves the room.

Then I see a look pass between DI Grafton and Dee. My brain whirs. Are they going to block this? Will it be deemed better that she stays here? I know I won't get the money until a formal ID is made. Is that the same for Pen?

Dee asks Isaac, 'Do you have children?'

He looks away and I feel suddenly awful that he has been put in this position.

I say, 'When I came to London, I started visiting Isaac's shop. I was thirteen. He's been the most constant thing in my life since then.' I add, 'I still work there.'

I first met Isaac when I was a surly teenager. I'd been in the care system for a few years by then and whilst I hated it – what the fuck is there to like? – one of the biggest challenges for me had been when we started being allowed to go out. On our own. On the whole, I was simultaneously desperate to be independent, to be free, and also terrified. I hadn't been by myself in all the time I could remember. My first few trips into London proper, I'd been accompanied by my 'key worker'. And I'd been surprised to find I liked it. I liked the whoosh of people going wherever it was they were going. The widening markets, the glaring shopping centres with their awful lights. The mishmash of interlinking roads and the lush, green parks springing up as if out of nowhere.

Before I went into care, all I'd known was the dark, dank countryside.

I saw a store with records in the window. I'd developed a love for punk music, perhaps because the brief explosive movement, well before my time, somehow reflected how I felt inside. I saw records in that window that I recognised and I stood and stared, fascinated.

On my first solo trip, Planet Pop was where I headed, with £5 stuffed in my pocket and a desire to own anything by The Slits. It was hidden down a side street and I struggled trying to find the bloody place but became utterly determined, as though my salvation depended on it and in a way, it really had. I'd had a childhood of complete isolation from the rest of the world; I knew next to nothing about subcultures or music, or clothes. All of my thinking had been 'done for me' in a gesture masquerading as kindness hiding the terrible truth. It had been drummed into me that everything man produced was an evil and the idea that we were better off without it all was hard to shake.

I did find the shop that day, though, and I liked the window display. I stared at it so intently that I didn't hear the door opening, or notice the black-clad figure coming out. It wasn't until he spoke that I knew he was there, and when he did, I almost jumped out of my skin, leaping around, hands held out in front of my face. God knows why. The tiny hands of a petite thirteen-year-old girl would offer little in the way of protection against any danger. Real or imagined. He looked at me with a frown. He had long hair, very bright eyes, and several rings in one of his eyebrows. He ignored my stance and said, 'Which one are you looking at?'

I pointed to The Slits record. He nodded, then launched into a heap of information about the band, their history, which songs were best and why.

At some point we moved into the store and he played me records for the rest of the afternoon, each one with an accompanying story.

It was the best afternoon I ever had. At first I thought him slightly scary, dangerous-looking, even. He was all studs and leather and tattoos. I'd never really seen anyone quite like him. But those afternoon trips where I gained my musical education also taught me how to love another human being. I was lucky, I guess, that he was who I stumbled upon. And also that I somehow knew not to mention to my social workers that I was spending all of my time with a man in a record store that also featured various kink toys and rubber outfits in its window displays.

Dee's face softens at my obvious love for Isaac. 'I read your file, Blue. You must be real proud of how your life has turned out.'

I swallow, unsure what to say.

Isaac clears his throat and takes a deep breath. 'I do have children, but the truth is I was a terrible father. Neither of them speak to me now and I don't blame them. You may or may not know my face but my breakdown and various addictions made the papers, so there's no point me lying to you about them. I've been sober since 1997, not touched a drink or a drug in all that time. I have my shop, which makes good money, and I still get pay-outs for records from back in the day. My children may not want to see me, but I've paid for both of their educations and deposits on their houses. If a day comes when they do want to make contact, they'll find me as I am now, which is well.'

Dee says, 'I do recognise you and I'm real glad to hear about your recovery.'

He smiles. 'Kind of you to say, and if I might be so bold, I can't imagine you'd find a better person to take care of a little girl than Blue, who knows herself what it is to be alone. And whilst I may not be the image that springs to mind of paternal support, I love her like she's my own and I'm on hand to help.'

Dee raises an eyebrow at the detective, who sort of shrugs. The she smiles at us both and says to me, 'And you have space?'

'Yes.'

'Where?'

I tell her and she grins. 'Oh good, Pen's school is an easy travel from there.' Which gives me an odd kind of feeling in my stomach. Pen is ten. For five years, she and Natasha had travelled to school almost past my flat. Yet our paths had never crossed.

Dee says, 'Pen has living family. I believe you know that?'

I nod, look at my feet. Hoping my heart doesn't smash through my chest. Flames licking my mother's face. Me shouting *I'm sorry* as I drop her hand. Pain in my arm, which didn't register for hours. Four children and a woman stumbling through the dark, dark woods.

Dee looks at her notes. 'Sienna and Brodie Dryden.'

My heart tremors a little. A yearning ache.

Brodie.

That whooshing sound in my ears. The crackle of burning wood, clothes, the smell of plastic catching light and going up in seconds. Natasha calm, grabbing my hand, pulling me away from my mother. From the flames. Brodie and Lisa on her other side. 'Time to go.'

Sienna outside on the lawn in her too-thin white dress on a too-cold night, slumped to her knees, watching the fire spread. Face paralysed and immobile. Jaw slack. We walked past her and Natasha didn't even glance her way. It had been Brodie who'd gone to his mother. Taking her gently by the elbow, pulling her up onto her feet. Adding her to our little ragtag band. The only adult and the only one being manoeuvred by someone else.

Tough.

The kids in that place were hardy. Yet to be chipped away at, made into whatever it was that Sienna had become. That my mother became.

I shut my eyes. I see Brodie's face, clear as day, his handsome, lopsided smile. That little squeeze of my heart that I used to get when I looked at him. A silly crush on Natasha's baby brother. But silly as it was, I now compare every man I go on dates with to the way I felt about Brodie and they all come up lacking. In an imaginary world I've often fantasised about what would have happened if Brodie and I ended up in the same place. Us against the Black House, the care system, the world.

Dee says, 'Are you all right?'

'It's a lot to take in. For anyone,' DI Grafton murmurs.

Dee shifts in her seat. 'I know and I wish we had more time. But . . . with everything taken into consideration, how do you feel now, Blue? No one would blame you if it all sounded too much.'

I say, 'Pen can come and live with me.'

Dee smiles. Is it genuine? Or just box ticked on what is likely a long list?

She says, 'We'll be supporting you.'

'What does that mean?'

'I am Pen's key worker. So I'll be nipping around.'

I frown. 'What, checking up on me?'

Dee is still smiling, but I greet it with a scowl, 'Not checking up,' she soothes. 'Supporting. Making sure everything is going OK.'

'And if it's not?'

She shrugs. 'I'm sure it will be.'

'But say it wasn't.'

Still smiling, she says, 'Then we'd reassess.'

So I have custody of Pen, but it can be revoked.

DI Grafton says, 'Can I ask why you're not placing the child with her biological family?'

Dee's face falls. 'Well. They live in Wales for one

43

thing, but mainly, her grandmother, Sienna, isn't very well. Mentally.'

I think of her. Many times she'd come and see to us children at the Black House, and she'd be bruised, battered. Not uncommon for the Aunts. Or for Amy, by the end. But no one discussed it.

Dee carries on, 'Over the years she's had several breakdowns.'

'And Brodie Dryden?'

'He works but is also his mother's carer.'

I look out of the window. Resist the urge to ask a hundred questions about him. What does he do for a job? Does he have any hobbies? What does he look like now? I see a flicker of his crooked smile. Squeeze my eyes shut and open them again quickly.

There is a faint breeze and a plastic bag bounces lethargically a few inches from the floor in its pull.

Carer. The poor fucker never got away, then. From one prison to another.

DI Grafton says, 'That's sad.'

And Dee nods.

I say, 'Natasha said in her letter they didn't know. About Pen.'

'No. They don't. Another thing we'd like to discuss with you in time.'

'Why?'

'We believe there is usually benefit for children in getting to know their biological families.'

I snort at that. No one says anything. Everyone in that room fully aware of my only biological family member. And the danger she'd put me in. The abandonment.

Dee asks, 'Are you ready to meet Pen?'

I don't say anything and the silence stretches. Dee and DI Grafton exchange another one of their bloody looks.

Isaac asks, 'Are you all right?'

I snap that I'm fine. He nods and I offer him a weak smile. 'Really, I am.'

I don't think it's entirely true. That I'm fine. I don't think I even like children, or at the very least I don't know any to have practised with.

DI Grafton looks like she's about to say something sympathetic, which honestly would be more than I can take right now. I stand. 'Shall we go, then?'

Dee says, 'Just you and me might be best.'

'That OK with you, kiddo?' Isaac asks.

And I nod because I feel I can't say no.

He tells me, 'I'll be here waiting for you both.'

You both. That easy.

We walk down a long corridor and I keep my eyes straight ahead, not allowing myself to be distracted by the bedrooms leading off from it. Or to look too deeply at the 'recreational room' we finally arrive in. It could be the temporary home I ended up in in Cardiff. Or my main one in London that I still pass from time to time and always avoid looking directly at. It could, I suppose, be any one of these places in any part of the country. But the difference here is the bank of computers at the back of the room and a games console in front of the TV. Children are huddled together in groups. French windows back onto a large garden area and there are more of them out there, milling around.

I see her before she's pointed out. Sitting on a large white chair in the corner of the room, curled up like a cat with a paperback balanced in her hands. She does look like Sienna. *Nenny.* It sounds like a comfortable sort of pet name but the way Natasha said it made her sound weak and ineffectual. All of the Aunts were 'Aunt', but she insisted on calling her mother Nenny. Always in a low, mocking voice. Sienna Dryden, broken by the time I knew her, must have been very beautiful in her day, just as her daughter was and so too is the child who looks up at me now.

When Pen's eyes lock on mine, my stomach does a sort of dropping flip-flop. I wonder if I'm going to be sick. That would be an unsettling introduction for anyone, of course. No hello, no preamble, just a pile of bile and vomit. I swallow, press my hand against my lips, push my feet against the floor and look away from her down to my toes. Carpet in here. A nondescript colour, which may once have been patterned.

I feel Dee move away from me.

When I look up, the little girl is there, book clenched to her chest, blinking up at me. Her eyes are a dark, dark brown and her face is set in serious lines. Dee seems about to speak, make introductions, but the girl says, 'Are you Blue?'

I nod.

Then she says, 'Mummy said you're good at drawing?'

Natasha had talked about me. Told her daughter details of my life.

I say, 'I'm OK, yes.'

She looks at my hand. 'Did you draw that?' Pointing to my tattoo.

'No. Well yes, but not onto my skin. Someone else did that. I did the design.'

She nods. 'Cool.' Then: 'Are you taking me home?'

I cough. More for pause than anything else. 'I thought you could come and stay with me? If you like.'

'OK.'

And that is that.

CHAPTER EIGHT

That, though, is not that. There is a lot of paperwork involved when you take someone else's child home – who'd have thought it? The final bits of admin won't be completed until DI Grafton has her definite ID. But for all intents and purposes and certainly for now, I am Pen's legal guardian. Pen comes into the office between Dee and I. DI Grafton makes her excuses and leaves, telling me she'll be in touch. I introduce Pen to Isaac. She stares at him and I try to see him through her eyes, which isn't difficult as I was pretty taken aback the first time I saw him. But I knew, even then, that the most benevolent-looking people could be pure evil. Joseph Carillo looked years younger than he was and he'd had the kind of cherubic face that encouraged almost instant trust.

Isaac looks dangerous by default. Something in the way his eyes are set. He also has a face full of metal and an outlandish collection of hats. He is weathered, looks like what he is – a man who has lived a full life. The only bit of him that doesn't look rinsed to fuck are his eyes. I like to think his eyes reflect the true him, corny though that is. They are beautiful, a deep brown. In his younger days, back when he was a famous singer, he'd been gorgeous. I can understand why girls up and down the country plastered their walls with his image. He is probably still good-looking, though I just see the man who is the father I never had.

He smiles at Pen now. 'Hey, I'm a friend of Blue's.'

She says, 'OK.' And goes to take a seat next to him. I sit on the other side of her. Dee is opposite. I am pleased to see her include Pen in the conversation. Maybe things within the care system have changed since my day, or maybe I had never been the kind of child who invited inclusion. Perhaps a combination of the two.

I sneak glances at the little girl, each time my heart catching with a fluttery kind of panic. I force myself to stay focused on Dee. Trying to keep my mind in this surreal and unlikely conversation.

She's talking about my flat and Pen's school. The logistics of the school run. Jesus.

Dee asks us if we're happy with everything. I look at Pen who shrugs and Isaac whose face is impassive.

I mutter, 'Sure.'

Dee smiles and picks up the phone on her desk, asking someone to pop into her office, then to Pen: 'May will come and take you to get your things.' And May appears, a young woman dressed like a children's TV presenter.

She smiles way too brightly at Pen and says, 'OK?'

Pen looks at me and sort of sighs. I suppress a smile.

Pen goes trailing behind May and Isaac says, 'Nice kid.'

Dee says, 'She is, yes, and I must say so far she's been coping far better than we'd have expected.'

I say, 'She knew she was coming to me?'

Dee says, 'It seems that her mother had discussed you in an abstract kind of way and the child knew the contents of her will in regards to her custody.' Dee shakes her head. 'A risky strategy in any event.' She means in case I hadn't taken her. But Natasha had known I would. I feel a prickle of annoyance at her assumption and that it was correct.

I don't particularly want to be responsible for a child. I've had to grow up learning to somehow look after myself but I can't even keep a plant alive in my flat. Isaac has been nagging me about it for a while, not the plant exactly, but being more nurturing, whatever the fuck that means. His latest thing is encouraging me to start dating again, or at least get a pet. Both things I've refused point blank to consider at the moment. Now there is a child coming to live with me.

Joke's on me, I guess.

Dee and May take Pen to say goodbye to the other children, though she doesn't seem keen, but goes along without complaint. Isaac and I stand outside by his car. He has a protective arm around my shoulders and the feel of the stiff leather from his jacket pressing against the thin material of my T-shirt brings me some comfort.

He repeats what he said to Dee: 'Seems a nice kid.'

I murmur, 'Fucking hell, though.'

He squeezes me to him. 'You're not alone.'

I blink back tears. One of the things that always surprises me about Isaac is his propensity towards sentimentality. I'd learned over the years that he was a man who'd move heaven and earth to help others when he could. When I'd started hanging round Planet Pop he hadn't said much, he'd played me endless stacks of records to start with, then at some point he'd have a sandwich and a can of Coke waiting for me, too. When he saw some of my scribblings on the covers of my schoolbooks he'd bought me a pad and a pack of pencils. I'd sit behind the counter while he worked, scribbling away, and he'd look at what I'd made and murmur encouragement.

Then when I left school, refusing to do A Levels and moving into a strange studio flat in a building full of care

49

leavers, he gave me a job. When I'd looked round my flat, wanting to buy my own place, and been short of the deposit, the exact amount I needed turned up in my pay packet as a 'bonus'. When I said it was too much, he'd ignored my protests and suggested we go and start looking at the tools I'd need to sort out the floors I'd bored him to death going on about.

Most importantly I suppose he'd given me love. He'd seen me through periods of bleak and desolate depression, and he didn't try and fix me, but he did take me to the doctor and said I had to look at it like I would any other illness. I'd read a lot of books about psychology in an attempt to understand myself, my childhood. A lot of them said if you had one person who loved you, who could be trusted and relied upon whilst you were in your formative years, you could overcome a lot of damage. I think Isaac was that that person for me. By my early twenties I was in my flat, off of antidepressants and OK. All thanks to Isaac and despite the odds stacked against me.

Pen comes out of the building with Dee, who hands me a file of the paperwork we have gone through together.

Pen looks at the car. 'What is it?'

Isaac's pride and joy. It's a Scirocco from the 1980s and he adores the bloody thing and has spent a fortune on it.

Pen says, 'It's from, like, the olden days.'

Isaac frowns and I find myself laughing. Then Pen is giggling as I take her suitcase, pop it in the boot and open the door for her.

Isaac gets in murmuring, 'Vintage.'

And Pen says, 'Doesn't that just mean old?'

He says, 'Jeez.' But I can see him smiling as he pulls away.

We don't speak. Isaac is fine with silence and I can't imagine ever being able to find the right words, though obviously at some point I'll have to find some, even if they are wrong. During this journey all the things I think of saying die before they make it to my mouth.

He pulls up outside mine and says, 'Would you like me to come in?'

I shake my head and step out of the car. Taking Pen's suitcase from the boot. She comes, stands next to me and looks at the building in front of us.

'Your house is small.'

'It's not all mine.'

'Oh.'

'I live in the top two floors.'

'OK.'

'It's bigger inside.'

Isaac looks at me. 'OK?'

I nod, waving him off, as does Pen.

She says, 'He seems nice.'

'He's OK. Let's go in.'

She follows me and we climb the stairs. I'm amazed that my hand turns the key steady and straight. I don't drop her suitcase and I manage some semblance of calm as I go in. But inside I am a mess and trying desperately not to show it. Pen seems relatively relaxed and wanders around, looking at the various sketches covering large sections of the hallway walls. She pauses at a set on a large piece of A3. Shit. I should have taken them down. Should have thought.

She reaches her small hand out and traces the outline of the face in the middle. Then she turns to me with a smile and says, 'It looks just like her.'

And I smile back. Relieved. 'She was a kid then, really.'

Pen nods. 'She still looks like that, though.' There is a slight quiver of her lip and she adds, 'Looked.'

Oh God.

'Do you want to see your room?'

'OK.'

I show her into it. It's a nice room with big windows and the walls are a bright blue. The covers and pillowcases are dark grey and I realise as soon as we step in that whilst I like the neat, subdued colours, it may not be to a little girl's liking at all.

I say, 'You can do what you want. In here, I mean.'

She says OK. Again. I am still clutching her suitcase, which I put on the floor. I open the wardrobe, the chest of drawers and ask if she needs help unpacking. We work in silence and once everything is emptied, she says, 'I left Boggles.'

I look at her. 'What?'

'My bear.' That lower lip goes again.

In the package of things I've been given is a key to Natasha's house. And Pen's. Not far from here. I'd known at some point I'd have to visit Natasha's house. But I don't want it to be now. 'It's probably back at the care home?'

She shakes her head. 'Nuh-uh. I forgot to pack him. Dee said I could get him when I went home.'

I say, 'We'll have to go and get more of your stuff soon anyway.'

'But Dee said today.'

A hundred things run through my mind. That things change. That we aren't staying at her house. But these things would hardly be comforting to her and she'd been pretty good about coming here instead of hers, too.

I stand, looking at her. She looks back at me. Brown eyes burning into mine. How funny that I should be scared of someone so small. But I am. There are so many feasible and likely ways I'm going to fuck this up.

I go back to the front door, grab my coat and keys, handing Pen's to her. 'Come on.'

The whole time I've been at my flat, Natasha has lived less than a mile away. Lisa had been a bit further out but still only a couple of stops on the tube.

It'd be a lie to say I hadn't thought of them. Of course I had. My childhood featured heavily in the cacophony of bullshit my mind can feed me when it wants to be a bitch.

But I didn't want to think of them. Or I forcibly tried not to. I'd made a decision after a year in care that I had to wipe the slate clean as much as I could, and that meant having nothing to do with any of them. What good could come of it?

I think I'd thought that if I cut all ties I could move on. Make it like it had never happened. It couldn't be that way, of course. You are, after all, just the sum of your experiences. The past festered within me and all around me. Chasing me out, hunting me down. I'd started off online looking very lightly at utopias, and alternative communities. The ideologies behind them, the many studies surrounding them. Reading other people's discussions on various forums. Now I was a full-blown expert. Despite myself I'd still grabbed out at the past in all its ugliness. I wasn't really free. Lisa had died, now Natasha, and I had been minutes away from them both.

I knew they'd come to London. Of course. Or I knew Natasha would and that she'd seek out Lisa, too. It had been our dream. So many nights awake looking at that blasted A to Z under the glow of torchlight. Thinking 'when' and 'if only'.

I try and push these thoughts away as I walk down the street with this little girl bobbing along next to me.

The house is big – it must have cost an absolute fortune – the doorstep is stone and stands out proud and grand-looking. There are two plotted plants either side. Tiny trees perfectly round. The door is a taupe colour with a large black knocker in the middle.

I open it and Pen heads straight in and up the stairs. I stand awkwardly in the hallway, staring at a photograph on a chest of drawers by the door. Natasha, Lisa, Amy and me. How had she managed to salvage it? I can't tear my eyes away. We could be a movie poster for a teen coming-of-age story. We could be happy, grinning siblings. We could be anything.

'I've got him.' I almost jump out of my skin but manage to stay calm, turning to Pen and smiling.

She points at the picture. 'That's you?'

I nod.

She says, 'Shall we take that, too?'

And I pick it up with a shaky hand, putting it into my backpack.

All the way home I feel the sharp edges of the picture frame knocking between my shoulder blades and at some point, Pen slips her little hand into mine.

CHAPTER NINE

It turns out that Pen has a pretty busy schedule. The first thing to sort out is her school. I have to go into a meeting with her headmistress. It's an independent school, in a pretty building with a small number of students. All girls. The first time I attended school, it was a large, state-run junior with an overwhelming number of children from all walks of life. This place feels more like a relaxing private members club but for children.

The head teacher – Mrs Williams – greets us at the front desk and suggests to Pen that she goes along to class.

Pen turns to me and sort of waves. I have an over-whelming urge to grab her and take her straight home with me. Though what we'd do all day is a mystery. Last night had been hard enough. She had the TV on until at about nine when she told me she'd usually be in bed by now.

After she'd gone to sleep, I barely slept a wink. Moving from my bedroom to the sofa. Unsure whether to check on her but eventually pushing the door open and stealing in. She looked even smaller, even younger, lying there in the newly made bed, her dark hair fanned out around her small face. Mouth slightly ajar and softly snoring. It was the first time I'd thought she looked a bit like Natasha.

I'd finally drifted off on the sofa at about three-thirty, waking with a start at five, showering, dressing and worrying about what time to wake her for school. I'd got changed three times too. So I guess I'm pretty nervous about the teacher meeting. Dee offered to come, as did Isaac, but I said I'd be fine. A lie that I am now regretting.

By the time we'd arrived at the school gates I was an exhausted nervous wreck, but Pen seemed OK. And now she's gone, that small wave all I'll have until pick-up. How the hell do people cope with this level of responsibility?

I push the thought away; Isaac would say *one day at a time*. And I can just about do that. I follow Mrs Williams down a long corridor where she points out various things: cups, awards, photos of girls on teams. Hockey, netball. A cheerleading squad, she says with a sort of chuckle, adding that one's popular. I nod. Feeling awkward and ill at ease.

Her office is comfortable, softly furnished and lined with books and beautiful pieces of art. I murmur at those, unable to stop myself. She seems impressed that I know who the artists are and asks if I dabble.

I shrug. 'I draw.' Then add, 'I work in a record shop mainly, though.'

She says, 'Oh.' And blinks. I imagine the parents of children here all have professional jobs far more sensible than mine. I am yet to find out what exactly Natasha did. All I've been told was property. Judging by this place and her house it must have been high-end. Certainly she has paid the fees here well in advance and there is more than enough in the sum she left me, which I don't yet want to claim even when I can, to see Pen through to adulthood.

I stand awkwardly in front of the paintings. She slips behind her desk gesturing to a chair opposite and I sit in it. It's too low and the back is too high. I feel immediately engulfed by the bloody thing as though it is trying to hug me into suffocation. I edge myself forward so I'm straighter.

She says, 'Penelope seemed a bit better this morning.'

'Oh?'

'Well. Since I last saw her. We got a call. Just before school ended last Friday.' She shakes her head. 'Unbelievable.'

And yet it has happened. The story of my life. So many things gone that have been unlikely. Unusual. Unheard of. Unbelievable. And yet . . .

I say, 'I only met her yesterday.'

Mrs Williams leans forward, all earnestness. 'You and Natasha must have been terribly close.'

I look away from her too-near gaze and back at the pictures hung on the wall. There is particularly beautiful nude. A slightly plump woman in charcoal, arms above her head, the faint beginnings of a smile on her face. Eyes half closed.

I say, 'We were once.'

'Oh?'

'We'd lost contact. It happens.'

'Indeed it does. Yet she left you her most precious thing.'

'Right.'

'And you're happy? To have her?'

The roaring in my mind. The faint crackle and fizz. Happy – what the hell has happy got to do with it?

I say, 'It didn't occur to me to say no.' Which obviously is no kind of answer at all and yet still the only one I have. I add, 'I'm sure we'll be fine.'

She nods. 'A period of adjustment for you both.'

'Right.'

There is a silence. An awkward one that stretches out around us. She seems to have many things to say but is unable to begin. I imagine words flooding onto the tip of her tongue and getting caught like fish in a net.

I stand. Done with this now. I tell her, 'You have my details. Pen will be at my address. I know what time to drop her and collect her and I have a timetable of her clubs.'

57

Mrs Williams stands. 'I'd rather hoped for a more in-depth chat.'

'I can't think there's one to be had at the moment. As you say, Pen and I are in a period of adjustment.'

I leave, knowing that she had expected more and that probably I had just been very rude. I'm useless at small talk. There was no place for it in my formative years. When me and the girls talked in our dorm, often long into the night, we'd speak in desperate, furtive whispers only. Everything we said outside of there could easily have been overheard. We had our most in-depth conversations at night – conversations that meant we knew each other so closely that when I left the Black House I felt like parts of me had been ripped out.

I walk quickly out of the school. I still hate institutions.

I suppose for Natasha, having a baby wasn't as big a deal as it might have been for some. She had practically raised Lisa and I, along with Amy. I learned very quickly not to bother the adults with anything, so it was Natasha or Amy I'd turn to with a scraped knee or a bruised elbow. Them that Lisa and I would tell tales on each other to.

There is no father named on Pen's birth certificate and I wonder if Natasha spent her pregnancy knowing it would be just the two of them. As I walk, the weight of Pen's care hits me again like a ton of bricks. I need to be back at school to collect her again at four-thirty. This is how each of my days will now begin and end. Punctuated by someone else's need.

Parenting.

The Aunts did most of the menial tasks involved in child-rearing. We ate in a big hall in the Black House. Mealtimes were one of the few occasions boys and girls mixed and where there were more than your close-knit little group. It meant I really only knew Lisa, Amy and Natasha in any real way. But the older children knew each other. When we hit twelve, we spent more time out of dorm between mealtimes and lessons. Lessons were in our own small groups. Delivered by different Aunts, I think so we didn't become overly attached to any one in particular.

Lots of bad things happened at the Black House. All the time. The Aunts were no exception but their day-to-day cruelties – slapped hands, a ruler across the back of your legs, the withholding of food – faded into the background in comparison to some of the other goings-on. It got so that I was numb to them and to my surroundings and surprisingly quickly, too. People say children can adjust to anything. I'd say they were right. I went from living in a sunny yellow flat that smelled of weed and incense and candles with Mum and going to a nursery school that had bunny rabbits and rainbows on the walls, to the dormitories that ran alongside a large black barn in the countryside of North Wales. It still smelled of weed and candles and incense but there was always another scent, too.

Fear – rank sweat and tears.

Lisa was my equal – a sister of sorts. Natasha and Amy did all the 'parenting'. I'd never thought at the time what the burden for teenage girls sharing a cramped space with two little girls must have been like. I was five when I arrived at the Black House. Natasha was eleven and a precocious eleven at that. Amy was ten. Lisa was eight.

Natasha was the only one of us who had another sibling, Brodie. Sons mostly stayed with their mothers or went to Carillo and his 'team', which consisted of two other men, for one-on-one training. They had lessons too, but often in separate groups to us. We knew more about the goings-on of the boys' dorms than other girls because of Natasha's connection to Brodie. He was four years younger than her and as far as I could work out, they got along fine. My crush on Brodie was never more than a secret. I suppose he was the only boy I ever saw in close proximity and those feelings are normal at that age. Maybe if I'd been at a proper school in a proper class, I wouldn't have even noticed him. But I did. He was a serious kid with the same dark brown eyes as his sister and floppy hair that fell over them. To me, he seemed the height of handsomeness.

When we stumbled through the woods that last night, he held my hand while I sobbed and hugged me before we were all separated. I still think about it now. If I daydream about romance, which isn't a pastime I indulge often, it's usually with him in mind and I often wonder how he grew up. The thought of contacting him regarding his niece fills me with both excitement and terror. I guess I don't have to think about it today.

Natasha was really the only one of us whose semblance of family life remained in any way intact and the only one who got out with surviving relatives. But Sienna Dryden had been Carillo's first member. A mother of two children whilst she herself had still been a teenager. Nothing about our lives was ordinary. Natasha was Carillo's favourite, and likely would have taken her mother's place as his main partner had things turned out differently. The thought makes me shudder. At the time, I didn't know any of this, though I understood she had more freedoms than others and, in turn, that we did too.

My phone pings.

It is an email. A message from a journalist. I read it, paused on a busy pavement as people push past me, heart hammering in my chest. He has heard about Natasha

Dryden's sad death. He is writing a book about the Black House and knows of her connection to it. He has spoken to survivors and managed to track me down.

I feel sick and press a hand to my mouth, my elbow shooting sharply to the side and connecting with a passer-by who frowns at me, muttering an obscenity just loud enough for me to hear. I can't form the words to say *sorry* or *piss off*. I turn on my heel, push my phone into my bag and walk quickly.

Questions fizz around my brain, waiting to form properly. No one should know who I am. Who Natasha was. After our 'rescue' we were separated, mainly to protect our identities. Our names were never in the press but our ages were and all of us arriving in one place would have been fairly obvious. It was also what the authorities thought would most help us to heal. For me, it had meant being wrenched from the only family I'd ever known. My heart had smashed into a thousand pieces for the second time in my young life. I grieved the loss of my sisters as I'd grieved the loss of my mother. Grief spilled from me for people still living. But I got used to their absence as I had steeled myself against my mother's rejection whilst she was still alive.

I had to learn the hard way on a particularly cruel winter's day. It happened in one of the 'classrooms'.

CHAPTER TEN

The children sit in rows. Today's class is mixed and Blue's eyes slip over to the boys. Before she got here, she had gone to nursery and there were boys there, but here it is different. Now she spends most of her time in this classroom, struggling to focus on what's being said and fighting the gnawing hunger in her belly. When she isn't here, she's in the dormitory. Always with Lisa, often with Amy and Natasha. They're nice, but all she wants is her mummy. She has cried herself to sleep for what feels like forever now. Calling out for her to come. To read her a story.

Tuck her in.

Her mummy never comes, but Amy has started reading her books and even lets Blue climb into her bed when she feels really sad.

But today her mummy is here in the classroom. She stands at the front, still beautiful but different, Blue thinks. It's the clothes.

Mummy loves jeans and floaty skirts and long, beaded tops. But now she always wears a long white dress and open-toed sandals. Her face isn't painted either and Blue doesn't like it. Not at all.

When she thinks of Mummy – and she does almost all of the time – colours come to mind. Beautiful, strong and bold.

Mummy is talking about things Blue doesn't understand and her mind drifts away from the alien words.

Social construct.

Poor ideology.

Lots of things that scare Blue about policemen who would try and steal the children. Governments attempting to brainwash them.

Horrible words that make no sense to the little girl who has just turned seven but doesn't even know it, because here birthdays aren't celebrated.

There is a pause in the teaching and a video is put on.

Blue braces herself but she knows better than to look away, has experienced sharp slaps and the feel of heavy rulers across her knuckles when she's tried to cover her eyes.

The videos are bad. They make her tummy feel like liquid and her heart ache in her chest.

They are of all the people 'out there' doing terrible things.

By the time it is finished Blue has tears running down her face. She swipes at them quickly before the lights come up and she feels something pressing against her arm.

She turns quickly.

It is Natasha's brother, eyes still facing forward, but holding something out to her.

She reaches for it, and feels it slipping around in her hand. When she glances down she sees it is a stone, just a stone, blank and flat and white. When she turns it over she sees a smiley face in jagged black lines.

She can't remember the last time she received a gift and her eyes well up all over again, her breath catching in her throat.

A voice, strident but familiar, says, 'Pay attention, Blue.'

She looks up, half-smiling. 'Sorry, Mummy.'

There is a frozen silence. Her mother looks slightly over her head, her face blank.

Blue says, 'Aunt . . .' and stammers on the word. 'I meant Aunt.'

She looks around desperately now but the other children have their heads bowed. Focused on their desks.

All kinds of things might happen.

Blue has seen it.

Life before here was not reality. Remnants of that life are gone forever, washed away along with the terrible sins of the outside world. Acknowledging the old order in any way is not allowed. Punishments may follow and they can be vast, varied. Often violent.

She is holding her breath but it does not stop her crying, sobbing.

Her mummy no longer her mummy, but Aunt, says, 'Class dismissed.'

And they file out.

Natasha goes straight to Blue and takes the small girl's hand. She looks up at her, bewildered. Then Amy is there. She and Natasha exchange quick, whispered words and Natasha tells Amy to take Blue out on a walk.

Blue goes, gripping the older girl's hand tightly and slipping the white smiling stone into her pocket.

They walk and walk for hours and by the time they get back to the dorm Blue's legs ache and she is exhausted. Lisa is there and so is Natasha, a bright purple bruise blossoming on her face. Blue gasps and Amy goes to her, wetting the awful tracing paper tissue they are provided with in the sink. She presses it to Natasha's face and they begin whispering again.

Blue starts crying, terrible, silent sobs.

Natasha looks at her, smiles and sort of winces. Every time she moves it seems to cause her pain. She says to Blue, 'I fell. Clumsy as anything.' Which Blue knows isn't true. Natasha is graceful enough to be a ballet dancer.

She doesn't know how exactly but understands that the punishment was to do with her saying 'Mummy' in class. Because there had to be one and she thinks that Natasha has taken it so she didn't have to. In that moment something within Blue hardens and she starts to feel hatred for Mummy, who could have not said anything. Who could have just left it.

Who could have never made Blue come here.

She goes to sleep with the little white stone in her hand and a hardness taking root in her heart.

CHAPTER ELEVEN

Brainwashed, people said afterwards. *Psychological warfare.*

Those videos stay with me. I learned later that some clips were from films, some were newsreels. None of it was appropriate for young, impressionable minds of course. It was endless hours of stuff that even adults would find disturbing and sometimes I wake even now from poor rest with images of starving children with thin limbs and distended bellies, or women held down by gangs and brutalised flooding my mind. Once you've seen something, of course, you can't unsee it.

That day in class had been a pivotal moment for me. Devastating, but also in some ways making my life there easier. Because loving her had been a lot more painful than hating her.

Family.

Natasha, Amy and Lisa became the closest thing I had to it. At the end of it all, Lisa and I were the youngest of the children left. We depended on each other because we had to. Afterwards, Natasha and Lisa and I were split up. I later learned that Natasha had stayed in Wales with Brodie and Sienna; Lisa was sent to Bristol for the same roundabout of care and foster homes as me. When they came of age, both had headed for London. They each made their files available to me by request. I didn't do the same. Both of them looked me up when they arrived in the city. I never knew how they'd found my details but figured it would have been Natasha's doing; she was nothing if not resourceful.

I ignored their messages.

I go and sit with Lisa now. I am freaked out and jangled inside, like a startled deer caught in the headlights of a car hurtling towards me at 80 mph. I don't feel like drawing today.

I just sit and cry.

For Lisa. For Amy. For Natasha. For Pen, who's lost her mother. Fiery, zesty Natasha. And now she gets me, a dull and subdued replacement. Not the caretaker that Natasha was. I had been the baby there, catered for and looked after. At the shop it is the same, with Isaac looking out for me. And as I cry, I just can't imagine why Natasha has done this. I can't reconcile the young woman I knew with someone who would willingly give up the life she'd fought so hard for. It just doesn't feel right and I keep thinking of DI Grafton telling us that the remains had yet to be formally identified. My own thoughts are too murky. Too difficult. The implications far too terrifying.

Because if it's not Natasha, then who is it?

And where is Natasha?

CHAPTER TWELVE

Annie Grafton is chewing gum, endless packs of shitty Nicorette. It literally feels like chewing cigarette butts and eventually she spits it into the bin and murmurs that she'll be right back. Her sergeant looks up, nods once. Everyone is busy, of course. Since there seems to be general warfare on the streets of London these days it's hard to find time for cases that aren't just shoving plasters over the terrible rise in gang crime.

Annie has felt disheartened for a while now. Not just at work, though the terrible effects of years of austerity and police cuts make her job close to impossible. But her personal life has also been a train wreck. Rather unwittingly she'd swapped a terrible habit of drinking too much for an even more detrimental habit of daily cocaine. Bad, for obvious reasons, and also likely to unhinge her career entirely. But she's been attending NA meetings for over a year now and seems to manage three months at least each time, before relapsing again.

The only really good thing to come out of trying to quit so far is her absolute clarity that she needs to divorce Ian. He's been annoying her for years, but until now he'd been nothing more than a minor irritation. During her new, mostly lucid state, she finds every single thing he does grating. And she's also come to understand that he likes her best when she's struggling or fucking up. Despite slow progress, she's determined to stop doing both.

Annie's standing outside the station puffing away when a message comes through from Dee: *'Penelope settled at school. Blue messaged to say she's fine. I thought Isaac was nice.'*

Annie finds she actually blushes, standing out here on the steps of the police station, thinking about Isaac. For fuck's sake. What a time to develop a schoolgirl crush.

She's still waiting on a formal ID of Natasha Dryden and when she gets back to her desk she emails to chase again. A message comes back straight away: *'Still no ID, I'm going as fast as I can.'* Complete with an eye-roll emoji. She smiles. Dr Simonson is a good guy, but he hates to be rushed. Unfortunately for him it's literally her job to hurry him the fuck up.

This case is bothering her, like an itch in the mind. None of it makes any sense so far. In theory it's a cut-and-dried suicide, but the cult links, the seemingly successful woman, good mother, no recorded history of depression killing herself like that . . .

Of course, looking over Natasha's case notes and the horrific abuse she'd suffered, it would be amazing if she didn't have some issues.

But she can't keep dwelling for too long. Another call comes in – yet another stabbing – and Annie finds herself swept up in the day.

CHAPTER THIRTEEN

We walk home from school and when we get in Pen gets her books out, lays them across my broad white table and starts doing her homework. I stand like a spare part for a while, just watching her. Unsure what to do. Eventually I sit awkwardly on my own sofa, scrolling through rubbish on my phone and sneaking glances at her.

After a while, Pen looks up and says, 'What are we having for dinner?'

'I don't know. What do you like?'

'I like Chinese takeaway.'

'OK.'

Pen lights up and grins. 'Even on a school night?' and I become aware that I am likely breaking some rule I have no knowledge of.

I shrug. 'There's not much in the fridge.'

Pen nods. 'I know. We'll have to go to the supermarket tomorrow.'

'OK.'

So we have takeout. Ordering more than two people could possibly eat. The expense doesn't matter; I have enough. Parsons said that eventually Natasha's money will transfer to me. I don't want it, and I don't need it. I've already decided I will put it away for Pen.

She eats with gusto. I rarely do. Eating is one of the things I still struggle with. It's not something I do often in front of other people if I can possibly avoid it. Aware that I eat too quickly, frightened still of the door opening and the punishment for greed.

But this evening, watching Pen shovel deep-fried chicken balls into sweet and sour sauce and then into her mouth, I enjoy both eating and not doing it alone. Pen actually talks quite a lot, it turns out. She rattles off stories about girls at school, her mouth full of rice, which falls out a few times and to which she says, 'Soz.' Wiping the bits from the table and dumping them unceremoniously onto her plate.

When we're finished, I say to her, 'I assume you have a bedtime?'

Pen narrows her eyes. 'Did my mum write you a note?'

I don't say anything, just wait, watching the girl who, I realise, is weighing up what she might be able to get away with.

Eventually she sighs, full of theatricality, and says, 'She would probably. She wrote notes for everything.' Adding, 'Eight o'clock. But later on weekends.'

'OK.'

'She reads me a story, though. At eight.'

I say, 'Do you have your books with you?'

Pen shakes her head. 'Don't you have any?'

'Not many. I read comics.'

'Oh cool.'

So I sit on the edge of Pen's bed, the girl all clean from her bath and in pyjamas, and we read an early *Tank Girl* that I realise as we go probably isn't suitable, thinking we'll have to go with something more age-appropriate tomorrow night.

It turns out she isn't listening too intently though and eventually, the kid reaches up, and wraps her arms around my neck, so close I can feel her hot breath on me. Then she murmurs goodnight, rolls over and goes to sleep. Just like that.

I try very hard never to think of Amy. But as I leave Pen and sit down in my living room, I am reminded of her reading us stories at bedtime. I think about Lisa all the time when I sit by her graveside and I've thought a lot about Natasha over the years, but Amy is a forbidden place in my mind. I'd forced myself to stop thinking about her even when we were still together.

She and Natasha weren't too far apart in age; they had both been at the Black House for many years. How many, we weren't quite sure, losing track of the days then the months.

They were different personalities, but had been through a lot of the same stuff, being older and further along in their 'training'. Amy was definitely softer than Natasha. Lisa and I went to Natasha for fun and Amy for cuddles. I loved her simply and wholly. Sometimes Natasha would be snappish and Lisa would whine, but Amy was always ready with smiles and affection and seemed to have limitless patience.

CHAPTER FOURTEEN

Some nights there are big impromptu feasts. Everyone has to attend. The women dance, the men watch. The grown-ups drink a lot, smoke their sweet-smelling joints, and Carillo moves through them like a god amongst mortals. Blue can't remember the last one. They seem to coincide with periods where the adults around them are generally easier on the kids, but she's learned the hard way not to let her guard down. Not to think she's safe. If she sees one of the Aunts coming towards her, she looks at the ground quickly, as Amy has told her to do. She understands now that the less attention she draws to herself, the better.

There aren't many men there but the ones that are look at her with an intensity that makes her stomach roil. They all know Amy and Natasha. Carillo himself singles Natasha out all the time and it isn't unusual to see her walking around the grounds with him of an evening.

Blue can't work out if this is a good thing or a bad thing. She understands that Carillo somehow favours Natasha and, as a result, their dorm gets certain compensations others don't. Brodie, for example, is allowed to visit his sister and tag along with the four girls, whereas the other boys really only interact with each other and the men until they hit thirteen.

At that age, plans are made for their futures. Blue has heard Amy and Natasha whispering about some of the boys and understands vaguely that eventually they are to be paired up, and off into new dwellings. Into the barn itself with the

72

other adults. The most important thing at the Black House is to keep everything going. Keep the community not just alive, but also growing.

Blue thinks Carillo has lots of children; the Aunts are often pregnant. A girl barely older than Natasha has just been 'married' to one of the boys. They were at the last feast together. No longer sitting with the children as they had previously, but grouped with the men and the Aunts now.

The girl – whose name Blue can't remember – had a softly swelling belly at the meal, concealed under her white, floaty dress. If Blue hadn't heard Amy and Natasha commenting in furious whispers, she wouldn't have noticed. Now, she is huge, blowing up, and it makes her seem oddly younger. A child's face, thin arms and legs and the full, ripe middle of a woman. Blue knows intrinsically that these are the things Amy and Natasha fear, but she doesn't understand them. Not really.

Blue wakes up one morning thinking about that night, the last feast. Not because of any particular interest in the pregnant girl, but because she is hungry. Her belly hurts with it. It's a hollow feeling and when she runs a cold hand over her stomach, it's hard, full of air. Things aren't good. Natasha and Amy are gone most nights now and come back tired and pale-faced. Amy climbing into bed sometimes without even speaking. Natasha glazed and distant.

The grown-ups are busy and the children haven't been fed for almost twenty-four hours. Lisa had cried last night and Blue had shushed her, telling her that Amy and Natasha would be back soon enough and bring something. But hey still aren't there.

The alarm had sounded, long and foreboding. Making any chance of staying asleep impossible. By the time it stops, it's been going off every five minutes for the past two hours. Blue wonders if the sound of it will ever stop ringing in her head. A phantom noisy call to . . . what? Nothing. They've been woken but not summoned to do anything. Be anywhere. Lisa is crying again and even though she's older than Blue, with the others gone, Blue feels she must do something. She tells Lisa she's going to find food. Lisa doesn't respond, doesn't even turn her head.

Blue pulls on jeans and her raggedy grey sweater. It's what all of the children wear. Day in, day out. They have two sets, often ill-fitting. She remembers her mum making her tie-dyed clothes that came out in swirly pinks and blues. She'd showed Blue how and together they'd wrapped white T-shirts with rubber bands and sunk them into vibrant, dark tubs of dye. She pushes this memory away. It is too painful to hold on to and she replaces it with her mother's cool, blank face. With Natasha's bruises the morning after Blue used the term "mummy". She feels herself steeling. Her insides turning from soft, bruisable things to hard, bulletproof metal.

It is a sunny day. Almost warm but not quite there yet. Blue likes the brightness and the leaves on the trees, turning now from green to golds and burnt oranges and browns. Her stomach tremors. Winter is coming. Winters here are harsh and unforgiving. There is no heating in the dormitories and loud five o'clock starts occur in the pitch-black.

The thought of what is coming steals any joy from the moment and she scowls at the leaves now. Pretty they might be, and autumn with her dressed-up low sunshine. Mocking her.

She feels that swell pressing inside like it's pushing the sides of her head. It isn't fair.

None of this.

Amy and Natasha being gone so long.

That girl with her growing stomach and the terrified look on her face. The boy, a man now, who she follows around, taking careful steps behind him. In his shadow as if she no longer exists.

The pain in Blue's stomach isn't fair. Lisa sobbing isn't fair. And yet it is all so.

74

She's thought more than once about just walking as far from here as she can. They've talked about it, the four girls, on days like this.

They've taken walks in each direction when the Aunts are too distracted to notice them. All they've ever found is nothing.

Confusing trees and tracks in the woods. Miles and miles of them.

Besides, what waits out there is worse than what's housed here. Isn't it?

She is far from her dorm now but still on Black House land, which as far as she can tell is never-ending. She reaches the food stores and takes a deep breath, looking furtively each way. This is where the adult dorms are, but they don't all rise at five like the children do. All clear, she forces her feet forward, her hand clutching at the chilled metal handle to the store, she twists and the door opens . . .

The first thing that strikes her is the sheer array of foods. More diverse than she's eaten in most of her time here. Enough for a feast every day. At the back of the large, slightly cooled room are several huge freezers. But she is not concerned with them. She sees packs and packs of biscuits. So many they could last a lifetime.

She means to only grab a few packs, shove them under her jumper and head back to her dorm. But as she picks up the first one, she can't help herself and her hand opens the first box. She fumbles with the plastic and manages to grip a cookie. By the time it reaches her mouth she is almost salivating. She eats fast, knowing from experience that her belly will cramp in protest but she's too hungry, too excited by this unexpected treat to care.

She eats one, two, starts on the third and is so engrossed that she fails to hear the door creaking open. But she does hear the gasp behind her and spins, dropping the packet and the biscuit from her hand. It smashes to the floor and she lets out a single, dry sob.

But it's only Amy.

Blue is so overcome to see her, so pleased as she steps over the crumbs, her relief intense, throwing herself into the girl's arms. Amy shushes her and murmurs, 'Blue, what are you doing?'

She looks up, shame-faced. 'I was so hungry. We were . . .'

Amy bends down. 'I'm coming. Natasha is coming. We'll bring food, OK? Go. I'll clean this up.'

Blue nods, and she feels dreadful.

The two girls get as far as the store door before rushing smack into someone else. A woman in a white dress. One of the Aunts, who looks down at Blue and levelly at Amy, who is tall for her age, and growing more so each day. Icy fear creeps its way down Blue's spine.

Immediately Amy says, 'It was me.'

They're banished back to the dorm. Blue stays clasped in Amy's arms, the two girls curled up on one bed. Her heart beats a frantic tattoo in her chest and she plays out how else that scene might have gone. How it should have gone.

In that version she's brave. Braver than she really is, and she steps out from behind Amy and tells the truth. That it was her idea to steal the biscuits.

But she's not brave and now they are here in the midst of the worst part of their punishment: the waiting.

Blue sleeps on and off. Hears Natasha come back in. She brings food with her, which she shares amongst the four girls. Blue doesn't eat. The biscuits she'd managed to cram into her mouth sit like hard balls of molten lava in her stomach. A reminder of her wrongdoing, and the punishment still to come.

When evening arrives, an Aunt knocks at the door and tells the girls to come out into the courtyard. Blue whimpers. Natasha and Amy exchange a look and it is Natasha who kneels down to Blue's level and says, 'No matter what happens, you keep your mouth shut, OK?'

'But Amy . . .'

Amy takes her hand, smiles down at her. 'Blue, whatever they do to me, I can take it. OK?'

Blue shakes her head. It isn't right. She should step forward.

Amy leans down now and says, 'Blue, you will not say anything. If you do, it will hurt me a lot more than anything they can do to me.' She presses a hand to her chest. 'In here.'

Blue nods but is unsure and more than anything – frightened.

They make their way out and stand with the crowd that has formed around the large black barn. The dream project of a maniac.

Blue rarely sees Carillo, but when she does her insides always feel jingly-jangly. He looks so kind, so soft. His voice is smooth and silky, like butter. Tonight, Blue thinks, he looks especially benign. Sad, even.

He calls Amy forward, along with the Aunt who had caught them in the act. The Aunt speaks in a voice empty of emotion, giving her account of what happened. Amy agrees with it. Carillo steps forward, an arm slung over Amy's shoulders now.

'Stealing from our stores is stealing from us all. And this girl, almost a woman, dragged a younger child into it with her. Imagine that, taking an infant along to your crime.'

Blue is crying, her hand stuffed in her mouth. Natasha has her held back, her firm fingers digging into the little girl's shoulders.

Carillo steps back, beckons to another woman. Blue realises with horror that it is Amy's own mother.

She forces herself to watch the woman, blank-faced and methodical, dole out Carillo's sanctioned terror on the thin, adolescent frame of her daughter. Even as Natasha tries to bury Blue and Lisa's faces into her body. Blue can't look away. Her body reacts to every one of the blows that should have been hers.

Amy's own mother.

Blue searches the crowd for hers. She is there, stood in a long line of Aunts. Watching impassively.

Amy's mother is dishevelled by the time she's finished. Blood from the girl she had borne on her hands which delivered the brutality, specks on her dress.

Carillo steps forward. 'Enough.'

Amy's mother steps back, her face settling back to blank as she stares impassively at Amy, a crumpled heap on the ground.

The men move to stand behind Carillo in dark, demented choreography. They are dressed casually, individually, in stark contrast to the Aunts who, like Carillo, could also pass for benevolent at first glance. A row of pretty young women.

Amy's mother joins them now. A messy smudge at the end of the line. The new Aunt – the pregnant girl – is the only one whose face shows anything at all. Blue can see that she is trying not to look at Amy, trying to stay focused, but she sees the girl's hand reach gently under her bump and a tremor on her lips that doesn't quite escape.

Everyone else – including the children of varying ages, who comprise most of the crowd – stays where they are. Blue looks over to the boys and catches Brodie's eyes. They are damp and wide and reflect the desperation in her own heart. Only the babies and toddlers are spared from these terrible events, though Blue notices there are fewer of them than last time everyone was gathered. Fewer adults, too, though she'd be hard pushed to name any of them. She has been forced to attend every punishment service since she arrived. She never gets used to them, in the same way she never gets used to watching hours of awful, violent footage. She is always horrified by their violence and public nature. Occasionally a punishment is mild, but more often unspeakably brutal. And they are always accompanied by rank fear. The fear of not knowing, and terrible relief once they're done.

Carillo goes to Amy's mother, leans down, picks up her hand and kisses it. She beams at him. Shudders of hatred ripple through Blue. She glances again at her own mother and feels them grow.

She shuts her eyes and thinks, not for the first time, that this life is unliveable. That quiet death would be better than the long agonising howl she finds herself in here. What good is her anger? An impotent rage she can do nothing about, because she is just a little girl, after all, and the people, the person, who should be taking care of her, isn't doing that now.

Carillo addresses the assembled crowd. The Aunts look at him with rapt attention. The men nod as he says things that Blue only half hears, her head buzzing with so much of everything that eventually the noise becomes a kind of droning numbness. She hears snippets about greater good, community and everyone being one. Adults clap, nod and smile. Their devoted faces turned upon him as though he is a warm sun on their skin.

All whilst Amy's crumpled, bloody form lies prone on the floor at their feet.

CHAPTER FIFTEEN

I sit on my sofa. I say aloud, 'You are here; this is now.' But I feel like I might throw up. Or as though I might crumble from it all. Any recollection of *her* always brings with it a sharp and stabbing pain. This memory that has never fully left me bites with sharp and hungry teeth.

Amy – a crumpled heap on the floor and the adults standing around watching while the woman who gave birth to her battered her down. There was no use in fighting back. Others had tried, and the result was a pile-on with consequences far worse than a beating from a single person. The adults often became wild on those nights, where boundaries were gradually pushed over the years until finally, they ceased to be. Things that were taboo became normal.

Beating your child.

Putting her on the pill so the madman you were in love with could train her up, prepare her for – if she was lucky – marriage to a boy her own age. If she was not, for so much worse.

These weren't the sort of things that could happen straight away. There was a slow and long erosion of trust and decency before they got to that stage. Madness takes time to nurture and come to full fruition. That's what they were – mad. What I perhaps might have become, too.

Completely, totally mad.

It was a strange place, a terrible place, but it probably hadn't started out that way and I still hold on to some of the behaviours I learned there. I'm still a vegetarian, for example. After all the footage of abattoirs, I can't imagine ever wanting to eat flesh again.

Not everything we were taught was necessarily bad, and Carillo hadn't initially intended for the Black House to become what it did. Surely no one ever hopes for disaster. But maybe I'm imbuing him with qualities he never had. Maybe destruction and death was everything he ever wished for, though I suspect a lifetime behind bars wasn't his ultimate goal. He was a master manipulator and, even if his intentions were honourable to begin with, his love of power, greed and lust ruined everything in the end.

Natasha was just thirteen when he decided she'd make a better 'bride' than her mother. By the time these decisions were being made, we were completely separate from the rest of society and all of the norms that went with it. We were one man with a big ego and a ragtag crew of damaged souls with vulnerable children in tow.

We were an accident waiting to happen.

Who knows how things might have played out if not for the fire? Maybe I'd have hit eighteen and left of my own accord. But not before the damage was really done. Not before I'd been trained to be someone's 'bride'.

I'm sorry that my mum died. I'm sorry for what she became and that she lost herself.

But that fire saved me.

Natasha had been part of the Black House since she was four. Amy since she was five or six, she was never sure At least two of the children, older than me, were thought to be Carillo's. Certainly there were babies that came later who were. The girl in the white dress whose name still escaped me.

I had arrived after five years of life, a lot of which I remembered. I knew there was something else out there, though with each day that passed, that something became flimsier, more opaque, less real. The world shrunk to a tiny, tiny thing.

The Black House. The people in it.

As I slide into sleep in my warm flat, miles and miles from the cold dankness of the Black House, my mind is filled with fuzzy memories of Amy and now Pen's little arms around my neck. Me reading to her as Amy had to me. I feel a swell of sorrow for the girl who never got a story read to her. Who never got tucked in at night. Who never made it to adulthood.

CHAPTER SIXTEEN

The next day after school is our supermarket trip. I am absolutely dreading it and relayed as much to Isaac as I sat in the shop talking about Pen. I found I had more good things to say than I'd expected to. He laughed at me and pointed out that he shared my hatred for pretty much all shops bar Planet Pop.

He said, 'If I had to shop for kids, I'd definitely do it online.'

I told him, 'She's adamant we have to go.' Then added, 'You only ever buy coffee anyway.'

He nodded, grinning. 'Simple tastes, Blue.'

One of the few bonuses of insomnia is that I usually do my food shopping when most other people are asleep. Just me, the odd shift worker, a few bored assistants on the tills and the shelf stackers. There is an unspoken rule amongst us all that small talk must be kept to minimum.

When I arrive now with Pen still in her school uniform, the place is absolutely heaving. She is entirely unperturbed, and beckons to me for a pound. She gets a trolley that's far too big and we make our way in. The lights are as awful and fluorescent as they always are, but accompanying them now is a cacophony of noise. People talking, children running around. More staff than seems to make sense until we wander past the awful-looking queues and I think they could probably do with a few more.

It's bedlam.

Pen worms her way in and out of various aisles. Picking up, squeezing and discarding fruits and vegetables. I let her choose what we get, aware that not much is adding up to proper meals as such, and wondering if I'm finally going to have to learn how to cook. As she throws in a multi pack of crisps, I suggest that we ought to get something a bit healthier. She sighs but makes her way back to the fresh produce section, asking me, 'What do you like?'

I shrug.

She rolls her eyes. 'Just like Mummy.'

'What do you mean?'

'She never cared what she ate either. Like, she fussed about my food all the time. Vegetables this and that, made us grow our own – that's why we had the allotment – but I always thought she probably wouldn't bother if it wasn't for me.'

My heart does a little chug at that information. I ask, 'Was she a good cook?' Genuinely curious as to what my old friend may have learnt to do.

Pen laughs with a snort. 'Oh my God no. She was bad.' Adding, 'But she did try. I'm good at food tech so I did a lot of the cooking.' She looks up at me. 'I taught her some things I learned at school.'

I nod. 'That's nice.'

She smiles. 'Yeah it was. She made it fun.'

She pauses then, her face more serious. People push around us. I need to say something. I should say something. 'I remember her being fun.'

Pen beams at me and relief pours in. 'She really was.'

At the till the woman tries to make small talk and I look at her blankly, eventually turning away and packing the bags with the insane amount of food from the trolley. Pen takes over and has the woman chuckling within seconds.

As we escape from the shop, calling a cab to help us home with all our bags, Pen says, 'You were a bit rude.'

'What?'

'To the woman, in there.'

I frown. 'I don't know her.'

Pen shrugs. 'Still.'

I don't know what to say to that and am relieved when the cab pulls up and we load up the boot of the car. Pen chats away to the driver, who tells her all about his children, who are at various universities, studying complicated-sounding subjects. As we get out, Pen eyes me pointedly. I pause, turn to the driver and say, 'Thank you.'

We take the bags up in two trips. As we go, she says, 'There, that wasn't so hard was it?' I open my mouth, shut it. She's looking at me intently. She says, 'Are you cross?'

'No.' I pause. 'I don't know. I've never thought of myself as rude. Just quiet.'

Pen sighs. 'Sorry. I'm blunt. Mummy always said it's better to speak plainly.' She shrugs. 'But I can be a bit too blunt.'

She is precocious, I suppose. But right now as she looks at me all I see is a little girl who's just lost her mother, her partner in the world. I give her shoulder a quick squeeze and say, 'You're fine. I'm just used to being by myself.'

She nods.

I ask, 'Natasha was a good mum, huh?'

She stares at me, her eyes glassy, and there is a long silence. Where my words stretch out between us. Words I shouldn't have said, because what good can they do? Pen doesn't answer. Instead: 'I think I'll go and watch TV in my room.'

I think about following her. But in the end, I settle for unpacking the bags, feeling again that wave of anger at my old friend. And also confusion. She was a good mother. She was fun. She had accrued wealth, made a life for herself far more successful than the one I had. Or Lisa had.

Why would she have done this?

I read Pen the rest of the comic book that evening, skipping over a few swear words.

She murmurs, 'I can read, you know.'

And I say, 'Maybe not the most suitable choice.'

She shrugs. 'I like her though.'

I smile at that. 'Me too.'

She asks, 'Your sketches are like these right?'

'Maybe a bit.' I say, 'I do tie-ins for big franchises.' Something I only did because Isaac had nagged and banged on at me about it.

'Will you do your own?'

'Maybe one day.' I add, 'I'm working on something.'

'A girl?'

I nod. She says, 'I bet she'll be cool.'

I think of the vague idea I have for a character and I smile. 'I hope so.'

She does that hug thing again and: 'Night.'

I figure I'm forgiven for my previous clumsiness.

After she goes to bed, I open my laptop and email the journalist back to ask what information they're looking for on Natasha.

He responds in seconds. *'Anything. Her death seems odd to me.'*

'Odd?'

'To go out like that.'

I close the chat and mark myself offline.

Like that.

The faint crackle and fizz. The smoke rising. The smell of burning flesh. I run my left hand over my right arm, feeling the uneven ridges.

It hurts to be burnt. And it marks you for life.

Lucky.

That's how the papers described us. Me, in particular. Protected by anonymity as we were, there were still some details that made it into the press. That a little girl aged ten was being treated in a local hospital, having suffered third-degree burns on her arm.

I snatch my hand away.

He's right. The journalist. And it is niggling at my mind. Even more so, seeing the wonderful job she's done with Pen. How can the two things align? Why wouldn't she want to stick around?

I think of DI Grafton's frown. *'The remains are hard to ID . . .'*

I google Natasha Dryden. The first thing that comes up is her LinkedIn profile. A picture of her fills the screen and my breath catches in my throat.

Still beautiful. Her slanted almond eyes stare out at me. Her hair is different. Highlighted to make it even fairer and certainly a haircut that cost some money. Everything about the photo screams success.

And yet she sat down in a shed. Set a fire.

She escaped Hell, only to go right on back.

I make a note of her workplace then google that, too. She doesn't have a Facebook profile, but she does have a public Twitter account. Various light-hearted jokes between her and a guy called Gareth Barnes. I make a note of his name. Google him. He does have Facebook and though most of it is set to private, some of his photos are public. There are a few of both of them, photographed with a larger group. They work for the same company.

My DMs ping. The journalist.

'Are you there? Can we talk?'

I ignore it.

My phone rings. It's Isaac.

I pick up. 'Hey.'

'All OK there?'

'Yes. Well, kind of. I was just wondering about stuff.'

'Like?'

'Why she'd do this.'

'We may never know her reasons.'

'I guess.'

'You're not sure?'

'No. Like, Lisa I got that. Wasn't surprised, you know.'

Isaac pauses. I can hear him lighting a cigarette. 'This feels different, huh?'

I sigh. 'You should see her house and the school this kid is at. It's like a mini Hogwarts but in Central London.'

'Must cost a fortune.'

'Right.'

'People can have money and still be miserable.' He adds, 'Look at me.'

I find myself grinning. 'Ha. But you enjoy your misery.'

'That is true.'

'Pen is a good kid too, and it sounds like Natasha was a good mother.'

He inhales and I hear the crackle of the cherry of his cigarette. 'You think something pushed her to do it?'

'Yes. Maybe. I don't know.' There is a pause. 'Maybe not something, maybe someone?' And it's out there before the thought fully formulates.

'Maybe.'

And I feel a little quiver of fear then.

He says, 'Maybe someone broke her heart, maybe

88

someone made her angry. Maybe she never really got over everything that life threw at her.'

I say, 'Perhaps.'

He laughs. 'You're still not convinced?'

'No. I'm not.'

He says, 'You might never know.' His voice is gentle, but the words still sting. I hate not knowing. I hate secrecy.

I tell him, 'I need to find out.'

CHAPTER SEVENTEEN

I walk Pen to school on our third morning together. I'm surprised to find we have naturally fallen into a routine of sorts already. I've understood the power of that ever since I left school and started working at Planet Pop. No matter how tired I am, I love starting my day with purpose. My routine is so different to the way things were at the Black House. Each day there began at five, but of course what occurred during the waking hours was down to the whim of a madman. Oftentimes we'd be left to our own devices and whilst many kids may have longed for such freedoms, the reality isn't so great. Boredom is still my number-one enemy. I thrive on routine and being busy.

And now my day has new punctuation in the form of the school run. For Pen's first two nights with me, I'd hardly slept at all. Every time I drifted off, I'd wake with a start and go in to check on her. Each time she was sleeping soundly, eyelashes fluttering on her cheeks, hair fanned out on the pillow. Last night, I was surprised to find that I'd drifted off in my bed around ten and had woken up at five. The often-elusive full night's sleep.

I ask Pen on the way to school whether Natasha liked her job. Pen says, 'Oh yes, loved it. And she was good at it. She wasn't just an estate agent, you know.'

I smile at that, can almost hear Natasha speaking through her daughter. But I say, 'No?'

'No. She helped super rich people build property portfolios.'

'Not the same thing at all.'

She nods sagely and I find I'm still smiling as I wave goodbye to her at the school gate.

I walk from there to the tube. Travelling through the rush hour throng, pressed too close to other people's bodies, and gasping for air.

Isaac is fairly casual about my hours at Planet Pop and though I like to think the place wouldn't function without me, I suspect that's not entirely true. I message him and Oren now to check if it's OK if I'm in a bit later. I get two thumbs up. I get off and walk to Mayfair and the office listed as Natasha's workplace. It is an old townhouse with a gleaming brass plaque by a large front door. I ring the bell and a tinkly voice says, 'Can I help?'

I pause then.

'Hello . . .?'

'I'm here about an employee. Well, an ex-employee.'

'OK?'

'Natasha Dryden.'

'Oh gosh, come in. Come in.'

The buzzer goes and I push the door open, stepping into a carpeted hallway. It's pretty in here, casual and homely. The woman who I assume buzzed me in is behind a wide table, white with ornate legs. She's in dark jeans and a patterned, floaty blouse. She looks polished but relaxed. This is money at its most comfortable.

Her face is screwed up in a perfect expression of unquiet. And she's standing, waving to an armchair.

'Without meaning to be rude, you are?'

'An old friend.' She's still standing, eyes narrowed. I add, 'I have custody of Pen.'

She sinks into a chair opposite mine then, hand to her chest, long, well-manicured fingers pressing into the sheer fabric, leaving small imprints as she moves the hand away. Dramatic gesture complete. 'Oh God. We'd all wondered what had happened to Pen. Is she well? As much as you could expect, anyway?'

'She's OK. I think. I mean I don't have kids of my own, but she seems fine.'

The hand goes back to the chest and now her face shows something else. Curiosity. I wriggle uncomfortably, looking round the large waiting area.

'Pen says you do property portfolios?'

The woman nods. 'Super houses for the super-rich.' Then grins. 'Gareth started it up, oh fifteen years ago now. He'd worked with Natasha at Baxter's and headhunted her to come here.'

I raise an eyebrow. 'That's quite a step up.'

She looks at me blankly.

I say, 'From Baxter's to this.'

'Oh I see. Well Gareth's dad was in property but they had some falling-out about I don't know what. Anyway the upshot of it was that Gareth had to go out and get a taste of the real world.'

'By slumming it at Baxter's?'

She laughs, that tinkly sound again, which I already find grating. 'Yes I suppose.'

'Lucky break for Natasha then.'

She nods. 'Yes, though she had already started investing in property herself. Purchased a few little places in what were then deemed bad areas. Kept hold of them. Worth a fortune now. Very savvy.'

Having seen her financial affairs in close detail, I can't argue with that.

'Is it a big company?' I ask.

'Here?'

Why on earth would I be asking her about somewhere else? I smile and nod, gritting my teeth.

'No, not really. Seven of us. Well, five now.'

'Oh?'

She nods. 'Ya-ha. Just before Natasha . . . you know . . . another girl left. Lyndsey.'

'Oh.'

'Awful for Gareth, losing two of his best team members, all of his sales team. I mean not as awful as . . . God, sorry.'

'It's OK. Don't be.'

'It's hard to know what to say.'

'Were you close?'

'To Tasha?' Tasha. I try that out and I think it works for her. Better than Natasha even. Tasha.

'Yes.'

'I mean we got along fine. She was super fun, but we weren't like BFFs. She was close to Lyndsey and Gareth.'

'Can I speak to either of them?'

She shakes her head. 'Well, Gareth yes, but not right now. Everyone's away until . . .' She stands, leaning across the desk and opening a large paper diary. 'Thursday.'

'OK I'll come in then. And do you have contact details for Lyndsey?'

She frowns. 'Well that's another thing – she's gone travelling. Like backpacking or something.'

'Oh.'

'I know right, like midlife crisis or what!'

She snort-laughs and I smile. 'Do you know where exactly?'

She shakes her head. 'No, here's the details we have.' She pulls out a business card with Lyndsey Dunmore's phone number, email address and links to various social media. She shrugs. 'You might be able to track her down. If you do, let her know Gareth's still pretty pissed.'

My phone rings. It's DI Grafton. She asks how I am and I say, 'Fine.'

'Are you sure?'

'Yes.'

'And Pen?'

I find I'm smiling then as I tell her about the little girl. 'She even likes comic books and records.'

'Well it's probably a much cooler job than other parents have.'

I think about that. I love Planet Pop and I love Isaac, too. I often weigh my life in the absence of things. No family. No background that I can speak freely about. Oftentimes no sleep. But the life I've built has welcomed this little girl into it; it's fun. Maybe I *am* cooler than the mums at her school, who I've noticed have identical highlights and far-too-big cars, unnecessary for Central London. Maybe I, with my worn, soft leather jacket, clumpy boots and tattoos, am a breath of fresh air for Pen. Maybe I'm just what she needs, like Isaac was just what I needed.

I say, 'Yeah I guess.' But I'm pleased at the thought of it. DI Grafton says, 'Dee Salisbury has been in contact.'

It takes me a while to catch up. 'Oh, from social services?'

'Yes. She wanted me to ask if you were happy to keep her as your key worker.' That surprises me. My experience of the care system and key workers and social workers and all the types of people who were in my life in an official capacity had been a severe lack of choice.

I frown into the receiver. 'I'm not super psyched at anyone poking their noses into my life, obviously.'

'Well no. But honestly she's there to help and you might need it.' I might. That's true. As if reading my mind, she says, 'Dee's definitely one of the good ones. Blue?'

'Yes. No, it's fine. I actually thought she was all right.' I add, 'It's nice to be asked.'

DI Grafton says, 'Yes. She figured if I asked, you'd feel OK saying no if you hadn't warmed to her and we could assign someone else.' You couldn't get much fairer. DI Grafton adds, 'I think Pen likes her, too.'

I smile. 'Pen likes everyone. Even Isaac.'

Grafton laughs. 'He's not as fierce as he looks.'

'Nope.'

'Dee wants to come and visit you both after school today if possible?'

It's one of the few days when Pen has nothing on. So despite the fact that I would really rather not I say, 'Fine.'

CHAPTER EIGHTEEN

Annie hangs up the phone. If she wasn't very much mistaken, Blue's voice had perked up when she'd talked about Pen. That's a good start. Better than she'd hoped for.

There are so many things about this case bothering Annie, she doesn't know where to begin. But she has found that she likes the young woman at the centre of it. Blue's background is extraordinary and yet she'd carved out a life for herself. But so had Natasha Dryden, which is what bothers Annie the most.

Her dramatic means of death, the links to a cult. Not just any cult, either. But the Black House was a far cry from most other cults, which were often fairly benign. The suicides were devastating but just as bad had been the years of abuse inflicted on mainly the women and children who had resided there. The abuse of children, carried out by their own mothers, and then eventually by Carillo, who sexually abused female minors for his entire time as 'leader'.

He'd started small. His first 'victim' was Sienna Dryden. But he'd been married before to a girl of just sixteen and the police had been called out to him and his wife not infrequently. Eventually he'd been the one who filed for divorce, on the grounds she couldn't have children.

Annie sighs, slides her phone into her pocket. She's at Natasha's dentist, having what is about to become a full-blown argument about the dead woman's missing dental records. She knows it's not the dentist's fault, nor her office manager, who seems genuinely baffled. Admin errors happen, computers fuck up. God knows, she struggles with her own back at the station, calling out IT at least once a week.

But the fact that there are currently no records for Natasha Dryden anywhere is making identifying the body very difficult, and adding to Annie's growing sense of unease about the whole sorry debacle.

The victim is the right size, right age. They have Natasha's carefully written will, complete with instructions for her solicitor to carry out a face-to-face meeting with Blue Sillitoe, indicating this *had* indeed been planned, in a scarily detailed, rational way. But the doc cannot pronounce formal ID until they have medical or dental records to match. Plus, now there's a query over whether the victim has ever given birth. Annie had managed to find Natasha's' hospital records for that though, and since Pen had been born via Caesarean and given the terrible state of a cremated body, that made some sense.

The office manager, visibly flustered now, her face red, tells Annie, 'I've never lost files before.'

'How many are missing?'

'A lot.' So not just Natasha's.

'And you've no idea what's happened?'

She shakes her head miserably. 'Please be assured I'm looking into it and we'll try and retrieve them any way we can.'

'Well, when you do,' Annie snaps, sliding her card over.

The poor woman nods and Annie backs down a little. 'It happens. Bloody computers, eh?'

The woman offers her a faint smile now.

Annie leaves, still frustrated. Still wanting what should have been a simple process done and dusted. This wasn't even supposed to be her case, but the call had come in and no one else had been available.

Now she feels responsible for Blue – God only knows why – and the kid.

She shoves an indigestion tablet into her mouth. She never should have been a copper. She simply isn't tough enough for it. She'd known it early on but figured she'd harden up with time. She never has though, and now look. Working overtime for a bloody suicide. Liaising with social services, and continuing to assist Dee Salisbury which she really doesn't have to do and could easily have passed to her sergeant.

The only saving grace is that because she is so married to her job, she's never done the family bit, which has made leaving Ian simple if nothing else. For her, anyway. He's rung twice in the past two days and she's ignored him both times. It has crossed her mind briefly that Isaac would be a good father, given how much Blue seems to rely on him, but she snuffs that thought out as quickly as it comes. She's heard him speak at meetings about his own children and he'd been a shitty dad in reality. Rock stars hardly ever make reliable parents or partners, she supposes. She blushes into the empty space of her car, mortified to find herself thinking of him again. Jesus Christ. Focus, Annie.

The job.

This blasted suicide.

Then she never needs to see Isaac again. If she needs a meeting, London is full of them. He attends the same three every week, which is kind of sad when you think about it. She compares his routine to the evening she has planned, which will likely consist of resisting the urge to call her dealer – of all people – and order a gram. She's done so well lately, too. Now isn't the time for a slip.

She makes a decision then and there that as soon as she gets the positive ID on Natasha Dryden, she'll allow herself a little R&R. Until then, no drugs, no booze. As much as she grumbles to herself about the hours spent going above and beyond, it isn't like she has much to go home to, anyway. She finds herself driving back to the station instead of her little flat.

CHAPTER NINETEEN

The girl at Natasha's company, whose name I hadn't even made a note of, had been perfectly sombre and obviously concerned. But I had seen something else in her eyes, too. Excitement. Back before I knew better, I'd entertained the idea of talking about my experiences at the Black House. I'd started my own research into the phenomena of cults. I'd bought a lot of paperbacks with lurid covers, watched some documentaries about cults, utopias, alternative communities. Then I'd become braver, more specific. None contained much information of use and I switched to the online communities, scouring forums for people talking specifically about the Black House, discussing it on Reddit threads, in Facebook groups, on podcasts. I found something I knew I couldn't be a part of.

Glee.

People are, of course, outraged by what happened there, but they are also fascinated. Like passing a car crash and being unable to avert your eyes. We were curiosos, us survivors. Artefacts from a disaster. Like the fossils of dinosaurs wiped out by who knew what.

We were an unruly gang of children emerging from hell. Ragtag, dirty little things who hadn't eaten dinner that night. Who hadn't gone up in the blaze that took everyone else. Who'd wandered the woods, traumatised, injured, wounded in ways we couldn't even begin to comprehend.

Me, Natasha, Lisa, Brodie and Sienna the Aunt.

Carillo left with the two other boys. Names were never released but seemingly their fate would have been similar to ours once the fucker was apprehended.

Care.

The barrage of society, school an alien concept let alone place. Then on into tricky adulthoods. I wondered often how they lived, the boys. I wondered how I did.

I check my DMs, take a deep breath and copy and paste the journalist's number from the message onto my keypad.

The relief when I get voicemail is overwhelming.

It's a sign. I'm not supposed to speak to him. What good can come of it? Curiosity killed the cat, right?

The research never got me anywhere good, anyway. I knew better than anyone that sometimes things had no rhyme or reason. They occurred, they were – just because.

Why is intangible, inexplicable.

I'd been over the whys so many times.

Why my mum?

Why me?

Why did Carillo pick her? Or us, I suppose.

Why Amy?

Why Lisa?

Why Natasha?

Why *not* me?

Those whys can build and build in your head like a swarm of disgusting, wretched, black, shit-eating flies. The buzz growing so intense it'll kill you.

Never mind why. Or even how. Just what's next.

When I reach the shop, Isaac is sitting behind the counter smoking and humming along to Mad Season, an album he plays on repeat. I look at him pointedly and he sighs, putting the cigarette out. Removing the ashtray and sliding it out of sight.

I tell him, 'It stinks in here.' And it does.

He says, 'No one's been in all morning.'

'That's not the point, is it? Unless you want to see this place closed down?'

He looks suitably castigated. I look in the diary and say, 'You have a meeting in half an hour?'

He nods, smiling now. 'You'll be OK here?'

'Keeps you out of my way.'

He laughs. 'Oren's due any minute.'

The door tinkles as if on cue and Oren comes in wrinkling his nose. 'Bloody stinks in here.'

'That's what I said.'

Isaac sighs. 'I've got a meeting. Make sure she behaves.' He points at me. I roll my eyes; glad the heroin addict is telling the kid who'd been out of prison less than a year to make sure I behave. For fuck's sake.

After he's gone, Mad Season finishes and I switch it for The Specials. Oren says, 'Sixty-five?' I shrug. We have a constant game going of attempting to guess Isaac's age, which is something of a mystery.

He grins. I smile back. He's a good-looking guy.

I say, 'I reckon he's been deeply pickled in vodka for such a large portion of his life, that he'll probably outlive us all.'

Oren grins. 'You might be right.'

I ask, 'How was your holiday?' His first with his girl-friend. He frowns and I laugh. 'That bad huh?'

He shrugs. Isaac makes a lot of jokes about Oren and I, but I had made it clear from the outset that I wasn't looking for a relationship. And I wasn't.

I dated in my twenties and found that it always got messy. Certainly getting involved with someone I worked with would be a big mistake. But I wasn't impervious to Oren's obvious charms, even if boyfriends weren't in my future. I also struggle with relationships with other women. So, most people, I suppose. I know the woman thing is my own mummy issues and fear of the Aunts, which I've never managed to shake. Obviously I know logically that the bad man behind all of my misery was exactly that – a man. Joseph Carillo. But my interactions had always been with the Aunts. My betrayal had been by my mother. In foster homes I never warmed to the mums, regarding them with guarded suspicion. It meant even when they were being nice, I was being a complete arsehole.

Oren's cool, but we are destined to be friends and nothing more. If anything, we are siblings, children of Planet Pop, and Isaac's habit of picking up waifs and strays. Besides, judging by his girlfriend who is shiny as hell looking at his Instagram photos, I'm not his type either.

He says, 'So Isaac tells me an old friend left you her kid in her will?' I laugh at the inappropriateness of it and he grins back.

'Yes.'

'Heavy.'

I shrug.

'What's she like?'

'OK.'

'You'll have to bring her in.'

I'm saved from anything else by what becomes a steady stream of customers, and before I know it, it's four o'clock and time for me to leave to collect the kid.

I have a voicemail from the journalist, and I'm shocked momentarily by a slight Welsh lilt. An accent I no longer have at all, having adopted the long flat vowels of London. By the time I listen to it I'm on my way to get Pen and feeling increasingly worried about the social services visit.

We are almost back at the flat when I tell Pen that Dee is coming and she looks up at me, outraged. 'I don't have to go back to that place, do I?'

'What place?'

'*The* place. The home, whatever you call it, with all the awful kids.'

I say, 'I'm sure they weren't awful, Pen.'

'They were – and scary.'

I can't argue with that. It's how I'd felt myself.

I say, 'You're not going back. You have a home. OK?'

She looks up at me. Nods.

Just seconds after we get in, the buzzer goes and I let Dee in. I am reminded as soon as she enters that I do actually like her. She says to Pen, 'Show me somewhere to sit, girl. My feet are killing me.'

Pen looks at me with a sort of surprised smile. I shrug and we head into the living room. Usually spotless, it is now comfortably filled with the detritus that Pen seems to leave in her wake. Her schoolbag is on the floor, some books in, some out; she had obviously forgotten to zip it. Since I'd gone straight from school to the shop, our breakfast stuff is still on the side. I hurry to it, swiping the bowls off and into the sink and rinsing my mug. Then I flick on the kettle and say, 'Can I get you a drink?'

I'm relieved when she says no, but Pen pipes up, 'Can I make a squash?'

'Sure.' I watch her spill sticky liquid on the side and then flood the glass in the sink. Making a racket while she goes.

I get a piece of kitchen roll and wipe up behind her, then I go and sit at the table. By this time Dee is happily cushioned on my sofa and she sighs. 'I've been on my feet all day it feels.'

'How come?'

'Lots of home visits. No point driving around London and I avoid the tube when I can.' I nod. I tend to do the same. It's one of the great bonuses of living in the city — you can walk and walk here and still remain in civilisation.

She says, 'So, I've come to see how you're both getting along.' She looks from one to the other of us, wrinkling her nose. 'Which is a bit weird, isn't it. But has to be done.'

She talks to Pen and the conversation is easy. After a while she suggests that Pen goes and plays while the adults have a chat. Pen rolls her eyes but does as she's asked.

Dee turns to me, face serious now and says, 'You OK?'

I nod. 'Yes actually.'

Dee says, 'She's a nice kid.'

'She is.'

'You've been into the school?'

'I have.'

Dee says, 'Has she mentioned her mother at all?'

I nod. 'A few times.'

Dee says, 'And how did she seem?'

I shrug. 'Confused, which is fair enough. I mean why *would* Natasha do this? It's very unlike her.'

Dee makes a clucking sound with her mouth. 'It's not easy to understand people's reasoning. Many children who grow up in that sort of environment . . .' She lets the words hang there between us. And I understand those people. I understand their reasons better than most; of course I do. But Dee didn't know Natasha. I think about telling her about the journalist, or maybe I should tell DI Grafton. But I'm not ready to do that yet. I don't even know if I'm going to speak to him.

Dee finishes up, says goodbye to Pen and leaves. I read a bit more from our chosen comic and she goes to sleep. I'm not so blessed with rest tonight though, and I sit awake, sketching, drinking endless cups of green tea and trying hard to imagine a scenario where Natasha just gave up. By morning I still don't have one.

CHAPTER TWENTY

NATASHA

My mother had me young.

That was mentioned often, as if it somehow excused things.

She'd been taken by Carillo when she was pregnant with my little brother, so it was thought.

Vulnerable.

Impressionable.

Not guilty.

A load of shit. I never gave her the benefit of the doubt, though I was urged to do so by many. My own brother included. There is freedom in forgiveness.

Ha.

No, thanks. Weakness, after all, is weakness. But I would attempt to entertain scenarios where I might have behaved as poorly as she did. They never felt realistic, though. I was tough. I was strong. I endured more than she ever had to, because of her. I was ninety-nine per cent certain I would never have behaved as she had. Never handed my own kin over for abuse, for what? Love? The day my daughter was born, I was certain – one hundred per cent, without a doubt – that I would never allow harm to come to her.

I loved her as much as I'd loved the little ones back then.

Maybe I even loved her a tiny bit more, or at least there was so much more hope attached to her. This little clean slate.

My little girls back then were damaged of course, as was I. No way for us not to be. But my baby, born of my own body, was fresh and untainted. Full of possibilities and goodness.

You are given something small and helpless to take care of, a living thing that relies on you. How do you behave? What choices do you make?

Nothing else matters.

No other job will ever be this important.

These are the things that define you.

The things at which my mother failed.

CHAPTER TWENTY-ONE

I drop Pen and go to the shop. Isaac and Oren are both in and the sudden silence that greets me lets me know they were talking about me. I feel my face burn as I hang my coat. More than anything I hate pity and certainly I don't want it from them. I can feel Isaac's gaze on me. Oren is trying to busy himself unpacking boxes.

Eventually I break the silence, snapping, 'Do I make good gossip?'

Isaac stares, impassive. Oren kind of freezes with records in hand, looking with more interest than is warranted at the display before him.

Isaac says, 'Too right. You've inherited a child for God's sake. There's nothing bigger to be talked about here today, is there.'

I laugh before I can stop myself and Oren looks from one to the other of us in relief. He's been the only one who's lasted here at Planet Pop, other than me. Isaac's other 'projects' either used again, leaving a tsunami of destruction in their wakes – the tills here had been raided more than once – or they moved on to something more suitable. But Oren seems to have got comfortable.

He gives me a tap on the arm now. 'We care about you, is all.'

I nod. He heads back to the stock room. I look at Isaac and say, 'He doesn't know . . . you know?' I shrug, face burning again, feigned nonchalance not even fooling me.

Isaac shakes his head. 'Blue, I would never betray your confidence.'

I nod, swallowing thickly. I know that, of course I do.

I'm about to apologise when he comes up and squeezes me to him.

'He's not stupid, but he knows when not to push, OK?'

'I know you wouldn't have said anything . . .'

I find it hard to put my feelings into words. I'd told Isaac about my life in stilted stuttering sections, between stacking and labelling vinyls, hanging posters, cashing up the till. He gave me space, let me speak and as I said the words, I had no idea that I had needed to hear my voice say them in order to make some semblance of sense. Isaac had said the right things when he felt he needed to. Most of the time he'd said nothing at all and at no point had he cack-handedly attempted to fix me. I knew that he didn't consider me broken and I think that is the real strong foundation of our friendship. One survivor to another. Isaac sees me as I see him.

I'd hated the group therapy sessions we'd been forced into after our 'rescue'. All wards of the state have to attend them. I also had to endure one-on-one as well. I'd feel poked at, prodded. Like someone was picking at my scarred arm, pulling open the wounds and dousing them in vinegar. One-on-one was preferable to group, but still awful. There were plenty of horror stories to be heard in the home. Terrible things had happened to children and every time I heard someone 'share', I'd feel that twinge. That awful fear that maybe just maybe, they'd been right at the Black House.

Imperfect though it was, worse things happened here it seemed. Outside.

That was before I knew the full extent of what had gone on in my childhood home though. Before the horrors became fully exposed. Leaving me sick to my stomach with rage, pain and worst of all, guilt. I'd been protected by my age from things Natasha, Amy and finally Lisa had endured. I'd been shielded. I'd got out 'in time' as various officials liked to put it.

In time for what, though?

That became the question that would keep me up in the early hours of the morning. My heart hammering, palms damp. Why me? Why had I been lucky? And why didn't I ever feel it?

It was afterwards that I found everything out. I was sat down by a busty woman with sharp features who was probably trying to be kind but stabbed me with her terrible words. Who told me my own origin story. One I never wanted. One I wished latterly I'd never found out, even as I knew I had to. I was always as sick as the secrets that pervaded my life. People need to know about themselves, though, even if it's a horror story. I assume it was decided by someone there that knowing would be best. But there is ignorance in bliss as only those carrying heavy secrets can attest.

I'd been hurt at the Black House, of course. My mother's rejection would have scarred me for life, no matter what. How can you rely on anyone when you can't rely on your parents? But plenty of people have that experience and they get over it. Get on. Besides, I'd had Amy and Natasha. What I learnt about what happened when they were taken away hurt more than anything else. That they had never said was what stung the most. That and the fact Natasha got me out in time. What I'd hated more than anything was that I lived only half a truth, I didn't know the full story. Not only were the adults lying, so were the girls I'd considered my sisters. For all of the right reasons, I'm sure. But I didn't feel saved, I felt guilty.

I'm about to tell Isaac about the journalist when the bell to the shop goes and customers come in. I've decided to wait until I have a chance to speak to Natasha's boss, Gareth, before I pursue any more information with the journalist, so it's not urgent. It just might put an end to my nagging curiosity. Perhaps Gareth will tell me that Natasha hadn't been herself, had been off for weeks and that he'd known this was coming. Perhaps he will reveal a reason, if not solid at least plausible, as to why Natasha would pull the plug on what seemed to be a perfect life. Not even in an all-things-considered way. Perfect because motherhood, money and a successful career was more than some people could ever hope for. More than some ever achieved. If it's what you wanted. Maybe there would be some light shed on why on earth Natasha would have survived that house of horrors, carved herself out a place in the world, given life to another human being and chosen now to give in.

My mobile rings. Isaac looks up at me.

'Hello.'

'Ms Sillitoe?'

'Blue.'

'Mrs Williams here.'

Pen's teacher. My heart hammers, 'Is Pen . . .?'

'Penelope's fine. But she has been causing some trouble, I'm afraid. We need you to come in.'

I think about calling Dee. I'll have to. It's part of the protocol of paperwork I had brushed through last night. Any incidents relating to school ought to be told.

I say I'm on my way, hang up and tell Isaac, 'Pen's school.'

He frowns. 'Is she all right?'

'Yes, but she's been causing trouble, according to the head.'

He's already getting his coat and putting his arms in, yelling to Oren to keep an eye on things.

I have no time to protest and realise, as he bundles me into his rickety little car, that I'm glad of his company.

CHAPTER TWENTY-TWO

Blue is tired. Wretchedly, awfully exhausted, and yet she can't seem to stay asleep for more than an hour at night. It's the constant disturbances. The Aunts who knock and take away Amy, Natasha, and last night Lisa, too.

Amy has been limping since her mother beat her. Her leg, tender with each step, may well have been broken. Still, she had to carry on, do her chores. Attend to Carillo and his mates. The men are getting lairier, Blue thinks. Whilst the Aunts and girls scurry about the place with their heads down now. She sees the grown ones reaching pawing hands out towards Natasha and Amy. In front of everyone. She wonders how much worse it is when they're in private. In the inky black middle of the night when the older girls are summoned and taken away. Returning in the early hours or well into the following day.

Natasha with hard, squared shoulders and Amy, quiet now, too quiet. Slowly disintegrating before Blue's very eyes.

And she doesn't know what to do.

How to stop it.

And she can't help but think that it was in some way her fault. That day in the food store plays in her mind on repeat.

Should have been bigger, better, braver.

It's been a hard winter. Long and endless.

More people have left, recently.

Blue has noticed that. The latest one to go was the girl with the belly full of baby.

Blue doesn't know where she's gone, what has happened to her. But she is glad.

The boy who was her husband according to Carillo, is sullen and moody. Blue has seen him lash out more than once at Amy as he passes. The older men, nudging each other, cajoling and egging him on.

Cruelty seems to be at an all-time high and each day Blue feels she is walking on eggshells. Head down, eyes glued to the floor, trying desperately to not be seen. She's found a hiding place between some of the dorms, one of them now mostly empty, and she's taken to stashing herself there whatever the weather, crouched down under the shallow cover of a white peaked ledge.

Today she is there. An escape from the unbearable sadness of Amy and Lisa who are curled up together in Amy's bed. Mourning secrets which Blue isn't privy to. She sits. Rain is coming down, but it is fine and thin. She'll be damp by the time she goes back, but not wretchedly soaked to the skin.

She hears footsteps, the breaking of twigs, leaves crunching beneath someone's tread and she leaps up, looking wildly each way. Trying to work out where she can run.

But it's only Brodie, his pale face looking around the side of the building. Blue is awash with relief first, but then she is unsure, because the division between boys and girls is growing and she hasn't seen him for a few weeks now.

He presses a finger to his lips and beckons her to him. She goes, following him out into the rain, getting heavier now. She places her feet where his have just been and they move towards the edge of the woods, where she pauses. Blue doesn't like it in there, is scared of its sameness. Of getting lost as she and the girls had before on their half-hearted attempts to find a way out.

He whispers, 'Come on. It's fine.' And takes her hand in his.

His hand is surprisingly warm and as they walk silently under the canopy of skeletal trees, she starts to feel slightly less scared.

Each step away from there brings small relief, but relief nonetheless. The Black House has a certain feel to it. Oppressive and suffocating.

Eventually they reach a river, which seems to spit a chill up with it. Brodie points to a set of rocks in the water and asks her, 'Can you make it across?'

She shrugs, frightened again but not wanting to admit that to him. She needs to be brave.

He says, 'Just step behind me OK?'

He goes and she forces herself to follow.

She finds she is holding her breath as she steps off at the other side and she lets it go in one long release.

He says, 'Come on.'

And she follows him into an opening on the other side.

It is rock face. Grey and bland and as they step in, she doesn't like it, pausing. There is little room to either side, barely any over her head.

He says, 'It's only for a minute.' And takes her hand again.

One second, two, three, thirty, she is unsure. She's on the brink of turning around when they step out into a large, open area. Light spills in from the other side where there must be a break in the rock, but above their heads is a long and wide roof of sorts. It's quite warm here and the light seems to glint and twinkle, making starred patterns on the walls.

It is beautiful and Blue stands still for a moment, taking it all in. When she looks again at Brodie, wide-eyed, he is smiling.

He tells her, 'There's a waterfall on the other side. That's what the noise is and what makes it look like this.'

She says, 'It's lovely.'

And he nods.

He goes to the darkest corner and gathers some things.

Blue watches him untie two blankets. He lays one of the blankets down and sits, patting the spot next to him.

She goes over and says, 'What is this place?'

'It's a cave.'

'How did you find it?'

He shrugs. 'I come out here, at night.'

'At night. Are you mad?'

'It's better than staying in our dorm after dark.'

She almost asks, knowing the boys are housed with a lot of the men, suspecting on many nights that's where Amy and Natasha go.

She wonders if he's going to say more and is relieved when he doesn't.

'I bring a torch and stuff and I found this place.'

'It's amazing.'

He nods.

She says, 'Does anyone else know about it?'

He shakes his head then says, 'I thought maybe we could share it.'

Blue feels tears prick her eyes and a lump in her throat.

She says, 'We have lessons soon.' And Brodie nods. He produces from his pocket a broken watch face. Crackled on the front with half a strap attached. He puts it down.

Lessons now are in the afternoons and they have about an hour until the first one starts.

Brodie lies back.

The little glistening lights sprinkle over the walls and all she can hear is the sound of rushing water.

Eventually she lies back too, and he takes her hand in his.

That afternoon in class, Blue zones in and out of the awful, terrifying lecture.

Today's session is led by one of the Aunts whose name Blue has never known. She has a booming fire-and-brimstone voice. She warns them of the horrors other children are subjected to.

How school trains your brain to be sick and ill, makes minions out of the children who go through its doors.

Blue wonders honestly how much worse it can be than in here.

She looks around and Brodie catches her eye; they swap a soft smile. She feels the swell of their secret in her stomach and a rare moment of happiness. In her pocket is the flat-faced white stone he gave her. The smiley face is all but gone from where she reaches in and presses her thumb into it.

But her happiness is fleeting as Blue's eyes settle on Amy. Her face is glazed, lips slightly parted. Eyes blank and staring ahead.

She is not the same as she was. At lunch she carries on sitting, staring at nothing, pushing food around on her plate and never eating it.

She is disappearing, Blue thinks, before their very eyes. She feels a judder of real worry.

CHAPTER TWENTY-THREE

In the car, I will myself to be calm, to listen before I react. This school is a place where Pen is happy. They are not my enemy. But my thoughts invariably sway to the Black House. Pen's teachers are not the awful keepers of outside trying to pollute innocent minds with wrongness. The classrooms here are nothing like the ones of my younger years and the teachers are not my enemy. Or Pen's.

I looked just this morning at the photo I'd taken from Natasha's house. The four of us, arms over each other's shoulders, eyes squinting in the sun. Remarkable in its ordinariness. By that time, Amy and Natasha's day-to-day existence must have been deeply unpleasant. Certainly, I woke often with a hard knot of fear in my stomach.

Amy still looked healthy in that photo. It was before she'd stopped eating and begun quietly withering away. A small and pointless protest, which made Natasha angry and me sad.

It was the visits to Joseph and the men. The things that happened whilst she was there stole her from herself. I didn't know at the time exactly what went on, but I knew it would be my fate too and I feared it.

None of us had attended school anywhere else, I had been due to start in reception the year we arrived there. All I knew was the Black House, with its weird doctrine and its stark division of male and female. My world was teeny-tiny and whilst I longed for freedom, once I had it, it tasted bittersweet. Frightening, mainly.

As my world expanded, so too did my fears, and I feel that fear again now as we pull up outside of Pen's homely-looking school.

I feel once more like a dirty child pulled from the mountains of Wales, like a feral wild thing, plonked into reality to be jeered at and stared by all of the proper people who'd been busily living proper lives.

As we come to a standstill, I find that my breathing is fast. My palms are damp and I feel untethered, as though I am not quite inside myself. I push my feet into the floor of Isaac's low-slung car and almost jump out of my skin as I feel his hand clasp mine. I look at him and he stares back.

'Breathe in deeply.' He demonstrates.

I copy him. Breathing long in and out. I sink back into myself, feel my hand clasped in his and the comfort that it brings.

Eventually he says, 'Ready?' And I nod.

Ready as I'll ever be, but feeling better bolstered by being with him, I follow his lead into the school. Pen is in the outer office when we get there, and I go to her, kneeling down. She looks scared, but I'm not angry. The first thing I ask her is, 'Are you OK?'

She nods. Then the head is there gesturing at me and looking at Isaac. He smiles.

I say, 'He's with me.' Quite stupidly because it's obvious.

She seems on the precipice of saying something but decides better and settles for, 'Very well.'

She gestures for us to follow her into her office, a frown at Pen to do the same. I take Pen's hand and squeeze it.

She looks from me to Isaac. He winks at her and I feel her hand soften in mine.

The head sits behind the desk, lips pursed and eyebrows raised. I don't like her very much I realise, and I take a deep breath in. Letting her speak is important. I will not butt in prematurely. Not all teachers are bad; she is not one of the Aunts.

We all settle down, Isaac pulling a chair from the back of the room and sitting unselfconscious alongside me. I am ramrod straight and Pen is looking carefully at her own feet.

The head says, 'Sadly, Pen hit another girl today.'

I look at Pen whose gaze is still concentrated on the floor area.

I say, 'What happened? What made you do that?'

Pen looks up, but the officious head interrupts, 'I'm afraid what happened prior to her infraction is of little importance now.'

I meet her eyes levelly. 'I'd like to know, though.' And she is quiet. I turn back to Pen. 'Pen?'

She looks up. 'She said you were a freak.'

I open my mouth, close it again.

Turn to the teacher who says, 'And I have spoken with the other student about her unfortunate use of language.'

I say, 'You shouldn't have hit her, Pen.'

'I know.'

'Did you apologise?'

She nods.

The head teacher said, 'She did apologise as soon as we intervened. But there's no excuse.'

No excuse.

I say to Pen, 'Why don't you go and wait out there for me, OK? Isaac can go with you.'

They leave. Pen still with her head down, shoulders hunched.

I wait for the door to close behind them, a soft thump, then I turn to the head. 'Whilst I appreciate there is no excuse for violence, I think it's clear that Pen is sorry and in her circumstances, I think we can afford to be lenient.'

The head's cheeks redden. 'That may be so, but the other girl's parents are very likely to be unhappy about this and who could blame them?'

'How badly hurt is the other girl?' Pen is, after all, petite even for ten.

The head says, 'That's not the point.'

I sigh. 'With everything she's been through, I'm certain you can cut her some slack.'

'With everything she's been through, perhaps this is no longer the most suitable establishment for her.'

The words hang heavy in the air between us. Pen likes this school. She has friends here. She has got along well here. I know that she has scored highly on the tests that she needed to pass to gain her place.

I smile smoothly. 'I'm sure this establishment wouldn't want to gain a reputation for giving up on students the second they have any troubles.'

Her face falls. I wonder what she'd expected. Agreement? Profuse apologies? Me to have a go at Pen, perhaps.

I lean forward now across the desk and she moves back, looking uncomfortable. Like she sympathises with the little bully who'd called me a freak.

'Penelope Dryden has just lost her mother. She comes home each day and the first thing she does is study. Her grades remain excellent, as you know. I'm sure if the papers found out you'd pushed out a child at a time she most needs support, your intake would slip.'

This place is lovely for all intents and purposes. The class sizes are tiny; the girls all seem happy. Pen speaks highly of her teachers. But it is still a business and that's what will play on Mrs Williams' mind. She hasn't thought this through, and she has severely underestimated me. A bad story in the press would be worse than a childish spat. I would never serve up that story but this dragon with her pursed lips and immovable hair doesn't need to know that.

She smiles back now. It is thin and reedy. Not meeting her eyes. But she says, 'This time, we will let it go.'

'With no further discipline.'

'With no further discipline.'

'Great.' I grin now. 'I'll let her social worker know.' And I see her face twitch at the mention of a social worker, which brings me an extra moment of satisfaction.

But best of all is stepping out into the office, taking Pen's hand and saying, 'Shall we go home?'

'I'm not in trouble?'

I shrug. 'I'm not proud with how you dealt with it, but you said sorry, right?'

'Straight away.'

'What more can you do? You're bound to be feeling pretty pissed off right now. Last thing you need is stupid comments.'

She looks at Isaac who shrugs. She says, 'Blue said pissed.' Trying out the word like it's a precious gift. We are all laughing inappropriately as we leave.

CHAPTER TWENTY-FOUR

The next day is Thursday. I talk gently to Pen on the way to school, reminding her that if she feels angry she should just walk away. I tell her about pressing her feet into the ground, taking a deep breath, counting to ten.

She says, 'You too, huh?'

And I laugh at that. For years my rage was a force all of its own. I had a reputation for violence in the care homes that had had to house me and plenty of foster families that had despaired. At the Black House there had been fights between kids from time to time. Nothing major that I'd witnessed myself, not between the children anyway. But there was always threat from the adults. Amy's beating remained forever burned in my mind, but there were plenty of other instances like it. Especially just before people started leaving. There was an escalation in violence then, and oddly it wasn't the acts themselves – always public and a sort of wicked relief by the time they occurred – that messed with my head. It was the impending threat. The menace simmering under the surface. The possibility. Never helped by the ever-changing rules which could be broken without you even knowing you'd done so.

I saw one boy await his punishment so scared that he urinated before it came to him. He'd been spared on account of his 'pathetic cowardice'. But he'd also been left standing there, red-faced with what must have started

124

as warm liquid drying into an icy streak as the day grew longer and the evening brought its ferocious chill.

I can't even recall his name, but I do remember spending the whole day looking out of the window and Natasha coming to move me away, shaking her head. I'd cried. At the cruelty. The helplessness.

But I'd never reacted with anger of my own. Not then, as I walked around numbly in an adrenaline-soaked daze.

It was months after I was out that it started to fizz up and out of me. Blinding and all-consuming. I would flip at any minor infraction. Leaping over beds in shared bedrooms. Chasing other children around, brandishing hairbrushes and cursing loudly.

Afterwards I always felt bad, always felt shocked. That I had it in me. Just like the Aunts. I vowed then that I'd never have children and during my vague forays into the world of dating I learnt fast that men could be a trigger for me, too. I steered clear of intimacy. Accepted that living alone was always going to be the most suitable option for me.

That the closest I might ever get to true love was lying on the floor of a cave, holding hands with a little boy whose eyes reflected the sadness in my own heart.

I was still raging when I met Isaac and he's been on the receiving end of it more than once.

But I have mellowed, and a lot of that has to do with Isaac's complete acceptance of me. I wonder if our paths hadn't crossed how I might be now. Anger is boundless and guaranteed to get you into trouble too. I've often thought that prison must be full of women like me. Unable to control themselves, unable to channel the energy anywhere. With no Isaac to calmly wait for the storm to pass.

Pen says, 'You fixed it now though, huh?'

And I smile weakly at her.

Fixed it? I don't know. I'd felt a simmer of it sitting in that office. I felt it when I thought about Natasha and her stupid final act.

One of the first comic book heroes I loved – genuinely loved – was the Hulk. Probably the least favourite outside of the under ten-year-old boy category. But I *got* him. I sympathised with him. Where the rage could take you and it wasn't even your fault.

I understood it was a psychological problem like any other that needed to be worked at, tamed. Of course I'd be riddled with those sorts of issues things that needed fixing and resetting, how could I not be? But I'd done the work, under Isaac's guidance. Work on myself that may not guarantee happiness exactly, but certainly saved me from unwieldy chaos.

He told me once, *'Anger is the noise that fear makes.'* And something in me got that. I shifted mentally. Those seven words were more powerful than any therapy I'd had, any group discussions with empathetic but ineffectual adults at the helm. Isaac got it.

Fear. Living with the almost constant threat of it. It'll eat you from the inside out. No wonder it had gotten into me. My bones, my flesh, my very fibre. Coming out as its corrosive counterpart.

Anger.

After school, I take Pen for ice cream at an awful place on the high street near mine. Sweets, it's called and it only serves sugar in a few million sickly, overly colourful varieties. She orders something that has cream, ice cream and some sort of baked good involved. I order a coffee. She looks at me sympathetically, 'Are you on a diet?'

I frown. 'No.'

She tucks in and when she looks up again there's a blob of cream on her top lip. 'Mummy took me here.'

There is a silence that hurts me a little and must be unbearable for her.

She breaks it. 'What was *your* mum like?'

I look away, watching a man at a table full of noisy boys of various ages, cowering over his mobile whilst they make an almighty mess.

'She died.'

'When you were little?'

'About your age.'

'I'm sorry.'

I look at her, passing a napkin across the table and pointing to her lip. As she wipes I tell her, 'Me too.'

When she finishes eating, we talk. She tells me about the girl she hit, says they'd never been best friends, but she hadn't been horrid before either. I ask if she regrets hitting her. She shrugs. And I get it, so I don't push. The human condition is a fragile thing.

She says, 'Mummy would have been mad. She dislikes violence. Says it shows a lack of control.'

I get an image of Natasha, blank-faced, staring at high, licking flames. The feel of her hands on me as she pulled me backwards. *'You can't do anything for her. We need to go.'* My mother. I couldn't do anything for my mother, though I had stuck my arm into flames anyway.

I've had many different thoughts about that over the years. About what I did to try and save her, despite the fact that if you'd have asked me, I'd have told you honestly that I didn't love her anymore. Not at all. And I'm yet to feel anything close to grief about her death. There are so many layers of anger that remain over how she treated me that I often think that maybe I will never get to the bit where my heart mourns her passing. I already grieved the loss of her when I was put into that dorm and began to see less and less of her. I hardened myself to it, though I do remember my heart breaking over and over at the time. That inherent, trusting part of me continuously smashed into a million tiny pieces. It got to the point where I wasn't entirely sure she was ever mine.

She was, though.

We were both DNA tested. After the fact. So there is absolute proof that I once belonged to her.

I think about what Pen said about her mother abhorring violence. Natasha could be spiteful sometimes. I guess we all could. I remember her pinching Amy once when she wouldn't stop crying. It got to her. The tears. She herself made a point of not sparing any. In all those years, I never saw Natasha cry. And one day she'd shouted at Amy to *stop stop stop*. And Amy couldn't. That was the truth. Some days she could do nothing but lie down and sob. We were so accustomed to it we barely reacted by then. But Natasha had been 'out' of dorm for a few hours. She'd come back jangled and she'd had enough.

I thought she'd been going down to hug her, but she didn't. Instead, she leaned over the bed, pressing a hand onto Amy's mouth, forcing her to be quiet. To be silent. Then she'd pinched her arm between her fingers so hard she left red marks for days after. Then the red marks turned into little round, blue bruises. Everyone had limits.

I'm glad she'd found her way into being appalled by it. Into teaching her daughter what was right or wrong.

I tell Pen, 'Your mum would have understood.'

CHAPTER TWENTY-FIVE

NATASHA

Girls – women – have to be tougher, stronger than men. It's a hard thing to take and unfair, but it is the way it is.

Crying might feel good for a few seconds, but it won't get you anywhere fast.

The world is trying to get you.

That's the thing. It's set up to take advantage, to make you think you're weak.

Even outside of the Black House, I soon discovered the wider world is just as full of peril if you don't know how to stand tall, how to make things work for you. Men have the upper hand in so many ways, but underneath all of their dominance and physical strength, they are soft and pliable things.

Joseph thought he was invincible.

Indestructible.

Above punishment and reproach. But it was his needs that made him weak, reliant as he was on the adoration of others.

I made a point of distancing myself from it all, from his pawing hands and painful, undignified instruction. I learned young the ability to spill my mind out of my physical body and elsewhere. So that agony, degradation, became a distant thing.

I told my sisters when the time came: this is what to do, how to do it. It's important not to let them take you, inside.

I have always abhorred weakness.

You have to be tough. You have to be strong.

You have to make difficult decisions and live by them. But you also have to be clever about it.

CHAPTER TWENTY-SIX

Gareth is exactly how I imagined him to be from his photo. He is that slicked kind of perfect. His hair sits in a manicured quiff, he has slightly rolled up trousers on, a blue blazer and loafers with no socks. The whole look screams effortless, but it's a uniform I've seen many times. Not original. Tried and tested.

He's also very good-looking and when he smiles, actual dimples appear in his cheeks.

He's smiling now as he shakes my hand, taking it in both of his and then sliding designer specs up his nose and saying how lovely it is to meet a friend of Tasha's.

When he says her name, the self-assured smile falters. He gestures to a seat opposite his desk and we both sit. The receptionist from yesterday pokes her head around the door and says, 'Tea, guys?'

He looks at me, eyebrow raised, and I say, 'Sure.'

The vibe here is casual. Smashual. A place that makes a fortune but is keen to give off an everyman vibe.

He shakes his head now. 'Still can't believe it, you know?'

I nod and say, 'She said the same, your ah . . . I didn't get her name?'

'Oh, our girl Friday? Gill.'

Girl Friday. Who says that?

He asks, 'How's the kid doing? Jeez. Can't even imagine that. I mean, kids aren't my jam.'

My jam?

He barely pauses for breath. 'You've taken her in, right?'

I nod.

'Wow.'

I nod again.

'That's mad.'

'Yes.'

Gill – Girl Friday – comes in then. Tea is of the green variety in little pots, pretty with small handle–less cups. She fills one for each of us, putting the tray in the middle and a cup to either side. Then she does that chest–clutching thing again and nods at me.

The insincerity levels here are high. I wonder if it's an estate agent thing. Obviously these guys are operating at a higher level than most, but still. A lot of the job involves clouded truths doesn't it? 'Cosy', 'lived–in', 'a doer–upper'. Smooth lies.

Looking at the pictures on the walls in Gareth's office though, nothing they sell here could be described in such a way.

Maybe it's the schmoozing.

When Gill's gone, Gareth takes a sip of tea and says, 'She was good at her job. Tasha.'

'Was she?'

He nods. 'God yes. Insanely so. She could sell anything to anyone.' He grins then, small crinkles appearing at the corners of his eyes. 'Which was great for us as we deal in million–pound properties.' Adding, 'And upwards.'

I nod, hopefully looking suitably impressed.

'She had a fair few of her own.'

I say, 'I know. I've inherited them.'

He lets out a low whistle. 'If you need someone to manage or help sell them . . .' The words hang in the air between us in a distasteful speech bubble.

I just smile then say, 'I hadn't seen her for a long time.'

He frowns. 'Yah, Gill said. Odd then, eh? That she left you the lot?'

'I don't know. I mean, I don't know who else she was close to now if you see what I mean.'

He nods. 'Right. I do, yeah. I mean . . .' He sighs. 'Look. I'm just going to be honest, yeah?'

I nod. 'I'd appreciate that.'

'I had the hots for that girl. I mean, you know, feelings.' He shrugs. 'Whatever.'

I say, 'She was very beautiful.'

He smiles, but it collapses quickly. His whole face seems to sag. For the first time since I arrived, he looks less like a caricature and more like a person with actual flesh and blood inside and real emotions. He wipes a hand over his face and says, 'God.'

I wait. He looks up at me and I say, 'You cared about her?'

He nods. Lips down turned. 'I did yes. For all the good it did me.'

'She wasn't interested?'

'No. Yes. Hell, I don't know. We . . .' he blushes slightly '. . . hooked up.'

'When?'

'A few times over the years. Every time, every single one, like a fool, I thought that would be it.'

'It never developed?'

He shakes his head. 'Nope and afterwards she'd act like nothing had happened. Light. That's how she was – always very light about everything, but sometimes I'd catch her looking serious or staring into space and I'd think, there's more there.'

I feel a wave of sadness for this man who was clearly in love with her.

He says, 'What I said about kids?'

I nod.

'I didn't mean it. I asked to meet her a few times, Tasha's girl. Nothing heavy suggested you know, to bring her in. Introduce us.'

'She never did?'

He shakes his head, 'She was the most private person I know, I think. We knew she had a daughter but that was it, really. We were away sometimes at conferences and such like and I never even knew who was looking after her. If the dad was maybe around.' He flicks his eyes to me, a question there.

I say, 'No one is named on the birth certificate.'

He nods. 'I think I always thought eventually I'd reel her in with my natural charm.' He smiles sadly.

I ask, 'Is that why you gave her the job here?'

He shakes his head. 'Oh no. She was good at what she did. Really I've never met a finer salesperson. To say she had the gift of the gab is an understatement. That woman had the Midas touch. I'd have been a fool not to hire her.'

'Were you the person who was closest to her, here?'

He sighs. 'I want to say yes, or my ego does anyway. But she was very pally with Lyndsey.'

'The woman who left?'

'Yes.' He frowns now. 'Leaving me right in the lurch.'

'Were you surprised? That she went?'

He nods. 'So abruptly, yes. I knew she wanted to travel; she went on and on about it all the time, and Natasha was very encouraging. She said she should spread her wings. But I didn't think she'd actually do it and if she did, I'd have hoped she'd at least give us a bit of notice.'

I say, 'She went just after Natasha . . .?' I swallow thickly. I still can't formulate what happened into any sort of semblance of reasonable language.

'Just before, actually. Like by days.'

'You discussed it with her?'

'Tasha?'

'Yes.'

He nods again. 'Told Tash I was pissed about the whole thing.' He smiles. 'She put her arms around me, kissed me on the cheek and told me I worried too much.' His face drops. 'Though now I'm here alone with Gill who, whilst very sweet, isn't going to be able to replace either of them.'

'I'm sorry,' I murmur. And find I am. For all kinds of things, none of which are my fault. But I can feel a peculiar kind of grief rolling off him.

We are not the kind of people you want to fall in love with, Natasha and I. That's for sure.

I collect Pen, pleased to find she's in a good mood. I may not like the head, but Pen's class teacher seems nice and that's who she has the most contact with, after all. I ask how things went with the other girl today and Pen shrugs.

'OK. I don't think we'll be best friends, but she hasn't said anything horrible.'

I nod. 'That's good.'

She sighs. 'I know. These things happen.' And she sounds like some sort of cartoonish little old wise woman. I find myself smiling.

When we get back to mine, Pen sees that I have put the photo from her house on my fireplace. She goes over and picks it up, running a finger across all of our faces.

She says, 'I miss Lisa still.'

And I am frozen for a moment. But of course, why wouldn't she have known her? Evidently Lisa and Natasha had stayed in contact. She'd said as much in her letter. Lisa died about what . . . four years ago? Maybe just under. Pen would have been six. Old enough to remember.

I say, 'You knew Lisa, huh?'

Pen frowns nodding. 'Of course. She was my godmother.'

'Oh.'

I sit down. I had moved myself out of their lives. Away from them. Had I missed out? Of course. Now both were gone and I'd never speak to them again.

I almost choke on the words as I tell Pen, 'I hadn't seen her for a long time.'

Pen nods. 'Mummy said you loved them both, but had to make your own way.'

'Did she?'

'Yup. She and Lisa argued about it once. I listened in.'

'What were they arguing about?'

Pen frowns. 'I'm not totally sure. I didn't understand all of it, but Lisa wanted to contact a lot of people – you were one of them. Mummy said the past was best left at that, and that if you wanted to see them, you'd have written back.'

My heart swells and contracts. Little pinpricks of pain seem to assault it from every angle.

She looks at me very directly and asks, 'They wrote to you?'

'Um. Lisa did.'

'Why didn't you write back?'

I shrug. How can I tell her things I don't have answers for myself?

Pen says, 'Mummy said you all lived near each other. In the countryside.'

'What . . . what else did Mummy say?'

'Not much and I'm pretty nosy. She and Lisa didn't like to talk about it. She said she'd take me to Wales one day though, to where you grew up. When I was older.' Her eyes get an awful shine on them. 'I don't suppose I'll ever get to go now, though, will I?'

This is where I'm supposed to say I'll take her. But I can't. The thought of that place makes me feel physically sick.

Instead I say, 'You have homework to do.'

She holds my gaze and I wonder if she's going to argue, and I try not to breathe. I have no idea how I'll respond. But eventually she scoops up her bag, lays out her books and pens and pencils, and gets to it, a funny little frown furrowing her brow.

CHAPTER TWENTY-SEVEN

Annie is getting increasingly irritated. Still no dental records for Natasha Dryden and much of her medical records are incomplete, too. It seems aside from giving birth to Penelope, she didn't visit medical professionals very often. Her last GP appointment had been for her cervical smear. Pen had all of her immunisations and everything else but also didn't visit often. Annie sifts through her mind, comparing this with the other first-time mothers she knew, who were plentiful a decade ago in her circle when everyone but her had started reproducing. What she remembers, from conversations had over sterilisers and lunches filled with muslin cloths and bleary eyes, was that they took the babies often to be weighed and that any little sneeze, cough or sniffle resulted in, if not a GP appointment, then various trips to casualty.

Could Natasha Dryden have just been the most relaxed mother in the world or did her learned distrust of authority follow her into adult life?

She hadn't travelled much, either. A few trips to France, work-related. Pen hadn't gone and thus far Annie couldn't account for where the child had been left. She'd ask Blue and Dee to find out.

The man at her work, Gareth, had said she was close to Lyndsey, who also worked with them, but Lyndsey herself had packed up and left England's shores for some, in Annie's opinion, ill-thought-out midlife adventures.

She jumps as her sergeant, Fiona McGrath, comes in. Popping a steaming mug of black coffee by her elbow, she says, 'Still can't find her records?'

'No.'

'Frustrating.'

Annie nods. 'It's not like anyone can offer an ID just by looking at her, is it?'

'No.'

The body barely even resembles something once human. And even their genius pathologist had found digging clues out from the charred bones difficult. A woman. Around Natasha's age. Right height, right build. Signs of birth inconclusive but couldn't entirely rule out pregnancy.

It's all the inconclusive bits that are getting to Annie.

Nothing adds up. It's all too neat and Annie doesn't trust neat.

She gets a call to her desk to attend a DV situation and puts the paperwork away with a sigh. Plenty of live ones to be focusing on, of course. It's not like her workload is ever lacking. She pauses a moment, though, and puts the files in her bag. She may as well have a quick look later on. Just in case anything jumps out.

CHAPTER TWENTY-EIGHT

I have no idea why I'd assumed Natasha would have told Pen about our childhoods. It would, of course, be akin to telling an infant a horror story at bedtime. If ever she were to learn the truth it wouldn't have been at this age, if at all. I also don't know why I'm surprised that Lisa was such a big part of Pen's life. I knew she and Natasha had remained in contact. I'dseen her once when I'd visited Lis'as grave. From far away, but I'd recognised Natasha. The way she stood had never changed: shoulders back, tits out, as she used to say. Confidence. The key to success. She'd tell us that a lot and use the Aunts as her key example of how not having it would ruin you.

By the end, we spent most evenings making whispered, furtive plans that we all suspected would never come to fruition. What we'd do when we were out. What we'd tell the police. By then we were all in agreement that no matter how bad they might be, they couldn't be as bad as the grown-ups there.

The journalist, David Belsham, has called twice and left his number again via text message. I type it into my phone twice, before deleting it both times. Putting my phone down on the side as though it might bite.

On the third attempt, I hit the green button and the call goes through.

A deep voice says, 'Hello?'

And I spit out, 'Blue Sillitoe.' Before I can chicken out.

'I'm so glad you called.'

I don't respond to that and I can hear my own breath echoing down the line.

He says, 'I'd love to meet.' The familiar lilt in his voice jarring to me.

I ask, 'What do you want?'

'Just to talk.'

'You're writing a book?'

'Yes. About the Black House.'

'Why?'

He laughs at that, but it's not a cruel sound. 'People are interested. What happened there . . . it was a tragedy. Tragedies make people curious, for all kinds of reasons.'

'Like we're some sort of freak show.'

'Not like that at all. I think people like to learn from others' mistakes.'

'Mistakes, huh.'

'Sorry, that was flippant of me.' I imagine him wincing. My hand grips my phone so tightly that my knuckles ache. 'But people are interested in how others come to be under someone else's control. What it feels like. And maybe most of all, how people survive it.'

I snap, 'I wasn't under anyone's control. I was a child.'

He says, 'I know.' Then: 'I'm sorry.'

'How do you know about Natasha?'

'I have contacts in various areas of law enforcement.'

'We're protected by anonymity.'

He pauses. 'Not all of my contacts are above cash bonuses.'

I smile slightly at that, even as it pisses me off. At least he's being honest.

'And you found me, too?'

'To be honest, I wasn't one hundred percent sure.'

I tell him, 'I hadn't seen her for years.'

'You lost contact?'

'Not exactly. She wrote.' I prickle with guilt as I tell him that. Something I hadn't been honest with Pen about yesterday, in case she was angry at me. How easily secrets spill out, how quickly tangled webs of lies weave around us. I add, 'She also rang a few times. Emailed.'

'You didn't respond?'

'No.'

'Understandable. Some things are best left in the past.'

'But you still want to talk about it, now.'

'Like I said I'd like an idea of Natasha's motivations. For . . . her death.'

My heart is pounding. He wants what I want, even if he doesn't know it. I ask, 'You were surprised?'

'That she killed herself?'

'Yes.'

'Very much so.'

I say, 'That's what you want to talk about really, isn't it?'

He sighs. 'I do, yes.'

I pause for so long that I think about just hanging up. But none of this makes sense to me and as I walk through this weird bit of my life with Pen in tow, assaulted by memories I can't get rid of, with suspicions about back then that I'd thought I'd made my peace with, I find I'm curious. About her, my past, Lisa.

Amy.

Everything.

And this man might know things I don't.

It is this that leads to me agreeing to meet up with him. At a public place to talk very definitely off the record.

CHAPTER TWENTY-NINE

Lyndsey's Facebook page is pretty public. I have an unidenti-
fiable account, mainly for things like this. I used it years ago
to see if Lisa, Natasha or Brodie had pages and to keep an
eye on any that were set up. I had often wondered if they
had done the same. Out of all of us, Lisa was the only one
who'd had her own page, as far as I could work out, but her
privacy settings had also been quite high. One thing I had
learned, and had been surprised about, was that she was listed
as being in a relationship. I've found the man's name, Mark
Savillus, and subsequently his address. I haven't pursued it,
though I look at the document now in which I've carefully
saved his details and ruminated on the possibility.

Natasha had emailed me about Lisa's death, and I hadn't
been surprised. Nor had I responded. I'd discussed it with
Isaac, who'd had no hard opinion on what I should do
either way. I had felt it was best left alone. But I'd also
felt terribly guilty. Like I'd deserted her not just once,
but a second time, even in death. It's why I visit her so
often now. But I have always steered clear of wondering
why she did it.

But now Natasha, too . . .

I haven't delved too deeply into any of it. I suppose a
bigger part of me doesn't want to know.

But now I am going in deep. I look over everything
linked to Mayfair Properties. I find pictures of Natasha in

the company photos. She's not tagged in them, though her full name is visible. Not hugely surprising. She did, after all, have a LinkedIn profile. Lisa's page is no longer active, but I find her tagged in a few posts. Pictures of her smiling shyly at the camera, eyes averted, squinting in the sun. One of her in Cardiff, a young woman still. A few in London. From what I can ascertain, they were tagged by the man posing with her: Mark Savillus. He looks nice. She looks OK. Not like she's about to kill herself, though the date tells me that one at least was posted shortly before she did just that.

It's hard to tell from pictures though, isn't it?

Many images from the Black House were released after the place went up in flames. Boxes of them salvaged from one of the outdoor storage sheds.

Images of Carillo surrounded by smiling, happy, healthy-looking people. I was transfixed by them when they hit the papers. One in particular. Just the women. The Aunts, all in their matching white dresses, long hair whispering around their waists, some barefoot. All smiling. And all of them so very young, which isn't how I remembered them at all. I suppose to a ten-year-old, people in their twenties are ancient.

They never smiled in real life. Or not at us, at least. Even when they weren't interacting but just scurrying past, alone, in small groups, even then their heads were bowed. Hands clasped in front of them. A stance Amy had adopted in later years when we were outside of the dorm.

There had been only a handful of images of the children and the single one I had of me and my mother. She'd given that photo to me wordlessly a week before the fire. We'd passed each other in the yard. Me avoiding her gaze, I'd assumed she'd been doing the same. When I heard my name, I looked up and felt that punch in the chest that I got if I ever thought about her.

Blue.

She'd come to me, reaching into a large pocket inside her full skirt and pulling out that single image, tattered around the edges. I'd taken it from her hand, little surprising shocks of love seeming to transfer from her to me. All in my head, I'm sure. By the time my hand had clutched it, she was already walking away, and she didn't look back. I'd glanced at the picture, then stuffed it in my own pocket. Knowing somehow I'd have to keep it on me at all times. Knowing that it was important.

She looked nothing like the woman she'd ended up being. That was for sure.

Brainwashed.

That's what all the experts said. I didn't like it. It felt like abdicating responsibility to me. My mother had been charmed by Joseph Carillo. She'd wanted to believe him, so she had. And my life was ruined because of it. But while she'd had some choice, some autonomy, I'd had none.

I feel bitter, I suppose. I didn't really know her. My memories certainly were in no way reliable. But that moment in class when she'd barely given me a second glance was, in my mind, unforgivable. Of all the physical punishments given out in lessons – slaps around the back of the head, a ruler wrapped over your knuckles with a sharp thwack and a crack as its blow landed – nothing hurt as much as my mother not even acknowledging my existence as her child. Had it not been for her handing me that single image, maybe I wouldn't have tried to free her at all. Would have just let the flames take her and not given her a second thought. My left hand presses into the curves on my right arm. I snatch it away. I blink, trying to clear my head and focus on the screen of my laptop.

Lyndsey doesn't use Facebook so much as Instagram and that's where I find image after image of her. Her and her cat. Her and various groups of women who look very similar to her. One of her and Natasha, all shiny teeth and lipstick. And a final one – a picture of a backpack, a passport and a folder from British Airways. Captioned #gulp #goingoffgrid #youonlyliveonce #followyourdreams

What I do manage to work out from various social media posts is the road she lives on, and the block of flats too. People are idiots when it comes to online privacy and she is no exception. Lyndsey has a captioned photo of her opening a parcel, the flap of it revealing her address for all to see. I make a note of the street name, then I send her a DM on both Facebook and Instagram. I also make a list of the 'friends' tagged on her social media.

The day is almost over and I find I'm exhausted. My brain has been tunnelling on at one hundred miles an hour, and sitting with Pen while she did her homework was a strain. I'm looking forward to doing absolutely nothing.

Pen gets out of the bath wrapped in white towels and asks quietly, 'How come you didn't go to school when you were little?'

I'd made some flip comment about why I couldn't help with her homework. I obviously hadn't thought about the words as I said them, but now the enormity of what I'd let slip registers. Pen being Pen, she doesn't forget anything.

I pause, walk into the bathroom and pick up the jug she has left discarded in the tub. I shake it off. Put it on the baths side and let the plug out.. I take my time, trying to think, unsure what to say.

One of the things I hated most growing up was being lied to. We were never given direct answers to anything that we asked. As a result, we just stopped asking questions, which was probably the point all along. We were Carillo's dedicated flock, accessories for someone else's life. It was not for us to question why, as we were told over and over again. Something I still buck against now. I don't want to lie to Pen, but for the first time ever I can understand why withholding some truth may sometimes be for the best.

Pen is looking at me wide-eyed from under turbaned hair, waiting. Not the kind of kid to let things go.

I say, 'What did your mum tell you about how she grew up?'

'She said you were all neighbours.'

I nod. I can't go against what Natasha said, can I?

Then Pen adds, 'But she was lying.'

I close my eyes, say to Pen, 'Go and get your pyjamas on and get into bed and I'll come through. OK?'

She looks at me with those deep, intense eyes. I meet her gaze levelly and tell her, 'I need a moment. To think.'

She blinks but goes.

I slide to the floor, my back pressed against the wall, my mind buzzing. I fire off an SOS text to Isaac.

Pen calls out, 'Are you coming?'

And I say, 'Give me minute.'

His reply is: *'Tell her you're not sure the truth is suitable and you need time to think about it.'*

I reply, *'That'll just make her all the more curious.'*

'Yes but it buys you time to speak to a professional.'

'Who?'

'Dee or the tasty cop?'

I send *'Tasty cop?'* with a vomiting emoji. He sends back a smiling devil.

He's right. Probably best that I speak to Dee. She knows my background and Natasha's. Her job is literally to oversee Pen's welfare. I only have to get through this evening.

I say thanks. He sends me an 'x'.

Pen is sitting up in bed and she looks particularly small and sad. I go and settle on the edge, pulling her covers over her knees and tucking it in at the sides. She turns her eyes to mine. 'Are you mad at me?'

I frown. 'No, why would I be mad?'

'Mummy hated me asking anything about before I was born.'

'She'd get cross?'

She nods and I feel a wave of pity for both her and Natasha. Of course a child will have questions. And this poor kid didn't know who her dad was, her grandparents, anything. In her own way, she was another victim of Carillo. I shut my eyes. That one man's warped desires can have such far-reaching implications for generations to come is an awful, tainted legacy. One that I am part of, that I will never escape, and I realise sadly, that Pen is touched by it too.

I ask her, 'What did Mummy tell you?'

'That you and Lisa, some other kids and her were all neighbours and that where you lived was pretty isolated, like not a town or anything so you all hung out a lot.'

'That's not untrue.'

'She said her parents died in a car accident.'

I look away then ask, 'How do you know she was lying?'

She shrugs. 'I asked all the time about her mum and dad and she said they were really nice people. But sometimes she'd get bits wrong.'

'Like what bits?'

'Once she said her dad was a schoolteacher and I asked what age, she said reception. Another time she said he taught science at secondary school.'

'OK.'

'And she didn't have any pictures of them.'

'Not even her mum?'

She shakes her head. I sigh.

'Pen. I don't want to lie to you.'

'Then don't.' Her voice is high-pitched now, a whine even. Natasha should have told her some version of the truth for goodness' sake. It was never her way, though. The consummate actress. She knew far more than I ever did about what had been going on at the Black House. I knew she didn't tell me everything and I suspected she made Amy keep quiet, too. I imagine that urge came from good intent and became habitual, always keeping bits and pieces back. I'm not surprised that she continued this into adulthood. Can even understand why she would. But I can't help but think she wouldn't have left Pen not knowing, likely to find out from me. I get that glimmer of unease again.

Natasha wouldn't have done this. She'd have wanted the final say, to make sure her child heard, if anything, her version of events. Because we all had different versions, didn't we?

When I'd finally found out the extent of it all – the terrible grooming and sexual abuse my friends but not I had been subjected to – from a stranger in a horrible council-owned room, it had broken me. I don't think I ever truly forgave Natasha for that, though I could understand her reasoning. I used to think if she'd spoken up earlier, done something . . .

Before Amy . . .

Well.

I close my eyes. 'Pen. I'm going to ask you to give me twenty-four hours.'

'Then you'll tell me?'

'Then I'll tell you what I can.'

She frowns.

I add, 'I won't lie to you, but there are some things I don't even know and some things that might be better kept aside. Just for now.'

She pouts. 'I'm not a baby.'

I smooth her hair back from her forehead, which is damp.

I say, 'Just give me twenty-four hours.'

'Did you know my grandparents?' she asks.

I pause. Perhaps some token information here would help. And it gives me a chance to prove I'm serious, about being honest. 'I knew your grandmother.'

'Is she dead?'

'No.'

She sucks in a deep breath.

I add, 'Sorry.'

Not sorry her grandmother is alive, though I don't care much about Sienna one way or another. But I'm sorry Natasha lied to her and that she's finding out from me now. My guess – or my hope – is that one day she'd have told Pen the truth. I can only imagine what it must have been like. Waiting for the right time. Not when she's a baby, or a toddler who can't understand. The days turn into months and the months into years.

Pen shakes her head and leans forward, putting her thin little arms around my neck. 'Don't be.' Then: 'I trust you.'

Those three little words rush through my mind. The gravity of her trust and whether or not I'm worthy of it.

CHAPTER THIRTY

I call Dee in the morning on my way to Planet Pop. She answers with a booming, 'Hello!' And then sounds genuinely delighted to hear from me.

I outline the issue and she doesn't speak for a moment then says, 'Why don't we meet face to face?'

I scowl. 'I'm at the shop so it'll be tricky to get away.'

She announces, 'I'll come meet you for lunch. Everyone needs a break, right?'

I tell her, 'Sure.' Though I'd honestly rather not.

She says, 'Perfect. Let's say midday. I know a good place near your work.' She reels off the name and address and ends the call, before I have a chance to protest.

Isaac is waiting when I get to the shop, which still has its closed sign facing out. Straight away he asks what happened with Pen. I tell him and that Dee is forcing me to meet her for lunch.

He says, 'Good.' And I frown. He grins. 'She seems all right.'

I am early to meet Dee by five minutes and unreasonably annoyed to find her already there, leaning across the counter and chatting animatedly to a man who looks so much like her I assume they are related. She grins at me, waving me over. 'Blue, this is Attlee, my baby brother.'

He grins and I say, 'You look alike.'

He laughs with the same booming guffaw as Dee and he tells me, 'I wear it better though, be honest.'

She rolls her eyes. 'Ignore him. But on the upside, this place has the best food around. All our mother's recipes.'

Attlee nods. 'She was the best cook in Jamaica.'

I raise an eyebrow. 'Is that so?'

He shrugs. 'She was also a woman you didn't argue with.'

Dee nods. 'It's true.' And I find myself more at ease than I expected, considering the nature of our meeting.

I say, 'Smells great.' Which it does.

She says, 'It is all good and today's special is goat stew, which I recommend.'

'OK.'

'Good choice. And drinks, ladies?'

Dee says sparkling water; I ask for a coffee. 'I need the caffeine.'

We make our way to a small table by the window. The place is busy and waiters and waitresses buzz around. It's loud but not unpleasantly so.

Dee says, 'You look tired. You not getting enough sleep?'

I shrug. 'I often don't sleep well.'

She frowns and I change the subject quickly. 'This is a family business, then?'

'It was my mother's dream but she never made it. She died ten years ago. God rest her soul.'

I murmur, 'I'm sorry.'

Dee grins. 'Don't be. But she left us money and Attlee wanted to do this. So this is where we put the cash.'

I say, 'You don't fancy working here?'

She shrugs. 'Maybe when I'm old and tired.'

I laugh. 'Isn't running a café quite stressful?'

She grins. 'Not compared to being a social worker in London.'

She's probably right.

The food comes along with our drinks. I take a mouthful of the special stew. It's rich, warm and tastes amazing. I've noticed under Pen's careful direction that I've actually started enjoying eating for once. The kid seems to endlessly consider what her next meal or snack is going to be and, as a result, I've been forced to as well.

We eat in silence for a bit and then she says, 'So, your sleep?'

I shrug. 'I never sleep well.'

She nods. 'Common. Amongst survivors.'

I laugh. 'You work with lot of ex-cult members?'

She says, 'I work with a lot of traumatised children.'

I look away.

We finish our food without speaking, but it isn't uncomfortable.

Attlee takes the plates away, saying, 'I'll bring more coffee, OK.'

I say, 'Thanks.'

As we wait for him to come back, Dee tells me that business at the café is booming and Attlee is pleased as punch with its performance. I say I'll bring Pen and think maybe I actually will – she'll love it. Attlee brings coffees two this time and a pot of cream.

Dee takes a sip of hers, waits for him to leave then says, 'Penelope doesn't know about the Black House, then?'

I shake my head. 'But she's a smart kid and she knows something is amiss.'

Dee nods. 'I'm not surprised.'

'What should I do?'

'Tell her the truth, but softly.'

I laugh, and it comes out like splutter. 'Tell her softly? I was in a cult that groomed children into a form of sex slavery then loads of people left and the rest drank poison and burned themselves to death?'

Dee shakes her head. 'You tell her your mother and Natasha's met a man who seemed nice but turned out not to be. That you all grew up together in a community that started with good intentions but became sick. Tell her eventually police and social services rescued you.'

I pause, thinking that over. 'That's a very sanitised version of events.'

Dee nods. 'And she'll no doubt ask you difficult questions.'

'How do I answer them?'

She smiles. 'Gently.'

'What if it . . .'

'Messes her up?'

I nod.

Dee says, 'Her mother is dead, killed herself, and has left her with a woman Pen had never met. She knows you both knew Lisa, who also met an awful end. Like you said. She's not stupid.'

'She's already traumatised. That's what you're saying?' My voice is rising. I can't bear it. The thought that Pen is somehow already damaged – that I can't fix her – is more than I can take. I feel my breathing start to speed up. The place begins to swirl. I feel dizzy.

Dee is there, her thick hands on my shoulders. Bending me forward. 'Lean down. Lean down.' She makes me put my head between my knees. One hand holding my shoulder, the other making small rubbing motions on my back. She's clicking her fingers and I hear her murmur, 'Water,' to someone.

'It's OK, Blue. You're OK.'

I feel everything start to calm and I sit up again, embarrassed now. I wipe a hand across my eyes, push my feet down hard into the floor. 'God I'm so sorry.'

A waiter puts a glass of water next to me and Dee nods thanks.

She reaches across the table and squeezes my hand. 'You, Blue Sillitoe, are what we would deem a success story.'

I frown at that. 'In what way?'

'In every way. Look what you endured. Look how far you've come.'

I say, 'Others had it worse.'

'Natasha?'

I nod, looking out the window.

Dee says, 'No one person has a monopoly on pain, Blue.'

I shake my head. 'I didn't do anything. To help.'

I don't even know which specific event I mean. Amy definitely, but Lisa and Natasha, too. I never asked what happened when they weren't in the dorm. When Lisa began disappearing, before the end, I didn't ask her about it. I could have. It had always been Amy and Natasha. Her and me. If I'd have asked her, she'd have talked. I always think about that. I don't think I wanted to know. I ignored their attempts to contact me. Because I couldn't handle it. What if I had lost a second chance to help? I blink away tears.

Dee says, 'Do you think Pen should be out there saving other people?'

I frown. 'Of course not, she's a child.'

Dee keeps hold of my hand, eyes set on mine. 'So were you, Blue. You were, in fact, almost six months younger than Pen is now when you got out.'

And maybe for the first time ever, I feel a glimmer of something unfamiliar. For the little girl that I was. Pen *is* a child, and I would do anything within my power to protect her from pain. No one did that for me.

I pull my hands away, pressing them to my face, covering my eyes. I take deep breaths, push the soles of my feet into the floor. Eventually I drop my hands and look back at Dee. 'I still can't sleep properly, and if I didn't force myself, I'd forget to eat.'

Dee shrugs. 'We are all works in progress.'

'What if I fuck up?'

She laughs. 'With Pen?'

I nod. She grins then and says, 'You're the best thing Pen has.' I think about that and she says to me, 'Think back to when you left the Black House.'

'It was pretty awful.'

She nods. 'I've read your file. You were pushed from pillar to post.' Then: 'How did you come to work at Planet Pop?'

I tell her about meeting Isaac.

She tells me, 'He made all the difference to you.'

'Yes.'

'Pen has an Isaac, but even better, she has that Isaac on call all the time.'

I let that sink in. Then I ask, 'What if I say the wrong thing?'

Dee shrugs. 'Then you say the wrong thing. I'm sure Isaac has; I'm sure every parent has at one time or another. Pen's not a delicate little thing. From what I can tell she's a lot like you. A tough cookie.'

I'm quite while I consider this, and Dee's face turns serious. I brace myself for impact.

'Now Blue, never mind all that, what are we going to have for pudding?'

CHAPTER THIRTY-ONE

Amy comes back into the dorm. Her clothing is torn. Her beautiful, auburn hair is tangled. Her eyes are red-rimmed, wild and unfocused. Her arrival has woken Blue.

Not just Amy coming in, but Natasha getting up. Moving to her side. Neither of them speak. Natasha helps Amy undress and as she does, Blue sees a litany of bruises covering her thighs and stomach, blood at the tops of her legs, still wet but starting to dry into a dark crust. Blue is tempted to pull her eyes away, to slip her body back between her sheets and covers, pull them over her head and sink into blissful darkness.

She doesn't though; she forces herself to watch. To bear witness and understand that this will be her fate, too. Lisa went last week. Gone like the others in the middle of the night.

Blue had, for the first time since she'd arrived here, been left alone. Lisa gets out of her bed, taking the clothes from Natasha, folding them into neat piles. Wordless.

Blue suddenly feels excluded. Left out. Her eyes stray to the stack of clothes, Amy's T-shirt torn and tattered, and she wonders why Lisa has bothered to fold them at all. They were ruined, sullied. Headed for the bin anyway.

Blue squeezes her eyes shut and is bombarded by a terrible internal show reel. A combination of the footage they saw in 'class' and the random acts of violence found in their everyday lives.

Amy still hasn't spoken. No one has. The only sound in the room is the ragged breathing of four frightened little girls.

Natasha, usually so calm, looks shaken at the brutality mapped out on Amy's thin, pale body. Blue forces herself to look again and realises there are cuts as well as bruising, old and new. Maybe they are the source of the blood at the tops of her legs? But Blue knows that's not true. She is reminded of war videos they had been subjected to. The weakness of women in conflict. The reasons they need men to protect them.

She shakes her head. Don't think it. Don't.

Natasha is using baby wipes now in an attempt to mop up some of the blood. Those wipes must be cold on Amy's skin, but she doesn't startle. Doesn't move. Just stares off into nowhere with a thick, glazed look in her eyes.

Blue clamps a hand over her mouth, to stop herself screaming or crying. Maybe in some vain attempt to push the bad thoughts down and away. She doesn't know. Lisa is sitting on the edge of her bed. Wide-eyed. Blue sees her own fears mirrored in the other girl's eyes and can't hold her gaze. Can't bear it. She turns away.

Eventually Amy speaks. Not to Blue, or Lisa.

To Natasha, direct and clear. 'I have to get out. I have to tell someone.'

Natasha shakes her head. Blue thinks she looks scared. Genuinely frightened. And that is bad, terrible, because nothing scares Natasha.

Amy cries then. Not loud sobs, just long, silent tears streaming down her cheeks.

She tells Natasha, 'It's getting worse, just because it isn't for you. It is for me and think of Lisa . . .'

A wet, sharp noise rings out through the little cabin room. It takes Blue a few seconds to realise it is the sound of Natasha's flat palm connecting with Amy's sodden cheek.

Natasha clamps the offending hand to her own mouth, wheezing. 'I'm sorry.'

Amy snatches for her pyjamas, climbing into them, wincing as she does. They are pale blue and thin. One of the blood marks from her skin immediately makes its way through the fabric. An irritated wound, starting off as a small, damp bead of red, blossoming into a more definite stain that Blue knows will never come out.

Amy gets into bed. Lisa climbs in next to Blue and Blue wraps her arms around her. None of them speak.

At some point in the night Blue stirs, aware that Lisa is snoring softly beside her. That's not what has woken her again though, it's the furious whispering, urgent and fast. Blue looks over and sees they are in Amy's bed, their bodies crushed close together.

CHAPTER THIRTY-TWO

As soon as Pen gets out of school she looks for me, her eyes full of questions. I nod once and tell her, 'Let's talk at home.'

She accepts that and she's quiet all the way back, her mind busy preparing itself to receive what I imagine must be long-coveted information. My mind is full of flames, hissing and spitting. The cave where Brodie and I used to hide. A brief respite from it all. A bright spot in what became terribly dark days.

When we get in, I make her wash her hands, eat a sandwich and then I talk.

I skim over as much as I can but once the words start to pour out of me, they keep coming. I am surprised at how much information I have retained and I'm surprised at how calm my voice is as it casually refers to, and then skirts around, horrors that ought to be unimaginable.

Pen listens, asking the occasional question and when I get to talking about Amy and reach a point where I can say no more – where my hand is pressed against my too-dry cracked lips – she slips off of her chair and puts her arms around me.

She whispers into my hair, 'She sounded really nice.'

I nod. 'She was.'

There is a silence then Pen nips to the bathroom, coming back with tissue for me and curling up on the overstuffed armchair that she seems to have made her own.

I tell her, 'This is hard for me to talk about.' And she nods.

I skip the months that followed Amy's death, where I was a ghost walking around in human form. Where I'd sneak down to the cellar to somehow punish myself if it wasn't doled out anyway. Survivor's guilt. Even before I was free. Because even then, I'd been the one still breathing, still walking around.

Natasha carried on as though nothing had happened. I don't know what I expected, what I wanted. But it wasn't that. Life wasn't the same. I wasn't the same. Even though we lived on a knife edge at the best of times, I'd found comfort in our little group. The three of them went some way to compensating me for the mother I'd lost. The one I still had to see on an almost daily basis. A shadow of her former self. Wandering around the Black House and staring at me through glazed eyes. The eyes of a cruel stranger.

I don't go into detail and I choose my words carefully. Dee's advice of gently echoing in my mind. I'm as gentle as it's possible to be.

I talk until I can't anymore. Aware that the story is incomplete, unfinished. She seems to sense it and says, 'It's OK.'

I don't know if she means me talking but I sink back, feeling tension I hadn't even known I was holding slip from me.

My left arm runs up and down the scarred grooves of my right and I pull it away, force it flat on the arm of the chair. But not before I see Pen looking.

She says again, 'It's OK.'

And I nod. Not because it's entirely true. But certainly it has been worse.

★

When Pen goes to bed, I take out the picture of my mother and me. I stare and stare as though the image may somehow have been changed by the years. Ready now to offer me some clue, some relief. But it never does. Always it's just an image of a stick-thin girl clutching a baby.

I go to sleep thinking about her, my mother, and about Natasha and I wake with a start, confused at a noise slicing through my sleep-addled brain.

It is Pen's alarm.

That means it's seven-thirty. I haven't slept this late since before the Black House. I don't get time to ruminate on it though, because Pen is in my room and talking already. On the way to school, she keeps chattering and when we get to the gates, she gives me an extra-long hug and waves like a loon.

I watch her go, my heart swelling with fondness for the little girl.

Then I turn and take out my phone.

He picks up on the first ring. 'Ms Sillitoe?'

'Yes, but Blue is fine.'

'Blue, then. I'm glad you called.'

'Do you know about Amy?'

He says, 'I think so, yes.'

We arrange to meet. I can't put it off any longer than I already have. My past won't let me go, however hard I try. I've never really left it behind. No matter what I might have thought, it has always been there chasing after me with flames licking at my heels and all of its awful secrets desperately whispering in my ear.

CHAPTER THIRTY-THREE

Blue isn't woken by the usual blaring five a.m. alarm, but by one of the Aunts. Natasha's mother, Sienna, is standing at the doorway to the girls' dorm. Blue jumps out of bed, pulling her grey sweatshirt on over her nightdress. Waking Lisa as she goes.

Sienna stands watching the children scramble. Natasha doesn't rush. She stands in front of her mother, stretching out, arms raised above her head in a posture that's almost feline, lifting her nightdress to reveal her naked body, all womanly curves and soft skin.

Blue is used to seeing Natasha naked. You can't live in proximity as close as they all do and be bashful, but she feels somehow embarrassed by this display, and looks away. Blue feels Natasha is making a show of her body and her eyes flick to Sienna's face. Her expression remains impassive, but Blue sees two red spots rise on the woman's cheeks.

Blue looks away entirely, concentrating now on pulling on knickers, jeans, slipping her nightdress off beneath her clothing. When she looks again at the Aunt, the red spots are fading. Her face betraying nothing at all.

It isn't until Blue is fully dressed that she realises Amy isn't there. Her bed is made, but empty. Her pyjamas are folded neatly at the end of it, the dark, red spot from the awful night before still there. The little girl can't tear her eyes away and a sense of dread rises within her at the sight of them.

Her heart hammers in her chest as Sienna says, 'Come.' And the five a.m. alarm starts to sound.

They are led to the large barn where everyone is assembled in various states of awakening. Blue feels sick and wonders if she's going to vomit. Or pass out. She half wishes for the latter, and a final passing, even. One where she shuts her eyes and never opens them again because surely nothingness would be better than whatever is about to come.

Many of the people look like they've dressed hurriedly. The children in their jeans and grey sweaters. The women in their long, white dresses.

Blue, Lisa and Natasha are pushed through the throng of people who part as they come. A line of three behind Sienna, who nods to the boys, gesturing for them to join the girls. The three become a group of six. Nick, Brodie, Martin. Brodie smiles at Blue briefly and she clutches the white stone in her pocket, unable to muster up more than a grimace in return. The nausea is overwhelming and she presses a hand to her mouth, which is bone dry. Her head hurts.

No one turns to look at the children as Sienna steps back, ushering them to the front. Blue is surprised, until she sees what all eyes are drawn to.

The horror of it is immediate and absolute. So overwhelming that at first Blue's brain doesn't register what she is seeing. It takes the image, files it away, but her hammering heart denies it vehemently.

As reality catches up, her limbs snap into action. She is moving forward, arms outstretched, running towards her dear, beloved friend.

Sharp fingers dig into her shoulder, pulling her back, scooping her up. One hand plants on the back of her head, burying Blue's face into her chest.

Natasha.

She is trying to help. Trying to save Blue from it. But two of the Aunts step forward, take Natasha's arms. Forcing her to

164

drop the smaller girl. Leaving Blue's eyes free to search out what will never leave her. What she can never un-see.

Natasha glares at the women either side. Neither one looks at her. They are unaffected by Blue's desolate heartbreak and Natasha's hot, seething anger.

Another Aunt pulls Blue roughly to her feet, keeping her facing Amy's crumpled, distorted and horrifyingly naked body.

Her head is crooked and wrong. Her neck painfully twisted and her eyes wide open.

The sharp colour of them looking out at nothing.

One of her arms is curled the wrong way, smashed to bits under the weight of her falling body. Her leg stands upwards at an impossible angle.

There is blood. Not much. Not as much as Blue thinks there should be. Though she doesn't know why its absence bothers her so.

Carillo steps out and up onto the steps of the barn, hands out before him. Beatific. He looks out at the crowd. Amy at his feet making a shocking, awful tableaux.

'One of our children has fallen.' He calls out, voice booming, 'Literally, figuratively. She made a choice, a bad one. When she came out here in the middle of the night, stole up onto the roof and ended something that didn't belong to her.'

Blue shakes her head and murmurs, 'No.' To what, she is not sure. That Amy is gone. Dead. That she would leave them at all.

That she is here and her mother is no longer hers.

That she is awake during a living nightmare.

Blue spins, trying to make eye contact with Natasha, Lisa, Brodie, but the Aunt behind her turns her head back. To make sure Blue doesn't miss a thing.

Carillo. The awful, awful man who Blue's mother loves more than she does her own child, is talking about evil. Guilt. Not being strong enough for this world.

Blue's sadness shifts, turning into rage.

'No!' again, but louder now. And again and again, and louder. The Aunt clamps a hand over Blue's mouth but still the little girl screams. Muffled but not stopped. She lashes out, arms and legs flying. Making herself impossible to get hold of, priming herself to get ready. To go. To run.

Anywhere but there.

But the Aunt is bigger, stronger, and two more join her. Taking Blue, wriggling, crying, howling, into the Black House. Down cellar steps, throwing her onto a damp, cold floor in a cramped, dark space.

When the door at the top of the stairs closes, Blue is left alone in the dark. Trapped in every possible way.

And worse than all of it, Amy is dead.

CHAPTER THIRTY-FOUR

NATASHA

Timing is everything. Don't you think? Life is like chess. You have to play a long game and be strategic about it.

Emotions muddy the water. Make it hard to make measured, careful decisions. It's OK to want to escape, but you have to do it the right way. At the right time.

We had a plan, Amy and I. If she wasn't tough enough for it, there was no reason for it to become my problem. Running before you're prepared is for losers. She didn't understand what would be waiting for her, how it would be with no money, no means. We had a job, a role within the awful system we found ourselves in. I took it seriously; it's what kept me going. Protect the younger ones.

All she had to do – all *we* had to do – was distance ourselves. You had to make it so you could separate your mind from your body. Crying didn't help. As Amy learned the hard way, it turned her into a victim. Her tears made the men feel guilty, which is why they took things out on her so badly.

She should have been more like me. I told her, and I passed it on to Lisa, too. Separate your mind from your body. Keep smiling.

Never let anyone know you're broken.

CHAPTER THIRTY-FIVE

I remember the feel of a damp, earthy cellar floor. Not being frightened of the dark because people were far more terrifying than the absence of light. But I was left there for over twenty-four hours. Just me and my thoughts. One image on replay – my friend's mangled body at the foot of a big black barn and a madman standing witness.

That image comes to mind now, and by the time I get to the café, I am full of anxiety as well as being nervous. Looking around, I see a man in a navy-blue jumper waving at me. With a deep breath, I go over to his table. He is younger than I thought he'd be. Close to my own age, I'd say.

I sit at the table and ask, 'You surely didn't cover the original case?'

He frowns. 'What? No, I'm just writing a book about it, like I said. Hence the research.'

I nod.

He smiles and I see he is very good-looking, 'Can I get you a drink?' Faint but it is there. That Welsh lilt to his voice.

I shake my head and he sits again, picking up his own coffee taking a sip.

I wait. Unsure what to say next.

Luckily he dives straight in: 'Amy Jenkins, thought to be sixteen at the time of her death, her remains were found buried on the grounds of the Black House. Injuries conducive with a fall from a height. Speculation by investigators concluded it could have been the eaves of the large barn and they were unsure whether her death was accidental, by design or by foul play.'

I clamp my fingers to my lips. He stares at the swirly colours coming out of my sleeve. Then sees me watching him.

He looks away. 'I'm sorry.' His face flushes.

I say, 'You know.'

'About your burns?'

I nod. 'How the hell would you know that?' My voice is rising. A man at the next table turns and glances at me with a frown. I glare back and he looks away.

I half whisper, 'My files are sealed. How the hell . . .'

He shrugs. 'I've been in contact with people at various places over the years.'

I blink. Once. Twice. 'Someone at social services talked?'

He shrugs again, looking uncomfortable. 'I'm sorry.'

I frown at that. 'I just thought . . .'

I don't know what I thought. That people coining in a paltry government pay cheque were above manipulation and bribery. I can barely even remember the names of people I saw in any official capacity. They all sort of blur into one.

He says, 'All the information I have, other than what was reported in the press, was hard to come by.' Like that makes it somehow better.

I ask, 'Amy's death wasn't reported? In the papers, I mean.'

He says, 'No. Her father specifically asked that it wasn't.'

'Her father?'

I am aghast. None of us had dads.

He tells me, 'He had filed police reports when Amy initially went missing.'

'Went missing?' I sound like a dumb parrot.

'Yes.'

'She was there with her mother.'

'Yes. But both parents had parental responsibility. They were separated but Amy's father still had a fair bit of contact.'

'So what, her mother . . . kidnapped her?'

'Yep. Pretty much. She started "dating" Carillo. All Callum – that's Amy's dad – knew was that she'd met someone. He said he was genuinely happy for her. Seemingly their split had been reasonably amicable. He'd remarried. Had been expecting another child when Amy and Pamela left.'

'Oh God.'

I rest my head forward onto my hands. Pamela. Amy's mother was called Pamela. An image of her blank face whilst she beat her daughter springs to my mind. Another of her standing by Amy's lifeless body. No expression at all, as far as I could recall. No heart-rending sobs for her beautiful, kind daughter. I wonder if I'm going to throw up.

David murmurs, 'I'm sorry. This is a lot to take in, isn't it.'

'No. No, I'm fine,' I lie. 'I mean; it is a shock. She never spoke about her dad. Amy.' I force myself to say her name, my tongue finding it difficult to form the word.

Amy.

He doesn't say anything. But I can see it on his face: he feels sorry for me. Amy never mentioned her father. Not once.

All of us had our secrets. Amy had been there longer than me. Not as long as Natasha. Maybe she'd just buried it away. What was the point in dwelling on things? Before she died, she was the most despondent when we talked about escape and I wonder now whether she'd made a previous attempt. If I'd had a dad or a sibling or anyone at all, I think I might have tried. As it was, I was nowhere near ready until I had to be.

I say, 'So you knew who and where we all were?'

He nods.

I ask, 'Lisa?'

He closes his eyes for second and I believe, perhaps optimistically, that he is sad for her.

He says, 'I was very sad to find out she'd died.'

I say, 'I lost contact with them.'

He nods. 'I know.'

I say, 'I didn't go to her funeral.'

'I know.'

'You were there?'

'Yes.'

Then it dawns on me, properly dawns on me. 'You were in contact with Natasha?'

'I met up with her at the funeral.'

'And she was happy to speak to you?'

He grins a sort of lopsided grin. 'Happy would be an exaggeration.'

'But she spoke to you?'

He nods. 'We became friends.'

I wonder if there's more to it than that. I think about Gareth and his lovesick puppy face. I ask him, 'How did she seem?'

'Honestly?'

'Yes.'

'Aside from the loss of her friend, she seemed happy and together.' He adds, 'Very private, though.'

'But you knew everything about her anyway, right?'

He grins. 'I'm a journalist, not a clairvoyant. Who actually knows everything about another person?'

'But you're surprised she killed herself?'

'I am.'

'And what information are you looking for now?'

He grins. 'If I knew that, I wouldn't be looking for it.'

I don't return his smile. This is, after all, my life and not a story I'm looking to sell.

As if reading my mind, he says, 'Look. I get that this must be weird for you on . . . all kinds of levels and I wade into it looking for a story.' He shrugs. 'It's my job. I worked on local papers for a while and they paid peanuts. I've been ghost writing for years to make ends meet, but I realised I needed to find something of my own to work on. Something that felt . . . unfinished. I'll admit that's what drove my formative research into the Black House. At some point though, I did start caring.'

'About what?'

He frowns and runs a hand through his thick hair. 'Shit, the whole thing. That many people dead. How the fuck did it happen, what were the parents thinking, how the hell did you get over something like that?' He pauses, takes a deep breath. 'I didn't have the best start you know, so trauma and recovery interest me, I guess. I didn't start out looking into this expecting to find any similarities.'

'But you did?'

'I did, yeah.'

I snort. 'So you survived a cult and a mass suicide?'

He shakes his head. 'I survived years of abuse at the hands of the people who were supposed to love and protect me. I felt an almost constant division between love and hatred. I felt uncomfortable in my own skin and wrong and like, why had I been born just to be so unloved?'

'I'm sorry, I didn't mean to diminish anything about you or your life. I don't know anything about it, and I know I don't have an exclusive on pain.' Dee's words spring out of my lips and I smile briefly.

He says, 'We all get an exclusive on our pain, though.'

I find I quite like him, despite myself. Plus, although my mind is reeling, and it is, I am glad to have found out about Amy's father. Glad that she had one parent who cared, even if it didn't do her any good in the end. My intense hatred for her mother spikes again. Pamela. What must it take for a woman to inflict and witness such cruelty on her child?

I say, 'It's been interesting talking to you.' Unsure whether I can handle much more right now, thinking that I have millions of questions but can't seem to formulate a single one yet.

I'm about to stand, leave and suggest meeting again in the next few days when he says, 'There was one thing I wanted to ask you about?'

'Oh?'

'Natasha had a kid.'

I blink, my mind racing. He knows so much but doesn't know much about this? I murmur, 'Wow.' Trying to give the impression I have no idea.

'I think you might know where she is?'

I stand then, and walk away. I'm opening the door and stepping outside when he catches up to me.

'I'm sorry.'

I look at him and don't speak.

'That was clumsy – you don't have to tell me anything.'

'I know.'

'Please do consider speaking with me again, though. We don't have to talk about that.'

I sigh and nod. 'Look. I'm trying myself to find out what the . . . circumstances were that led to . . .' I wave my hand around '. . . this.' Meaning Natasha's death. 'So, let me know if you find anything out about Natasha, yeah?'

He looks relieved. 'I will.' I'm walking away as he calls out, 'It was nice meeting you.'

I wave without turning back.

I check my phone and see three missed calls all from Pen's school, one from Dee. Heart pounding in my chest, I listen to the voicemails and then I'm running as fast as I can.

I've not got very far when a car beeps next to me. It's David, who says, 'Do you need a lift somewhere?'

Without having time to consider the implications, I nod and wrench the passenger door open.

CHAPTER THIRTY-SIX

NATASHA

The most important job you could ever have is being someone's mother. I knew that even before I became one.

There were many things I could, if not forgive, at least understand. Men are simple creatures, I think. Beasts some of them, but not complex. Never as complex as they themselves think they are. I watched Joseph work my mother and then others. She was the first, for a time the most devoted. But his attentions turned to me fairly early on. My body betraying me, becoming something shinier, newer than my mother's. She turned a blind eye, of course. They all did.

I hated her for it, but I also knew that no matter what, I wasn't going to end up like her. A servile, lovesick fool.

Nor like Amy: broken into a thousand unfixable pieces.

When I was pregnant, the only thing I was slightly scared of was having a male child. I so desperately wanted a girl, you see. Someone just like me.

Girls, women, are tough when we need to be. We are strong, intelligent, complex. We can subdue our base desires in ways men cannot. Ways that always leave them weak.

Joseph's lust proved to be his downfall and I led him there happily enough. I led them all on that merry dance towards the end and now I'm dancing all over again and, as always, it's my turn to lead.

CHAPTER THIRTY-SEVEN

Dee and Mrs Williams are in the office when I burst in. I look from one to the other and glare at the headmistress, taking a step towards her. It is Dee who stops me, pressing a hand onto my arm and shaking her head.

'Take a seat, Blue.'

Her voice is so firm and I am so scared that I do as asked. Mrs Williams asks who the gentleman is. I'd raced from the car in such a hurry I hadn't even noticed him following me. I mumble, 'A writer.'

He smiles and puts his hand out. Dee turns to me with raised eyebrow.

I say, 'Journalist.'

She says to him, 'I think you ought to leave.'

He says, 'Of course. Sorry, I wasn't . . . I mean I'm not going to like, use this for a story, or anything.' I feel a moment of sympathy for him but it's overshadowed by fear for Pen.

Dee adds, 'DI Grafton is on her way,' and gives David a withering look.

I tell him, 'Keep this to yourself.'

He nods. 'I will, just . . . let me know she's OK.' My heart sinks. He had known Natasha had a child and seemingly suspected I may be the one who knew her whereabouts. This not only confirms it but also that I am in charge of said child. He now knows her name and which school she's at.

He's hurried from the office by Dee who looks none too pleased.

When she comes back in, I say, 'I met him for coffee to find out what he knew.'

'Which is?'

'A lot more than he bloody should.'

The headmistress gasps – I assume at the word bloody – and I glare at her. 'Really? You've lost a fucking kid.'

She opens her mouth as though about to speak. Thinks better and shuts it.

The door knocks and DI Grafton comes in. 'Was that David Belsham I just saw leaving?'

I groan. 'You know him?'

'He's been hassling us for comment.'

'I met him for a coffee, told him nothing, then he drove past me running to get here.' My voice is rising and my breath becomes a bit laboured. Jesus wept. I push my head down into my hands.

DI Grafton kneels beside me. 'It's OK, Blue. Our only objective right now is to find Pen.' But her lips are thin and pursed and I get the impression she's none too happy about it.

I nod. 'Please.' And a million awful thoughts clamour at the front of my mind. 'God, please.'

The head says, 'She left at the beginning of lunch.' Adding, 'We saw her leave on the front gate camera.' Dee and DI Grafton exchange a look. The head adds, 'So just over an hour ago – she couldn't have got far.'

I jump up out of my seat. Dee places a hand on my arm. It is cool and soft. I sit down. Desperately working on keeping my mouth closed, so as to avoid a torrent of abuse pouring out. I press my fingers to my lips. Pen is fine; I can't entertain anything other than that. We'll find her. She'll be back at this school. I ought not to piss this woman off any more than I already have.

DI Grafton turns to me. 'Blue, do you have any idea where she might have gone?'

I shake my head slowly, thinking hard, and then it dawns on me. I start to talk very quickly.

The time in the office seems to move like liquid. Seconds dragging, minutes racing by. I feel in and out of myself. Finally, DI Grafton rings. I stare at my phone until eventually Dee picks it up, putting it on speaker.

'I found her sitting on a train at Paddington.'

Pen is fine; she is safe. The relief is overwhelming, but it is quickly replaced. Pen left school. I told her the truth and it had repercussions. I have worked very hard to keep my life simple. I have had more upset, more drama than one person can reasonably be expected to endure.

But now I am livid. Absolutely deranged with it. But outwardly I am surprised to hear myself speak, cool and calm, to Dee. 'I don't want to speak to her and she's not coming back, either.'

Dee takes the phone off speaker, speaks to DI Grafton then hangs up, standing to get her coat.

I tell her, 'You take her away. Back into care. I'll pack her bag.' And I stand to do just that.

Dee puts a hand on my arm. 'I'll keep her tonight. I won't tell her anything. You take time to think about what you're saying right now.'

I say, 'I don't need time. The whole idea was stupid. I never wanted a fucking kid. I knew I wouldn't be any good at it and she's not exactly helping, is she?'

Dee stands, stoic and solid. 'Blue. Stop. Take time. You have my mobile number. I'll take her to school in the morning then I'll come and see you. We can talk then.'

I go home, stomping all the way from the school to my flat.

When I get in, I go straight into Pen's room. Get her suitcase out from under her bed and start putting her clothes into it. Then I pick up her pencil case, schoolbooks and large pad. It falls open on a page where Pen has started drawing. It's a crude representation of me, but actually not bad. And surrounding me are hearts and stars that she's gone over in bold felt-tip pen.

I sit on the edge of her bed and start to cry.

CHAPTER THIRTY-EIGHT

The little girl has managed to get as far as Paddington and is sitting, waiting to leave, on a train heading to Cardiff. Annie has driven to the train station at an alarming speed, calling ahead to the transport police and asking them to keep the train there. Once she arrives, she and three officers search the length of the train and eventually Annie finds Pen, sitting alone in her school uniform in a large empty carriage.

The girl looks at her through wide eyes, which relay her young age, but her mouth is set in a grim and determined line.

Annie sighs and sits down next to her. 'Hello, Pen.'

Pen looks out of the window. 'The train isn't moving.'

'No, it won't until we get you off it.'

'I want to see Wales. Where my mum grew up.'

'And you can. But not like this.'

She pushes her lip out, a caricature of stubbornness.

Annie says, 'Blue is beside herself.'

Pen's face softens. 'Is she?'

Annie nods. 'Of course. I'm going to call her now, OK?'

Pen nods but her face is white.

Children, thinks Annie. Resilient, odd little blighters. The girl must have decided on this course of action at some point over the last twenty-four hours, not mentioned it to a soul and then spent until lunchtime getting ready.

Blue picks up and Annie immediately says, 'She's fine. Do you want to speak to her?'

There is a pause and then Blue says, 'I don't want to speak to her and she's not coming back here, either.'

Dee comes on the line.

She tells Annie, 'Blue isn't ready to talk to Pen yet. I'll come and meet you both there, OK?'

Annie frowns into the handset. 'OK.'

She hangs up and Pen's little eyes are wet now. 'Is Blue mad at me?'

Annie pats her on the shoulder. 'She just needs some time to cool off, I suspect. Let's get you back.'

CHAPTER THIRTY-NINE

At some point I pick myself up, pour a large glass of wine and down it. I don't drink often and it goes straight to my head. I decide this isn't such a bad thing and immediately pour another one, then a third. I stand as the effects of the alcohol catch up with me. The room starts to spin and I remember now why it is I never have more than one glass.

I grab the bottle and the glass and head to my sofa. The long-stemmed glass wobbles dangerously for a second when I try to put it down on the coffee table.

I sit, enjoying the buzz and a blank mind. I pour another drink, swig it. My mind, though, has other ideas, thrumming to life, intruding on the short peace the alcohol gave me. I think about Natasha and Sienna. 'Drippy Nenny' as Natasha would refer to her. There was always something between the two of them that I didn't understand. Later when I considered it, I tried to imagine a woman so in love with a lunatic she gave him her daughter. Would there have been jealousy on Sienna's part? Certainly there was anger and contempt from Natasha. She hated Sienna with her body and soul. Considered her weak and ineffectual. I knew if Brodie hadn't insisted on bringing her that night, Natasha would have happily left without her. I've thought often about how it must have been for them afterwards. There are some wounds from which you can never heal.

I pour another drink, contemplating this. Drink as I wonder if any of those tensions played out between Natasha and her own child. They say that don't they? Patterns can repeat themselves.

I don't think so, though. Can't really entertain it, and surely Pen herself is proof that Natasha had done a good job. A great job. Pen is brilliant.

My eyes sting with tears. I feel vaguely nauseous and slightly drunk. This is what people do though, right? Numb it with alcohol. I pour another glass and down it, then another, and lean back as the room starts spinning.

I must have drifted off because I come to with my phone ringing and my head pounding. I grapple to pull it out from my jeans pocket, surprised to hear my voice sound slurry when I say, 'Hi.'

I am assaulted by a wave of nausea. And sink backwards into the cushions.

It's Isaac who says, 'Annie rang. Are you all right?' Annie? I frown at the handset.

'Not really.' And I find myself talking, my words jumbling into each other and not making much sense.

There is a pause and he says, 'Are you drunk?' I hang up the phone. It immediately rings again and I switch it off.

People do this sort of thing all the time. I never have more than one glass of wine but why shouldn't I? I didn't ask for any of this shit.

Bloody Pen. Bloody Natasha. I lean forward, finding I almost can't stop.

I think I need to lie down and I crumple into the sofa. I must drift off because the next thing I know Isaac's face is an inch from mine as my eyes snap open and I scream.

He jumps back, staring down at me, wide-eyed. My

head feels like jelly and the room is spinning. Isaac looks at me. I look at him and he holds up a key. 'I let myself in.'

I try to nod but instead I feel awfully sick. I push past him and into the bathroom. I get to the toilet just in time and throw up twice, with noise and an awful vigour.

When I get back out to my living room, Isaac points at a coffee on the table and my stomach lurches again.

I murmur, 'No thanks.'

I no longer feel dizzy but I do have a splintering pain in my head and my mouth feels like I've been licking sawdust. I wince as I sit down.

Isaac says, 'You're a lousy drunk.'

'You'd know.'

He grins. 'I would have drunk you under the table.' I smile back, but my head splinters again and it turns into a grimace.

He says, 'Annie said Pen isn't here?'

I shake my head. 'She won't be coming back.'

'Want to tell me what happened?'

'But Annie has filled you in, right?' I can hear the pettiness as I emphasise the word *Annie*. I hate the thought of being discussed and I hate that he's calling DI Grafton by her first name as though she's a friend instead of just a terrible imposition. It takes me back to the days where adults would speak about me and my future in barely concealed whispers.

Isaac says, 'I'd like to hear your version.' I tell him roughly, anger building afresh as I say it all. Ending in: 'She decided to nip off to Wales. So Dee got it wrong, too. I shouldn't have told her. She's not mature enough to deal with it.'

He doesn't say anything, though I give him the space for agreement.

In the end I ask, 'What's the time?'

He looks at his watch. 'Almost five a.m.'

I wipe a hand across my face, 'God.'

He says, 'You were sparko when I got here. Figured you'd be best left.'

'What time did we speak on the phone?'

He shrugs. 'Midnight, half past.'

I murmur, 'Sorry.'

'Get in the shower. We'll get some breakfast and go to Dee's.'

I'm shaking my head. 'No.'

He looks at me, not speaking. I meet his gaze, stubborn, resolute.

Eventually he says, 'She's a child and you're what she's got.'

I shake my head again. 'She'll be better off there. Everything about those places has changed since my time. I don't remember people like Dee.' And it's a good point, I think.

'No.'

I stare at him aghast. He doesn't look away, doesn't back down. I say, 'Isaac, please.'

'No, Blue, I'm not going to agree with you that you should abandon that child.'

I burst into tears. He sits and lets me cry it out, and when I'm done, he says, 'When you started showing up at Planet Pop you were a lost little thing.'

I snap, 'I hadn't had the best few years.'

He nods. 'You'd had a terrible time. A very unfair start.'

I snort. 'That's an understatement.'

He nods again. 'It is, yeah. Life can be a bitch.' The words hang between us. He goes on, 'I watched you grow from an angry, awkward young woman into who you are today.'

'An angry, awkward grown woman?'

He smiles but shakes his head. 'No, Blue. I mean, you can't handle your booze and you could do with getting out more.'

I laugh. 'Coming from you.'

He shrugs. 'I know you get bouts of depression and I'm not judging you. But you were never meant to be miserable, and you were never meant to be hard.'

I shake my head. 'Isaac, I was so scared, when I got that call. That something had happened to her.'

He nods. 'Yes. I bet you were.'

'I'm mad at her.'

'You'll get over it.' We don't speak until he says, 'I'm going to have a fag on the balcony. Get in the shower.'

CHAPTER FORTY

I come out, scrubbed, dressed and having taken an ibuprofen, feeling slightly less wobbly.

Isaac is on the phone. He says, 'Yes, she's ready. We're on our way.'

I frown. 'Who are you talking to?'

'Dee.'

I scowl at him, but he just shrugs. 'I got her number from Annie and called her last night, while you were out of it.'

'Oh terrific.'

The fucker grins. 'Come on.'

We get to the home and I am furious right up until the moment Dee swings open the door to her office and Pen is sitting there, head down, in her crumpled uniform from yesterday and looking so small and helpless that I swear my heart cracks down the middle.

I say, 'Pen.'

She looks straight up at me and promptly bursts into tears.

I go to her and put my arms around her, pulling her little, stick-thin body to mine.

She sobs, 'I'm so sorry.'

I pull away, shaking my head. 'No. I'm sorry.'

'What for?'

'For not coming to collect you last night.'

'You don't want me to leave?'

I know Dee hasn't said that to her, because Isaac told me. Apparently they'd all been quite certain I was just having a moment. Despite the fact I was certain of no such thing. But she doesn't need to know I wobbled and I see again then how sometimes the truth isn't always the best thing.

I say, 'Pen, look at me.' And she does, her watery little eyes cutting right through me, her lower lip stuck out in an almost comical parody of sad. 'Your home is with me. OK?'

'I'm sorry for leaving.'

'I know and I'm not happy about it.' I look at Dee and Isaac then back to her. 'I just needed to cool off, that was all.'

'Are you cool now?'

I say, 'Baby, I'm always cool,' in a silly voice. And she grins. I add, 'But we need to get you home and ready for school, OK?'

She nods. I take her hand.

Dee says, 'A quick word?'

Isaac says, 'I'll get us in the car. Meet you there.'

She shuts the door and I turn, expecting a bollocking or something, but all she says is, 'Are you OK?'

I nod. 'I think so. I hope so.' Then: 'I don't normally drink.'

She smiles. 'No, Isaac said.'

I groan. 'I don't really remember him phoning.'

She shrugs. 'Lucky he did.'

'You didn't tell her, what I said to you?'

She shakes her head.

I ask, 'Why?'

'I figured you'd come around.'

I head down to join Isaac and Pen, marvelling at the fact that they all seem to have a lot more faith in me than I do myself.

CHAPTER FORTY-ONE

Once Pen is at school, I say to Isaac, 'I need to do something. Can you open the shop?'

He says, 'What do you need to do?'

I tell him and he stares at me for a minute. 'The shop can stay closed. I'll drive you.'

I say, 'It can't stay closed – that's a whole day's takings.'

He shrugs. 'I'll message Oren.' He taps out a quick text. As we climb into the car, his phone pings. He shows me the screen. 'See, Oren will open up. No dramas.' And then: 'It's only money, anyway.'

I roll my eyes. As we drive, I tell Isaac about the agency where Natasha worked. My doubts about why she would have killed herself. The journalist who was actually quite nice.

By the time I'm finished I say, 'You think I'm being weird?'

'Not at all.'

'Really?'

He shrugs. 'Really. Annie isn't happy with all the details, either.'

'Oh?'

He says, 'She mentioned it when we spoke yesterday.'

'What's she unhappy about?'

'Mainly the same as you – a feeling. And they still haven't been able to ID the body.'

'Oh?'

He nods. 'I'm sure they will.'

I'm not, but I don't say it. Instead I ask him before I have a chance to censor myself, 'Did you find being a parent, a dad . . . difficult?'

He is quiet for so long I start to worry that I've over-stepped the mark. I'm about to apologise when he starts to speak.

'You know Gill already had a child?'

I nod. 'Your stepson?'

'Yes, Jacob. I loved that kid; he was easy-going on the whole. Missed his dad, who'd died in a motorcycle acci-dent. No one's fault, just one of those shit things. Gill was a good mum, a good person.'

I think about making a quip about her taste in men but it's not the time.

Isaac says, 'We got married and honestly – I felt like some kind of hero, I guess. She'd been on her own, broke. I was in the band and we were selling shitloads of records. I had money coming out of my ears.'

'Sounds tough.'

He smiles but keeps his eyes on the road. 'She got pregnant and I was set to tour. I made vague noises about staying behind, but she insisted and it wasn't difficult to persuade me to go.' He shrugs. 'I was into drink and drugs by then, usually not around her and Jacob, though I'd be lying if I said never. Honestly I travelled so much it was easy enough to hide and when I was home I drank a lot more than she ever knew about. But I had the excuse that those periods were my weekends and I used it.'

'I guess she married a rock star.'

'She married an immature arsehole. I was already on my way down when I met her and she was like the last beacon of sanity.' He shrugs again. 'I thought her and

Jacob had fixed me. That I had it all under wraps. Then came Jackson. My tour finished. There was Gill with Jacob who'd just turned six and a new-born. Too busy for me, which is perfectly understandable, except I felt left out.' He sighs. 'The band were falling apart, that was to be our last tour, but I'd picked up a heroin habit on top of everything else by that point.'

'I'm sorry, Isaac.'

He smiles, glances at me, then: 'Me too. I wish I had a different answer to your question, but I don't. The truth is, I was an awful father. I put Gill and the kids through another ten years of hell before I walked out. The only decent thing I did was leave her the house.'

'And you got sober, got well.'

'Yeah, but too late for them.'

I know that Isaac has reached out a few times and that Gill won't entertain him. I can't imagine him being anything other than the fantastic man I know now, but he isn't a liar and if he says he put them through hell, then he did.

He says to me now, 'There's this thing we say in recovery – that one day you'll get to a stage where you don't regret the past anymore. I'm at peace with it and I know I'm better, but I do regret losing them.' Pulling in to park outside a block of flats, he says, 'This is it.'

I take his hand, squeeze it. 'Thank you.'

He nods. 'Go on now, unless you want me to come in?'

I shake my head. 'I'll be fine.'

I get out of the car and head up to the house, realising my stupidity as I do, ringing the bell with her name on isn't going to help me. I try two of the other flats in the block before I get an answer. An old lady's voice comes through the intercom, thin and faint.

I say, 'Hello I'm looking for . . .' Then I pause, what am I looking for? 'It's about Lyndsey Dunmore.'

She inhales then and: 'Come in, please do come in.' The buzzer goes and I deduce she's one of two flats on the ground floor. She stands by her green front door at the end of a well-maintained communal hallway.

Despite her somewhat wispy voice, she is a tall, sturdy-looking woman with very long hair that is a pure white colour. She has a nice face, but it is screwed up in concern right now. There is a large ginger cat sitting just behind her.

She says, 'Come, come.' So I follow her inside.

Her flat is too warm, but she is still wrapped up well.

She says, 'Tea, coffee?' And I shake my head. 'Sit, sit.' I do – onto a sofa coated in fur. She sighs. 'Sorry, that's Justin.' She points to the cat. 'He likes to leave bits of himself everywhere with common disregard for everyone else.'

I smile, hopefully politely.

She tells me, 'Little bugger's taken up home here and I've not the heart to kick him out.'

'He's not yours?'

She frowns. 'Are you a friend of Lyndsey's?'

'No.'

'Then what . . . Why are you here?' Her voice is rising.

'God, sorry. I'm a friend, was a friend of her friend. Natasha.' I am jumbling my words and the thought flashes across my mind that I'd have been a terrible detective.

She relaxes slightly at that. 'Ah. Yes, I knew Natasha and her very cute daughter . . . Penelope, is it?' She's smiling and I realise with horror that of course she mustn't know. Why would she?

I blurt out the truth, hardly managing to spill the words coherently. I hear *dead, tragedy, suicide* and *custody*. And hope I've got it all out in the right order. She has a hand clutched to her chest. Almost an imitation of the receptionist at Mayfair Properties. But on her, it is genuine.

I murmur, 'I'm sorry.'

She leans forward and touches my knee once. 'No, I'm sorry for you. As I said, I didn't know Natasha well, though she and Lyndsey were thick as thieves. Gosh.'

There is a moment where she takes everything in and I sit awkwardly, looking at the cat. Fat, smug, unperturbed by news of death and suicide and . . .

'What would you like to know? About Lyndsey?'

I say, 'Well.' Then falter. 'Um, I was told she left, rather abruptly.'

She is nodding now, leaning forward. 'It was very strange indeed.'

'In what way?'

'We are, well I considered us, friends of a sort . . . a familial kind of relationship even. I'm not sure if you know, but very sadly Lyndsey's parents both died in a car crash when she was in her early twenties.'

'No, I didn't. How sad.'

'Yes and no siblings. I sort of took to looking after her a bit I suppose.'

I smile. 'That's nice of you.'

'Well.' She shrugs. 'My children are grown and gone, busy lives. Lyndsey was just there.' She waves a hand. 'Anyway.'

'She didn't tell you she was going?'

'She said she was planning to go sometime in the next year or so but the first I heard was after I'd been hammering on her door for a week with no response.'

I say, 'Oh.'

'Yes, and I'd realised Justin here couldn't get in.' She shrugs. 'Eventually I found a note, which had ended up wedged under my doormat.'

'What did it say?'

'That she was going travelling, wouldn't be able to look after Justin and hoped I could. She transferred some money to my account. For his food and whatnot.'

'That must have been tough.'

She frowns. 'It was just . . . weird.'

'That she didn't tell you herself?'

She nods. 'Yes. We were close, you know. If not a visit, which honestly, I would have expected, then at least a phone call.'

Her eyes tear up and she laughs, wiping at one. 'You must think I'm a silly old lady.'

I say, 'Not at all.' And mean it. People can be thoughtless and cruel. But there's something about this that I don't like. I ask her, 'Was the note definitely in her handwriting?'

She shrugs. 'Looked like it, yes. She was a bright girl but could be very childlike sometimes. You know, and perhaps a bit impulsive, so although I was surprised when she went . . . well, it wasn't beyond the bounds of possibility.'

I say, 'She sounds lovely and your friendship sounds very special.' I think of me and Isaac. People who find each other in place of anyone else.

She smiles. 'Perhaps, I mean, I thought so.' Then: 'If you do find out anything . . .'

'I'll let you know.'

CHAPTER FORTY-TWO

I call DI Grafton. She tells me Lyndsey still owns her little flat and that the mortgage payments are all up to date. They – the police – haven't been able to get hold of her yet either, though they had been told by several acquaintances that Lyndsey had responded to some contact via social media. I make a note to tell her neighbour, not sure whether it will be of comfort or not.

When I go to collect Pen, her face is pinched and worried-looking. She looks at me through wide eyes as though she has the weight of the world on her shoulders.

I say, 'What's up, kiddo?'

She says in a voice so small I have to lean down to listen, 'Are you still mad at me?'

I frown. We start walking. 'No. We've talked. Also, I'm sorry, I meant it when I said that.'

'I deserved it.'

I stop walking, bend down in front of her and wait for her to meet my eye. When she does I say, 'Actually, no you didn't. I behaved like a sulky child.'

She tells me, 'Mummy used to leave me at Lisa's when I was naughty.'

I still at that, trying to keep my face impassive. I don't know what she means. 'Oh really, naughty like how?'

She shrugs. 'If I didn't do what she said, or I lied about something.'

'Did you do that a lot?'

She looks away. I stand stiffly, and we start walking again. I stay quiet and eventually she says, 'Not really. But I did other things wrong. If I'd done something I knew would make her cross, I'd get scared sometimes, though I wouldn't know exactly what I'd done.' She kind of laughs. I don't join in. Not finding what she's saying amusing at all.

I remembered Natasha's anger when we were children. It was a very quiet thing, something that lurked in the shadows waiting for the right moment to surprise us. It had been particularly hard on Lisa, who was sensitive by nature. I'd learnt since that silent treatment was a form of abuse in and of itself. Natasha had been a child then, though.

Pen says, 'I lied once about looking through her stuff.'

I say, 'Oh yeah?' Trying to keep my voice even and casual.

She nods.

I ask, 'What did you find?'

'Articles, a book. Some old photos.'

I take her hand and squeeze it. 'You had some idea? About the Black House?'

She nods. 'I'm sorry.'

'Why are you sorry?'

'For snooping, for not telling you.'

'That's OK. It's natural to be curious.'

'It made Mum mad.'

'How was she when she was mad?' I ask hardly wanting the answer. My heart pounding now.

Pen sighs. 'She could be kind of mean.'

I put an arm across her shoulder, pressing her little body to mine. We walk the rest of the way in silence.

CHAPTER FORTY-THREE

NATASHA

Joseph, of course, got so many things wrong. But one thing he did understand, though he never implemented it well, was the need for discipline. Of the mind, the body.

You have to be rigid in your approach to things, rational. Not let feelings cloud your actions.

I love my baby girl. God knows I adore her, as I had Blue and Lisa, too. But I had to protect her, train her. And in that I also had to protect myself.

She was always a curious child and I tread a delicate tightrope between encouraging it, and making sure she didn't push too far into my affairs.

I'm her mother, in charge of her. Not the other way around.

The day I watched that place burn, I vowed never to be under the control of another human being. Never to be at anyone's beck and call.

Never to be manipulated like the stupid Aunts and drippy Nenny.

It was important that I raised her to be enough like me to manage, but not to the point of rebellion, of course.

I knew what was good for my own child, after all.

I knew she'd grow to be fierce. Like Blue.

My other success story.

Not like Amy. Not like Lisa.

Amy with her broken heart and her attacked body. Lisa of all things, falling in love . . .

CHAPTER FORTY-FOUR

Two days after Amy died, I had my first panic attack. I woke up before alarm had sounded, heart racing, palms sweating, absolutely convinced I was going to die. I tried hauling in air, gasping as I did so. The more I gasped, the worse it became. At some point my hands curled into fists and I couldn't straighten them back out. I've since learnt this is a physical response to hyperventilating. At the time, I thought I was having some kind of seizure that would kill me.

Natasha slept in a bunk over my bed then and she'd woken, probably pulled from sleep by the sound of me thrashing in my bed.

She'd dropped down, leaned in and taken my hands in hers. She'd said things to me. I couldn't remember what and I'm not sure I heard the words even at the time. But her tone was soothing and the feel of her calm, cool hands, softly holding my clawed, clenched ones, was helpful. She made me breathe with her until eventually my body was doing its own work again and I was able to fill my lungs with air. My hands relaxed, my limbs relaxed, my heart slowed to a normal pace.

From that day I would become very unsettled if Natasha was out of sight. I'd trail around after her and when she was 'taken' in the evenings I felt a sort of isolated despair.

Lisa had started to withdraw and though we still chatted, still tried to make each other laugh, we were also careful to skirt around the topic of Amy.

Looking back, it's weird that we never discussed her. I know Lisa tried and Natasha had told her very firmly to stop. One time when I'd mentioned it, Natasha had knelt down in front of me and said, 'You can't change the past, you can only try and erase it.'

I'd said, my voice full of stubborn grief, 'I don't want to erase Amy.'

Natasha had smiled, but it wasn't a warm expression and she hissed, 'She's gone. Focus on what you have.'

She meant her. She was what I had and what Lisa had. We both knew that Natasha had a harder time than us, that whatever it was she was taken for, was what had ultimately killed Amy. We tiptoed around Natasha. We needed her. I needed her. We were careful around her then. Dialled into and reactive towards her moods. She was all the safety and we clung to her like drowning swimmers reaching for a life raft.

I'm lying awake long after Pen is asleep, thinking about all of this stuff. Out of all of us, Natasha was a survivor.

I can't believe she is gone and that she would have done it to herself. An old familiar thought crosses my mind. Natasha whispering furiously to Amy in the middle of the night, telling her not to go. Not to run. Not to cause trouble for the rest of us. A few hours later, Amy's naked body at the bottom of the barn. The question has crossed my mind more than once: Did Amy jump, or was Amy pushed? A thought so terrible I don't allow it to sit and fester. Pushing it far, far away because I can't handle all the other questions that one raises.

As the night creeps on, dark turning to light, I become sure of Natasha's own suicide as an impossibility.

And if she didn't kill herself, then who did?

The next morning I wake with a start and a head full of deepening suspicions. After I've dropped Pen at school, I call David Belsham. He doesn't hesitate in agreeing to meet with me straight away. I tell him I need to do something first and we arrange a time. I text Isaac saying that I'll be late.

I double-check the address on my phone, Mark Savillus's place of work. He is a chef at a hotel I know but have never visited or eaten in. I walk there, hands deep in my pockets. My head thrumming with thoughts not fully formed, or clearly defined.

Maybe he's not working today. Maybe he won't want to talk to me. I don't know. I somehow want these things to happen almost as much as I want to know what he has to say.

I force myself to go in anyway. It's an up-market place and I stick out immediately. A maître d steps forward with a silky smile. I ask to speak to Mark. She frowns. I add, 'I'm a friend of Lisa's.' Almost choking on the words that no longer feel true. What kind of a friend ignores you? Blocks you from their life? I had always felt that I had to. That it was self-preservation. But I'd owed her more.

The maître d goes over to a man I recognise from the Facebook pictures. He is mid-chop, a large knife raised over some vegetables. He turns, putting it down. His eyes search for me, meet mine. He nods.

I follow him out the back to a staff room of sorts. It's empty, just tables and chairs.

He says, 'The coffee machine is terrible.' Half in apology.

I shrug. 'I'm not thirsty.' He glances at his watch. 'And you're busy.'

He smiles. 'A kitchen is always busy, but I can spare ten minutes.'

I nod, grateful, nervous. Unsure where to start, what it is exactly that I want to know.

I say, 'You were Lisa's boyfriend?'

'Fiancé.'

My eyes widen. He smiles but it's sad, mournful.

I murmur, 'I'm sorry.'

'Me too.'

'What . . . what happened?'

He sighs. 'God. I don't know. I knew about . . .' He waves a hand around. He means the Black House, of course.

I ask him, 'Do you know who I am?'

He nods. 'Yes.'

Tears spring to my eyes. 'She tried to contact me.'

'I know.'

And that's all there is of that. He doesn't bother with any platitudes and I'm glad. Being ignored would have hurt her. I know that. Knew that at the time. But I still couldn't handle it.

He says, 'I've seen your pictures. At her grave.'

'Oh?'

'They're pretty good. She would have liked them.'

And I feel all kinds of things then, mainly warmth. He said something kind when he needn't have. When I'm not even sure it was deserved. I'm glad then, that Lisa had him, even if it was over too soon.

'Lisa always said you were the one most likely to be OK in the end.'

I raise an eyebrow at that, 'Looks like Natasha did all right for herself.'

He snorts. 'Natasha was a bitch.'

The words hang there between us. Inappropriate and brutal. Particularly in light of recent events.

He pushes his chin out. 'Sorry if that hurts you to hear.' He shrugs. 'But it's how I feel.'

'Can I ask why?'

'She was a control freak and she had a hold over Lisa that made her run herself ragged trying to please her.'

'It's hard to explain what we went through together.'

'I get that, got it. Never tried to become between them, and I loved Pen, too.'

'She's a good kid.'

'She is, and Tasha used to dump her with Lisa every time she annoyed her.'

I swallow thickly. 'Annoyed her how?'

He shrugs. 'By not doing as she was told.'

'Natasha . . . she went through a lot. I imagine parenting raised its own challenges for her.'

Mark snorts and I frown, feeling an urge to defend someone I hadn't seen for years, could hardly claim I knew well.

His face softens. 'I'm sorry.' And he looks it. He runs a hand through his longish hair. 'I just always felt that Lisa would have been better off away; it was like she was unable to move on. Like Natasha didn't want her to.'

'Natasha didn't like you?'

'She did to start with. Too much, if anything.'

'Oh?'

He nods. 'Yup, flirted outrageously. Touched me too much. Always dolled up to the nines.'

'She hit on you?'

'Yes.'

'You turned her down.'

He nods again. 'And she'd done it before. To show Lisa that men she got involved with didn't care. In some fucked-up way, Lisa seemed to think Tasha was doing her a favour. Shit, I don't know. They were close, but oppressively so. They were on the phone to each other all day every day; Tasha was in and out of Lisa's place. When I joked it would have to stop once we were married, Lisa was appalled, and I . . . I backed off.'

'Were they getting on, when Lisa . . .?'

He sighs. 'Lisa wanted to reach out, to other survivors.'

I think of Brodie, Sienna. The other boys who'd made it out, Carillo himself. I press a hand to my lips and ask from behind my fingers, 'Did she?'

He nods. 'Yes, she emailed and heard back from a few people. Natasha was livid.'

I shut my eyes. Run my hands over my face. Push my feet into the ground beneath me.

Mark's phone beeps. He murmurs, 'Shit.'

Then I feel his hand on mine and I jump. 'I've got to get back.' I see nothing but concern in his face. 'I'm sorry, if anything I said has hurt you.'

I shake my head, smile faintly. 'No. It's OK. It's just . . .' I shrug. 'Do you know who else she was speaking to?'

He frowns. 'Nicholas something? And she had an email from Natasha's brother.'

Brodie. Just thinking his name makes my heart squeeze.

Nicholas, though . . . I vaguely remember himI knew some of the boys had survived. Was I glad he had? God, I don't know. I'm sorry anyone died. Which is enough, right?

I thank Mark and he gives my hand a quick squeeze and is gone.

CHAPTER FORTY-FIVE

I'd arranged to meet in a coffee shop. I go in, fully expecting David to laugh in my face at what I have to say, but when I tell him firmly that something really isn't right about Natasha's untimely demise, without having any clear idea or the vocabulary to express what exactly, he agrees with me. Which leaves me . . . I don't know where that leaves me. I don't know whether his agreement makes me feel better or worse.

The coffee here is good, and I caress the cup in front of me, thinking about how much caffeine I've ingested over the years. How many mornings I've woken from thin, shitty sleep and whether Natasha had been doing the same. Whether even back then, when we were children, she was masking a silent inward scream. You can never truly know another person.

I ask him, 'How did you two meet?'

'I sent her an email just before Lisa died, saying I was planning on writing a book about the Black House. I'd given up hope of hearing from her to be honest, and getting her side of the story, but she responded.'

'That's what you wanted? Her side of the story?'

He says, 'I wanted the truth about the Black House.'

I say, 'The truth is subjective.'

He nods. 'It is, yes.'

'My mother would have told you Joseph Carillo saved her from the horrors of the real world.'

He sighs. 'Coercive control.'

'Weakness.'

There is a pause, a silence. I become aware of the sounds around me. The gurgling of the coffee machine, the low murmur of other people having conversations. The sound of the blood rushing around my body.

'So she came to you wanting to talk?'

He smiles. 'We met face to face at Lisa's funeral. I felt sad for her, thought that she was vulnerable, and I suppose she must have been. Lisa was her closest friend.'

I wince at that. The little group pared down eventually just to the two of them. I hear Mark's words echo in my mind. *Obsessive* was how he'd portrayed their friendship. Suffocating, with Natasha in the driving seat. But her job as she saw it had been to take care of us. Me and Lisa.

I say, 'You became friends?'

He shrugs. 'It started out as me trying to find things out, which was our arrangement. I think she got more out of me than I did her, looking back, though. Even then.'

That sounds more like the Natasha I know and I smile. 'She was always pretty bossy.'

He laughs. 'I can see that.'

I tell him, 'It was her who got us out, that night. Moments before the fire spread to our dorm.'

He asks, 'She saved your life?'

I nod, look away from his gaze, out of the window onto the street. People rush past in both directions. Going about their business, not a care in the world.

It's not like that though, is it? Not really. Everyone has war wounds. No one gets through unscathed.

I force myself to look at David. 'She did, yes. She was obsessive about it in the end. Escape.'

'And you made it.'

I nod. 'We did.'

She saved my life. And I diligently removed her from it.

'Is that why you think she wouldn't do this?'

I shrug, trying to make my thoughts get into order. 'Amy . . .' And that one word fells me for a moment. Tears spring into my eyes and I stare down into the mug in my hands, watching the dark liquid and white foam swirling into one.

And there is another silence between us. I hear every noise from the other tables amplified in my mind and blood rushing through my body, my heart pounding.

I say, 'Amy was sad; she was fucked up.' I add, 'You can understand why.' In a tone more defensive than I mean it to be.

He says softly, 'I'm sorry for what happened to your friends.'

I kind of nod. The last of four. Only me left. I look out of the window, blinking back tears, watching people bustle past in pairs and little groups.

There have been so many times I've thought about Amy over the years. So many moments where I'd wished she'd been free to see what I was looking at, to walk down a street alone, or around a museum or to sit in a café sipping coffee and looking out of the window.

Part of the reason I'd allowed contact with Natasha and Lisa to drift into nothing was that the memory of her absence was so sore. Even today I can shut my eyes for a second and see her crumpled body.

I ask him, 'What happened to Amy's . . . remains?'

'She was dug up. Her father buried her.'

I nod, swallowing thickly.

I desperately want to be out of here. I desperately want to get to Isaac. Planet Pop. My life now with light and love and laughter.

David asks, 'You don't think she jumped?'

I look back down into my mug. I see Amy's pale drawn face, recall Natasha leaning over her bed whispering to her. Saying what? Pull yourself together? It'll be OK? I'd never know now.

CHAPTER FORTY-SIX

Natasha shakes Blue, rousing her from a deep sleep. The first thing Blue notices is the smell.

Something is burning.

Natasha says, 'Get dressed.' Getting Lisa up, too.

The two small girls dress in silence. Natasha takes each of their hands and leads them out. There is crackling, fizzing, popping. There are flames, licking sky-high. Up and up.

They can hear a boy, shouting.

Natasha calls, 'Brodie, come here.'

He is yelling, but not his sister's name. He is saying 'Mummy', over and over again. Natasha sighs, dropping our hands and heading towards him. Towards it.

The fire.

Lisa stands, frozen with her mouth open. Blue looks urgently towards the licking flames. 'Come on.' But Lisa shakes her head.

Blue races forward. Towards the burning building. The barn.

She sees in through a smashed window. The grown-ups lying down on the floor.

They could be sleeping. Or they could be dead.

Blue feels whispers of fear and horror. Then she hears her name, sees the top of a familiar head, a hand reaching up towards the window.

She knows who it is. Thinks of walking away. Slips her hand into her pocket. Feels the white stone. The photo her mother had pressed into her hand. The one she had looked at a thousand times now.

She leans closer to the window, feeling the heat of the flames on her cheek, until she can see her.

'Mummy?'

The woman smiles, her face full of . . . emotion, movement. 'Blue.'

Blue leans further.

'Don't come too close.'

'You need to get out.'

'I'm stuck.' And Blue follows her mother's pointed hand. Her leg trapped beneath a fallen beam. The smoke is dense and getting more so. Flames licking forwards.

'I'll get you out.'

The woman shakes her head. 'You go. I'm glad you're OK. I love you.' And the red and yellow heat shoves forward. The woman screams.

The noise is more than Blue can bear. She strains on her tiptoes, leaning through the window, feeling the hot wooden frame on her stomach, reaching her arm desperately into the worst, most acute pain. Gripping for less than a second her mother's fingers before the fire takes her. Eating her alive.

Blue jumps back, her skin in agony, her heart smashing apart. The sound of her screams mingling with her mother's.

She runs, stumbling, calling for Natasha, calling for Lisa. And she smacks into Brodie, hysterical, in pain, wounded. He grabs her, pulling her to him, whispering into her hair. 'It's OK. You're OK, Blue.'

Behind him stands Sienna, dazed and unfocused.

Natasha glares at the woman, pulls Blue from Brodie and says, 'He had to save her.' Her voice loaded with rage and disapproval. She frowns. 'Lisa?'

Blue turns. 'Back there, I think.'

Natasha nods, says to Blue, 'Your arm?'

'I tried to get my mum.'

Natasha snorts at that, 'We need to go.'

And they run. Into the woods. Away.

Blue feels her heart cracking as she thinks of her mother back there in the Black House as the fire rages, turning slowly into ash. But she also thinks of Carillo, and Amy's mother, and fear nips at her heels, forcing her on. Staggering into the dark, dark woods. Natasha dragging her along. Brodie, Lisa and Sienna just behind and the whole world waiting on the other side.

CHAPTER FORTY-SEVEN

I walk into the shop and find Isaac hidden behind a large stack of records. I only know he's there because I can see smoke rising from his ever-present cigarette.

I shut the door forcefully and he calls out, 'Can I help?'

He steps around the side of the counter, face breaking into a smile when he sees me.

I frown. 'You can't smoke in here.'

He looks like he might attempt a denial – stupid, as a fag dangles from his mouth. Instead he jumps behind the counter and stubs it out. 'I know, love. I was gasping.'

I say, 'Then step outside.'

'Sorry.' Then: 'I will.'

We stand like that for a moment. Isaac head down like a scolded child. I go over and start helping him label records.

I ask, 'Discounting?'

'Yes. We need to make some room.'

He shrugs. Sheepish. He has a habit of ordering large amounts of stock during moments of exuberance. It's something I've gently tried to pull him up on many times, but the man seems completely unable to let a bargain go, so I just accept that often we'll have more vinyl than we can fit in and during those periods we'll have big sales. It means the shop is busy and also that we'll be doing a few fairs, which I always enjoy, despite myself.

One of the things I've always loved about working here and with music is the passion people feel for it. When I lived in the Black House I always felt that enthusiasm was a dangerous thing and too much of a good thing invariably turned bad. Even Carillo, I'm sure, hadn't set out to be a mass murderer, but he was (you could use the word suicide all you wanted but I'd never be convinced). And women like Sienna, like my own mother, hadn't packed up their small, sad, lonely little lives and headed to Wales for punishment. To lose their own personalities and their children. It was meant to be a utopia. It hadn't worked out.

I suspect if I'd never met Isaac, I'd have felt the same bitterness towards any human endeavour that I did after the Black House.

But he and his array of colourful friends, geeky musicians, and well-worn, ex-drug addicts, had taught me people were all right. They could care and form communities that weren't toxic. The record fairs were lovely – people joined by a shared love of the same thing. And if arguments over the merits of 'Germfree Adolescents' and The Slits got intense, they were always resolved in a friendly manner.

I tell Isaac I met with the journalist again. His eyes narrow, almost imperceptibly.

I say, 'You think I shouldn't have?' My voice more defensive than I want it to be.

He shrugs.

I snap, 'Spit it out.'

He sighs. 'I don't know. That's the honest answer. It feels like maybe digging into things that might be best left alone, and Annie said . . .'

I explode at that. 'Annie said! *Annie*. What the hell is with you and that woman?'

He looks at me open-mouthed.

I say, 'You're supposed to be on my side, not backing her.'

He shakes his head. 'I'm not backing anyone.'

'But you thought taking Pen was the right thing to do? How is that leaving things alone? I was done with my past, happy to leave it there, but now it's back and I can't run, Isaac. I can't escape it.'

I feel my voice rising, my face getting hot.

He comes around the counter and takes me under his arm, squeezes me to him. 'Kiddo.'

I blink away surprising tears. He's always called me kiddo. Always treated me like I was his own child. God knows I love him more than anyone else I know. He is my anchor in an unsteady sea. I am jealous, I realise, my usual distrust of women rearing its ugly head. But Annie . . . DI Grafton, is not one of the Aunts. She isn't trying to hurt me.

'Blue. Look at me.' I meet his eyes. 'I know you, and I know myself the pain of not doing the right thing.' He shrugs. 'Taking Pen was the only thing. You'd have lost sleep over it. Got down over it, been back to a place I never want to see you again. You may not have asked for it, but it happened anyway and sometimes, kiddo, that is the way the cookie crumbles.'

I nod. He's referring to the year after Lisa died. I'd ended up in a sanatorium. Or a nut house, to you and I. Isaac had paid for it without batting an eye and without ever mentioning it again. My mind had broken, shattered into a million unfixable pieces. But I'd worked through some stuff in there. Got a bit better. Slowly, slowly.

I say, 'You think David is bad news?'

'Who am I to say? I just think he has his agenda. It may not align with yours, and An . . . DI Grafton doesn't like him.'

'Police never like journalists, though, do they?'

He laughs. 'You watch too much TV.'

I say, 'Joking aside, wouldn't you have wanted to know what he knew, if you were me?'

'Probably, yeah.'

I add, 'I'd never have found out about Amy's dad.'

'Are you glad you know?'

I think about it. 'Yes. I'm glad someone other than us loved her. She was very special.'

Isaac nods. 'She sounds it. And you're right. I've no place to judge.' He adds, 'I'm sorry.'

I tell him, 'I've decided to see Brodie again, and maybe even Sienna.' Adding, 'Dee suggested it.'

'OK.'

'You don't think that's a bad idea?'

'They are Pen's family. I think you have to explore it.'

'Natasha never did.'

'And who can blame her.'

'But I should?'

He takes my hand again, squeezes it. Picks up his box of cigarettes, which I frown at. He puts them into the drawer with an eye roll. 'Explore it. That's all. You said you liked Brodie at least?'

I nod. 'Dee located them. I have an email address for him.'

'So drop him an email.' He smiles and his eyes crinkle. 'I need to smoke; you finish these.'

I mindlessly label the records. Pretty much the whole stack has been reduced to £1.99. I used to worry about Isaac's profit margins until I realised that royalties from his 'big in the 80s' band still paid out pretty handsomely. He had used a large royalty payment and purchased the whole building that housed the shop outright. He'd also bought and paid for his ex-wife's house and seen both of his children, Jacob and Jackson, through costly private education and universities despite their unwillingness to have anything to do with him. I'd learnt that money wasn't an issue for him. It also meant I was grossly overpaid, as were the wrecked charity cases he bought in to do the grunt work. Most people Isaac welcomed through the door left better than when they started though, and I could count some of those washed-up drug addicts amongst my friends.

I finished the stack in no time. Isaac was in and out, taking calls. Addicts usually, and he was known by a lot of local services as someone who may help out when others wouldn't.

At four o'clock I tell him I need to go. He asks me what I'm going to do, and I say I'll email Brodie. He grins and I feel annoyed and full of love at the same time. I roll my eyes at him, so he knows I'm not a complete pushover. But as I'm walking around the counter, he surprises me by grasping me to him. I hug him back, breathing in the familiar smells. Leather, fags and a faint whiff of patchouli.

I collect Pen and we eat together. She's been somewhat subdued since her aborted trip to Wales, but she seems more like her usual self this afternoon and I'm glad. I decide not to mention anything to her about her grandmother and uncle, realising that this is the very definition of withholding truth. Understanding again that it is not always a black and white thing.

I do think Natasha should have spoken to Pen more. Pen speaks of her mother with almost reverence but Natasha sounds like she was as much a mystery to her own daughter as she had been to me.

After Pen is in bed, I open my laptop, type in the email address I have for Brodie and stare at the blank message box.

I have reason to contact him. I am sure he is reeling right now. His sister is dead. There is a child, his niece, to consider. It turns out, according to DI Grafton, that he'd known about Pen all along, but respected Natasha's wishes to be left alone. The police told him custody had gone to me and he hadn't contested it, nor tried to get in contact. I'd asked them to tell him I didn't want to be contacted and he has respected that, though it must go against his natural impulse. Or maybe it doesn't? Maybe he is glad to see the back of her. Maybe he is someone different to the boy I remember. Last time I saw him, after all, he was a child. So was I, and one who had a crush. That skews perception, doesn't it? Perhaps I have imbued him with all kinds of characteristics he never had. Her will specifically dictates that the details of her burial and funeral fall to me. Pen needs closure. I feel that surge of annoyance again. She has gone. Leaving me behind to sort out her mess. Tell Brodie and drippy Nenny if you like. Bury me however you see fit. Raise my kid . . .

Her remains still haven't been released for burial, but DI Grafton thinks they will be shortly. They are still awaiting formal identification and I know they have liaised with at least Brodie about it, if not also Sienna. I haven't pushed for information, though burying my head and hoping it will all go away isn't working. I don't feel at all prepared to even guess at how she might have liked things. I don't feel at all prepared to speak to Brodie. Even by email. To which he may not even respond.

In the end I write:

Hello Brodie,
    I don't know if you'll remember me: Blue Sillitoe.
From Wales.

I'm sorry about Natasha. She mentioned me in her will, though it's been many years since we spoke. Perhaps we could arrange a phone call?
All best,
Blue

From Wales. I can't quiet bring myself to type the Black House. But I hit send and less than thirty seconds later, a message pings back.

Blue,
I'm so happy to hear from you.

He has attached his number.

I stare at it for a while, until the digits are burned in my mind. Then I close the lid of my laptop and go to bed.

CHAPTER FORTY-EIGHT

The next morning, Isaac looks up and sees Annie Grafton come in. The bell over the shop door tinkles and she frowns at it as though it had done so intentionally to irritate her. She turns her hard stare on him and he smiles at her, amused. 'Hello, Annie.'

She sighs. 'Isaac.'

'How are you?'

'I've had better days.'

He nods. 'Can I interest you in a coffee and a cigarette?'

'Hell yeah.'

He heads out back and puts the kettle on, making them both a cup of instant Nescafé. When he gets back onto the shop floor, he finds her rifling through seven-inches. She jumps as if caught in some sort of underhand act when he comes out. He asks, 'Anything take your fancy?'

She shrugs. 'I don't have a record player anymore.'

He says, 'Terrible pity.'

She grins. 'I'm hardly ever home anyway.'

'You work too hard.'

'Better than having too much time to fill.'

He nods again. 'True enough. Now we have to go and stand outside to smoke. I cannot endure another pious lecture from Blue or Oren.'

She waits while he locks the shop then they head out with steaming mugs to the little courtyard out the back.

She says, 'You live here?'

'Yes, upstairs.'

'Easy commute.'

He laughs, lighting a cigarette and passing her the box. 'It is, yes.'

They smoke and sip coffee.

Eventually, Isaac says, 'Is this purely a social call?'

And she frowns. 'Of course not.' But he catches the hint of red rising on her cheeks. She looks away and her copper hair falls in a wave across her face. She seems very focused on stubbing out her cigarette and Isaac suppresses a smile. She's a good-looking girl, but could do with loosening up a little.

She says, 'You kind of adopted Blue?'

He laughs. 'I think we adopted each other.' He says the words lightly, but for him they are full of gravity. Blue had been like the missing piece in his new life. He was religious about his sobriety, but when she had slunk into his store, he'd learned that actions were important and he'd spent the early days of recovery perfecting them. Get up, go to work, stay out of people's business unless asked, don't use, don't drink. He'd done a lot of it on autopilot, staying safe, protecting his already smashed-up heart from any further pain. Blue had reminded him that feelings mattered, too. In taking care of her, he'd somehow learned to also take care of himself.

The sun is high in the sky, glinting off of the corners of the shop's back door. It's a nice day, he thinks.

Annie says, 'They were split up on purpose.'

'The children from the Black House?'

Annie nods. Isaac doesn't say anything. She tells him, 'They thought fresh starts would be best.'

'Maybe they were right.'

Annie runs a hand over her face. He finishes his cigarette.

She shakes her head. 'I don't know. It must have been a terrible wrench and very frightening.'

He thinks of Blue coming into his shop, head covered by a too-big hoodie, angry eyes fixed firmly on the floor.

Annie asks, 'What was she like, when you met her?'

'She was scared, and cross. Which you couldn't blame her for.'

'Of course.'

He sips his coffee.

Annie asks, 'She told you about the Black House?'

He nods. 'In dribs and drabs. I never pushed her.'

Annie takes out her own pack of cigarettes, lights one and passes it to Isaac.

They smoke in silence. Eventually Annie says, 'We don't think it's her.'

'What?'

'The body from the fire. We don't think it's Natasha.'

CHAPTER FORTY-NINE

I walk back slowly from school after dropping Pen off. It's warm but cloudy, and I've overdressed based on how it looked from my window. The big jumper I'm wearing is too hot and by the time I get back to my road, I'm covered in a thin film of sweat and feel as though the wool is like wire.

Standing outside of my building are Isaac, Annie and Dee. I speed up, fearing the worst, and then reconsider. I literally just dropped Pen off. She's fine. So . . . what?

I stop in front of them and the conversation they were halfway through slips into silence.

Isaac says, 'Let's go in, eh.'

We head up the stairs and into my flat. I say, 'Can you excuse me for a moment?' The heat from the jumper has become unbearable. I mutter to Isaac to put the kettle on.

In my bedroom I tear my top off and the bobbly wool snags slightly on my scarred arm. An odd feeling that I should be used to by now, but still makes me wince. I put on a soft long-sleeved burgundy T-shirt, spraying deodorant on first, then I nip into my bathroom, splashing my face with cold water.

By the time I get back out to everyone, I feel slightly better, but then I am aware of all of the bodies in my living room, which feels smaller for the addition of them. And the impending news, which I'm assuming won't be good, since a policewoman and a social worker have turned up to deliver it.

Isaac watches me closely as I head to the kettle. He says, 'I'll do that; go sit.'

I do as I'm told whilst he makes four cups of tea. Dee asks how Pen is doing this week and I say, 'Fine.'

She murmurs, 'You're doing a great job.' Just as Isaac arrives with a tray of drinks. I'm not thirsty, but I say thanks and wait whilst everyone else takes the obligatory first sip of their too-hot drinks.

Isaac has taken the seat next to me and although I'm comforted by his presence, I'm starting to get twitchy now. I snap, 'Well?'

Looking first at him, then to Annie. The fact they exchange a look annoys me further.

I say, 'Obviously you've all been talking about me. Feel free to let me in on it, eh?'

DI Grafton takes a deep breath, pauses and then says, 'The body we found doesn't belong to Natasha Dryden.'

I'm glad now that I hadn't picked up my tea. I think I might have dropped it, like some kind of stereotype from an episode of *Law and Order*. Scene: shocked relative/friend.

I stare at her, she looks back. She has a nice face, though it's set almost permanently in a slight frown. The frown deepens as she looks at me now. I turn to Isaac. Open my mouth. Close it.

Dee says, 'This must be a terrible shock.'

I laugh then. It bursts up from me as if out of nowhere. It's over as fast as it started and confusion sets in in its place.

I look at Annie. 'How do you know?'

She says, 'The pathologist was struggling to work out whether she'd given birth. Well, the body we have has never been pregnant; further tests have confirmed it.'

'Jesus.'

Annie nods. 'I know. To be honest, I was alarmed when it turned out her dental records were missing, and an ID that should have been quick and simple became way too complicated.'

I look at her, then Dee. 'I've just emailed Brodie.'

Annie says, 'There is an officer on the way to speak to Brodie and Sienna Dryden.'

No one says anything for what feels like ages, but is likely only a few seconds.

I feel Isaac's hand pressed against my back and lean into him until I am slumped, his arm around my shoulders. I ask DI Grafton, 'Is she alive?'

'We don't know.'

'She left a suicide note.'

'She did.'

'And careful instructions. She'd thought about this.'

'She had.' My brain whirrs with possibilities. None of which seem feasible or satisfactory.

'Who does the body belong to?'

'We don't know yet. But we're working hard to find out.'

But I think I already know. 'I might have an idea.'

CHAPTER FIFTY

It takes DI Grafton all day to piece together what she can. I end up going into the shop with Isaac until I have to pick up Pen. The thought of being alone all day with only my mind for company is too much. Oren is there, so obviously I'm not needed, but he doesn't comment and I'm glad. I keep wondering how the conversation with Brodie and Sienna went. *Your sister/child is dead. Nope, not really . . .*

When I do collect Pen and we get in, she gets straight on with her homework. I haven't told her about any of this and am aware that as it all gets more complicated, my dishonesty grows. Lies seem to feed each other, like fat maggots swelling as they feast on rotting food. I wonder at what point the mass of them will be big enough to burst. Where does the truth become so pressing that it must be spoken?

Dee rings and I take the call on the balcony, door shut, keeping an eye inside to make sure Pen doesn't come out.

We talk in hushed tones about the implications. I put it to Dee that Natasha may still be alive. Dee says, 'If she is, and this is some kind of sick stunt, I'm not sure Pen will be going back to her anyway.'

Sick stunt. I say, 'What if it's murder?' Shuddering even as I say the words.

Dee says, 'You can't speak to Pen about this until we know more.'

'I know. But I hate lying to her.'

'It's not lying; it's just not telling her everything.'

'Isn't that the same thing?'

'It's the same spectrum for sure.'

'Dee, I'm not an idiot.'

She sighs. 'I know that, and I know it goes against your instinct, but this really is for her own good.'

We hang up and in my little kitchen I break a vegetable stock cube into a pan of water, which I set to boil for pasta. The thought of attempting anything more complicated than that is too much right now.

I watch the water turn from its quiet stillness with little fragmented bits of the stock cube bobbling about, to a hot pan of boiling bubbles. I turn it off, fill it with penne and olive oil and turn the heat back up. *Your own good.* That was something we were told over and over. What we (the adults) do is for your own good, and you (children) must do this for the greater good. You are a small part of a larger mass.

I get an email from Brodie.

'The police have been here. They are saying it's not her — what's going on?'

I read it for the fifth time since I arrived home and start again to type a response, giving up in seconds, locking my phone, sliding it into my pocket.

Sienna was hailed latterly as something of a hero, though that description of her never sat well with me. All I really remembered of her was that she was very tall and very pale, though Pen reminded me of her and I couldn't say why exactly. Pen is solid and Sienna was ghostly almost; her white skin coupled with her vacant disposition made her seem more apparition than living, breathing woman.

Carillo's first recruit. She'd been just fifteen when she had Natasha. Carillo was newly divorced. He'd been married for less than a year and his wife filed on the grounds of cruelty. Something that would come up later at his trial and again and again in news articles, podcasts, and documentaries. The warning signs had always been there.

Two years later, Sienna was his second wife, pregnant with Brodie when they met, a different father to Natasha's and another man who was gone. Carillo had started running a yoga centre in Wales. It turned out he was sleeping with the woman, Deborah Softley, who funded it. She would become his third 'wife', though his only legal remarriage was to Sienna.

Boys in the cult were 'tutored' directly by Carillo or James Malachy, an ex-prisoner who'd served a long sentence for a string of rapes; again information none of us had at the time and which came to light long after.

Deborah owned the Black House, and several other properties, which she signed over to Carillo with no question. She, Carillo, Sienna and James moved on site with Natasha in tow and Brodie secure in Sienna's belly.

Over the next two years, Carillo recruited. First Amy's mother, then others. He drew people in with his promises of communal living, shared childcare, forest school for children and a strong emphasis on self-sufficient, communal living. What underpinned all of his 'theories' was the idea of radical self-reliance and a group of people who were spiritually aware but free of religion and the constraints of modern society. The Black House insisted that everyone was responsible for their own choices and happiness. That we looked after ourselves.

What this meant for us children was severe neglect interspersed with uneven abuse. What it meant for the men and women who followed him was complete subservience under the guise that everything they did was through their own free will. It was all an illusion, of course. Joseph Carillo got there by picking out vulnerable people. People who'd lost their way and were isolated from family. He then love-bombed the hell out of them. Then the gas-lighting began.

It is hard to describe or even conjure up to outsiders just what living within a closed community is like.

In my day-to-day life now, I interact with a dazzling array of people, despite not being what you would call socially inclined. But there are people in shops, on transport, in cafés. People who live on my street, my neighbours. There is television, the radio, billboard posters, graffiti. Letting the elderly and infirm sit on trains, even. Little social kindnesses like that didn't exist at the Black House. We were encouraged to do things like grow our own food, but mealtimes kept us all in short supply. I remember constantly being just a little bit hungry even in the beginning, before they started starving us. So any food we grew and dug up we often hid, kept for if not ourselves then our tiny units.

Amy, Lisa, Natasha and I were our own pack.

Later on, it turned out that Sienna had actually helped several of the boys and their mothers to leave. I never knew whether she hoped they would get help and lead to her rescue, or whether she'd been planning to go next. Maybe she was scared for Brodie. Certainly it was too late to save Natasha from the worst of it. Carillo had a regime of torture for boys who were unwilling to comply with his program, his overall vision, for those who refused to lead the women and children by whatever means necessary. Those means were harsh physical and emotional punishments and sexual abuse. Not everyone had the stomach or taste for it that James and Joseph shared and some boys – and girls

– were groomed more easily than others. Whilst the adults had been picked for certain traits, experiences or just parts of personality that made them pliable, the children often baulked at things they didn't want to do. The mistake Carillo made, when I look at it dispassionately, was that the children and adults lived rather separated existences there. He assumed our compliance would come more easily and yet it wasn't the case. We were young, sure, but we were also in pain and confused and angry.

In the Black House the adults were only the people Carillo had handpicked. The women were looking for someone to be in charge; the men were usually drifters with bad temperaments. Streaks of evil ingrained. Never cleverer than him, though, and with nothing to draw them back to the outside. He himself always seemed benevolent, kind even. But nothing there happened without his say-so.

I have watched Isaac, over the years, working with various addicts and misfits who'd come through the door of Planet Pop, for casual work or something more formal. When they arrived, they were rattling, desperate, and would do anything they could to get through the day. I knew that Carillo targeted rehabilitation centres and I could see how that responsibility Isaac took so seriously and worked so gently, could easily be abused. But I still couldn't fully forgive the grown-ups at the Black House. Because unlike me and Amy and Lisa and Natasha and Brodie, and Nick and Martin they had been given a choice.

I email Brodie back and tell him I'll call him later on.

My phone rings and its David Belsham.

He asks how Pen is and I say tell him she's fine. There is a pause and some crackling on the line. He says, 'The reception here isn't very good.'

'Where are you?'

'Wales.' My heart hammers faster. He adds, 'I was planning to go and speak to Brodie and Sienna, but I thought
maybe I should run it past you first.'

The body isn't Natasha's. Brodie and Sienna know this,
but David doesn't.

I think quickly and tell him, 'I'm coming.'

'To Wales?'

'Yes. There are things . . . well. I need to speak to them
before you do. OK?'

'OK. No problem.'

I hang up and call Isaac and Dee.

CHAPTER FIFTY-ONE

Annie looks at the charred remains that barely even resemble a human being. Blue was right. The blackened bones do belong to Lyndsey Dunmore. Which leaves her with more questions than answers. That's the way with this job, sometimes. She thanks the pathologist and lets the young PC know to get back to the station, update the files and start searching for a next of kin.

He mumbles that he's already looked and she snaps at him to 'Look harder.'

He nods, lips pursed in a thin line, which irritates Annie, but he heads off to get on with it.

Her mind is whirring. She'd known something was up with this case. Hadn't liked the ease with which Natasha had so neatly and efficiently tied up her life, or the mess she'd left in its wake. But this? The implications of this are far broader than she'd anticipated.

And for Annie, everything is further complicated by Isaac. She'd seen him at meetings for the past year, and it had crossed her mind that she found him attractive more than once. She'd dismissed it as her usual appalling taste in men. She had a long, sad history of bad taste, as her two divorces and soon to be third, would attest. She'd made a point of avoiding him in meetings, which had been easy enough as there was an unspoken rule in twelve-step fellowships that it was men for men and women for women. But she'd always found herself listening intently when he shared, and she liked him as a person, too. Still, no bother, but having their paths cross like this has thrown her.

Add to that the fact that she also likes Blue, and now feels somehow more responsible than she should for any of them.

She thinks about calling Isaac with the information, but that wouldn't be right. It's Blue who gave her the heads up and it is Blue she must call now.

CHAPTER FIFTY-TWO

Isaac comes over early and is in my flat and drinking coffee by the time Pen stumbles out of bed, hair in disarray and eyes half shut. When she sees him, she snaps fully awake in that way that only children can and wanders over, throwing her arms around him. She murmurs, 'You smell of cigarettes.' And then frowns. 'Why are you here so early?' Then she looks at me, taking in the fact that I'm fully dressed with a bag by my feet.

I tell her, 'I need to go away, hopefully only for one night, maybe two.'

'Where to?'

'I'd rather not say yet.' She stares at me and I meet her gaze evenly.

She says, 'You're going to Wales.'

I let out the breath I'd been holding and nod.

'You said you'd take me.'

'And I will, I promise. But not this time.'

She narrows her eyes. 'Why?'

'Well, Pen, it's a school day.'

'So we'll go at the weekend, then?'

'It's only Thursday.'

She smiles. 'Well let's say if you're still there Friday Isaac can bring me after school.'

'Like Isaac has nothing better to do?'

He's grinning. 'Don't mind at all. Oren can cover. I love a road trip plus I'm concerned about this one's musical taste. Have you heard of The Vamps?' He grimaces. I glare at him.

He carries on, 'In fact, we'll definitely do that. I'll stay here until Friday then we'll come on up. I'll book an Airbnb. OK?'

'Sure.'

She looks at Isaac. 'So you're looking after me?'

He nods.

She grins. 'Cool, I told Marianne that I knew a rock star. Can you come right into the playground?'

He smiles. 'Why not.'

'Can I have chocolate on toast for breakfast?'

He's about to say yes, when I interject, 'Weetabix, no sugar.' I lean down and kiss the top of her head. 'I'll see you at the weekend.' And to Isaac: 'And you too.' With a frown. He grins back.

As I make my way across London I'm surprised at how calm I am, and that it lasts all the way until the Cardiff train, where talk from the conductor of various stops leading nearer and nearer to my final destination, and my past, are called out.

I had brought a book with me, thinking I'd catch up on some reading on the journey, but I don't even open my bag. My eyes remain glued to the outside view, watching as the city that I now think of as home changes to rolling fields and hills and eventually, the landscape of my childhood.

I am transfixed by it, held still by it. Large swathes of countryside. Fields and hills backing onto woodland, where I know from experience you can walk for miles without seeing another living soul.

I get off at Cardiff. A city I've only been to in my childhood. I spent a miserable month in a home here, waiting for the powers that be to decide my fate.

That that was to be London, and Isaac and Planet Pop, is one of the few things from my formative years that I am truly grateful for. I have never been back here. I have never wanted to, and I hope that this visit will be brief and maybe my last one. I get off the train on shaky legs and stand outside the train station, jumping as people start to bustle past me. I've booked a hotel, nothing fancy but I'll go and check in. I am glad that there are hours between now and when we have arranged to meet.

The taxi driver makes gentle conversation, which I don't respond to and eventually he stops. I over-tip him as some sort of compensation. I am not normally quite so rude, managing at least one-word answers, but here in this land that nearly broke me I find I have no words at all.

I check into the nondescript chain hotel and head up to the blank room.

I lie back on the bed and shut my eyes. Images of Brodie as a child spring to the forefront of my mind. I think of the cave. The handful of occasions we met there. Trying desperately to recall everything we'd said. Though that wasn't what mattered. What had mattered was being there together. If Natasha had been tough with sharp edges, Brodie was as soft as butter. His eyes always seemed to convey so much emotion. After Amy died, he was the only person I spoke to about her. Sitting in our damp hideaway with glimmers of light from above. He encouraged me to remember events, specific things. Those conversations I could remember, at least.

I knew Sienna hadn't been charged with anything and because she'd helped others escape — her big betrayal, she was made into a media star, cancelling out the abuse she allowed to be visited upon her children in the eyes of the public. Of all people, it turned out that drippy Nenny was something of a hero. It's one of the things I'd have liked to have been able to discuss with Natasha. I remember reading it in the papers and toying with the idea of contacting her.

I never did, and now I wouldn't be able to. A thought flashes in my mind that that may not be true and I allow myself the possibility – likelihood, even – that Natasha is still alive. Sitting somewhere, laughing her arse off at us all.

Or is she? Pen is well looked after. She loves her mother; I can hear it when she talks about her. She wouldn't have deserted her any more than she would have deserted us.

I open my eyes, boil the kettle and drink a cup of too-hot tea with awful thimbles of long-life milk in small plastic containers. Then I face the inevitable and text to say I'll be there in half an hour.

CHAPTER FIFTY-THREE

I'm ten minutes early, dressed more carefully than I would usually be and with perfume on. He is already sitting at a table at the back. I watch him through the large pane of glass. His hair is still a dark, dark brown and slightly too long at the front. He shakes it a few times, his hands resting in front of him next to a round mug, and my heart contracts at the familiarity of the movement. I press my fingers to my lips and they come away with a thick, glossy pink on them. I wipe them on the inside of my jacket pocket, still looking at him. He is now even better-looking, and he is grown up, but essentially he is the same and yes, I still find myself attracted to him. Dammit.

His eyes look up, meeting mine, and I see that he recognises me, too. He sort of stands, then realises the pointlessness of it – he's inside and I'm out, after all. It's up to me. I force myself to move through the door, raising a hand pathetically and then dropping it, in front of him in just a few short strides.

I say, 'You look exactly the same.' Before I can stop myself. Brodie smiles. I smile back and some of the tension seems to ease.

'Sit sit, let me get you a coffee,' he says, and his voice has the hint of a lilt to it. That accent I worked very hard to get rid of.

I watch him as he goes to get me a drink. He is very tall, over six foot I would say. They were a good-looking family; I remember that. All the women at the Black House were. Carillo, in true predictability, only picked young beauties to join him for his spiritual enlightenment.

Brodie comes back, places a large round coffee cup in front of me and another on his side, moving his empty one away. I wonder how long he has been there. Touched that he turned up early for our meeting. He unloads a tiny jug of milk and a spoon from the tray.

He sits, saying, 'It's just filter but it's the best coffee in the city I reckon.'

I add one sugar and the milk and take a sip. 'Not bad.'

He nods. 'One of life's great pleasures.'

I hear a rushing in my ears, the faint fizzle, crackle, *pop* of fire burning loud and bright. I take another sip of my coffee, push my feet down into the floor. This is now, that was then. I'm safe. The past can't get me; it is not a living thing.

I look up and he says, 'This is weird, huh?'

I nod.

He looks out of the window. 'A policewoman called. Grafton?'

'Yes. She's all right.'

'They all are, aren't they?' The words hang there. The unreality of everything we were taught. Police are the bad guys. They want to harm you. He says, 'The body isn't my sister's.'

'No.'

'It's a friend of hers?'

I nod. 'Lyndsey Dunmore. I went to her flat.'

'You knew her?'

'Oh no. Sorry. After all of this. Her neighbour was concerned. Other than that, she led quite a lonely life, I think. From what her neighbour said, she was her closest friend.'

238

'How awful.'

'Yes.' I ask him, 'You weren't in contact, with Natasha?'

He shrugs. 'Not since she left home at seventeen. I'd get emails for a bit, sporadically. I don't know how much you know?'

'Nothing. I got put into care in London.'

He frowns. 'But you spoke to her?'

I shake my head.

'Oh. What about Lisa?'

Another shake.

He sighs. 'Natasha only told me about her death afterwards and by email, which was a bit shit of her. That made me sad. Lisa always seemed all right.'

I focus on the empty packet of sugar on the table. The corners of it are curling up. A few grains have spilled out, making a little line on the table. I use my napkin to wipe it, collecting the granules, rolling it all into a ball.

'Yes.'

'Sorry, I know you were all close.'

I shrug. 'You still live with your mother?'

A sigh then, followed by a grin. 'I do, yes. We can't seem to escape each other.'

I don't know what to say to that, so I stay silent.

He tells me, 'I was glad in a way, when Natasha left for the city. They were never destined to get along. My sister is . . . was . . . incapable of forgiveness.'

Is the implication there that he has forgiven his mother? I ask him, 'Did you miss her?'

'At first, yes. She'd always looked after me, I guess. Especially in light of the fact that our mother wasn't always capable.'

'Is she now?'

He raises an eyebrow. 'Of looking after me?'

I laugh at the absurdity of this nice, adult man needing care, though if he's anything like me, he still does. My mind wanders back to Isaac. 'No, I don't know. Of anyone, herself included?'

'Not really. She's never fully recovered. From everything.'

It's my turn to look away, sideways at the street outside. It's a warm day but grey and drab.

I say, 'So Natasha still emailed sometimes?'

He nods. 'That was my lot, though. I suggested I come to London to visit her a few times. I kind of guessed her problem was with Mum, not me.'

'She didn't want you to visit?'

He shakes his head, smiling, but it's forced and I can see it causes him pain. I murmur, 'I'm sorry.'

He shrugs. 'She was always a hard one, wasn't she.'

I think about it. Natasha's defiant resilience. Her refusal to shed a tear, her frustration with Amy for doing just that, for eventually breaking. I think about myself ignoring emails from her and Lisa. Even the day of Lisa's funeral, being unable to make myself go. Hardness can protect you, or at least keep you cushioned to some degree.

I say, 'She was, yes.'

'I often think that was her biggest problem.'

'What do you mean?'

'I don't know. No man or woman is an island.'

My memories of Brodie are of a soft, confused child with chocolate brown hair and sad brown eyes.

I find that my feelings towards him seem to be the same as they always were. I like this man sitting in front of me and I don't consider him to be a risk.

I say, 'You knew, about Pen?'

He nods. 'She told me in an email. Asked me not to tell Mum.' I frown at that. Natasha had been quite clear to me in her letter that Brodie didn't know, certainly Pen hadn't been told about her uncle or her grandmother. Secrets. Lies? Or just Natasha trying to protect her daughter. I myself had avoided the past for so long.

'And did you tell your mum?'

He shakes his head. 'No. I asked to meet her and all she said was one day . . .' There is a pause where he looks like he's struggling with what to say. Eventually he blurts out, 'So she's with you?.'

He smiles at that and I feel an unexpected rush of relief. I didn't think I had been seeking his permission or his blessing. But Pen is his niece. His blood relation. Not that that means anything to me, the lone Sillitoe.

I say, 'She left really clear instructions. She also told me you didn't know.' I shrug. 'I'm sorry.'

He takes my hand and I feel little zings of electricity ping up my arm. Confused, freaked out, desperate for him to do it again? I don't know but I snatch it back, making a big thing of picking up my coffee.

I take a sip, put it down and ask him, 'You're not pissed?'

He shakes his head. 'No. You're a good choice. You seem remarkably together. Despite . . . you know. Everything.'

I grin. 'So do you.'

'Appearances can be deceptive.' But he's smiling. 'On the whole I'm OK, I think. I always thought Natasha was the tough one but honestly I think the fact that I cried and grieved, forgave Sienna, maybe meant I was happier on the whole.'

I look out of the window, watching people bustle past. I think of Isaac, whose own children still want nothing to do with him, and all that they are missing out on. The secret file of anger I have ferreted away. My rage at my mother, like a little pocket of poison within me. I savour it still. Get it out to play with when I'm feeling bad. The anger is, of course, inverse. It is as much directed towards me as it is her. Because if your own mother can't love you . . .

He says, 'She wouldn't give me any other details about her life really. Nothing substantial other than that she had a child, but I have found things out.'

'Oh yeah?'

'I hired a PI.'

I laugh. 'No way – like in the films?'

He grins. 'I guess. He wasn't very glamorous though.'

'But he did a good job?'

He nods. 'He found her address, social media presence, my niece. Penelope Dryden.'

I say, 'Pen.' Softly.

'That's a nicer name for a little girl.'

'She's a good kid.'

'I'd love to meet her.'

I nod. 'We'll sort it out.' And as I say those words, I know that is the right choice.

'I'd love that. Is she here?'

I shake my head. 'No. She has school.'

He nods. 'OK.'

This weekend she'll be here, but I need to run this idea past other people. Dee. Isaac. Pen herself. Brodie can wait a day; he's waited this long.

There are so many things I want I ask him. So many questions bustling at the front of my mind. But the words don't come and silence stretches out around us.

He says, 'How long are you staying?'

'I'm not sure yet.' And then: 'This is the first time I've been back. To Wales.'

His face is serious now and he looks at me so intensely I feel overwhelmed, flustered. He takes my hand and squeezes it.

When I get back to my bland hotel room, I pour myself a whisky from one of the tiny bottles in the mini bar. I am full of conflicting feelings and with a tight ball of confusion sitting in the pit of my stomach.

At the Black House, boys disappeared.

When this stark, awful phenomenon was discovered, it became the most discussed, most reviled of all the reported horrors. Eclipsing the consistent sexual abuse of female minors.

Murder.

When boys were deemed uncompliant, they would be there one day and gone the next. Carillo didn't kill any of them himself, of course. He was only convicted of coercion, control and rape. A string of child rapes. But James was the one who killed the boys. Mercilessly and brutally. I didn't interact with him much myself, but I knew of him, was scared of him. He was a tall man, stick-thin with straggly long hair and a mean face. He watched us children with hard eyes and I saw him strike out at some of the Aunts in an almost offhand fashion. More for sport than any particular reason. I knew that Amy flinched every time he walked past and suspected he had doled out his fair share of pain to her. I'd seen him administer a public beating once, and he did it with a smile on his face. When reports came out that he was thought to be guilty of murder, I wasn't surprised.

The bodies of two male children were found buried behind the big yard.

Next to Amy.

I'd wondered more than once if he'd had anything to do with Amy's death. If not the one who'd physically pushed her, at least one of the men who'd taken her to the brink of her own mind. Just as Carillo had favoured Natasha, it was no secret James considered Amy one of his. On the endless, stretching nights when I was unable to sleep, I would play various scenarios out in my mind. He became an almost mythical character. Cartoonish in his devilment. But all of the adults there were like that to me. The men were more animated than the Aunts but the Aunts were no less terrifying, with their blank faces and wicked hearts.

Was he bad? Before Carillo?

Hard to tell. He was an ex drug addict, had been to prison for a string of petty and somewhat pathetic offences. In and out of care homes throughout his growing up. Ripe for the adulation of a man like Joseph, who took him in and helped him get clean, as he had many others before him. He weaned them off of hard drugs and replaced their idle hours with hard work, tender care and a purpose.

We were going to build utopia.

It was the children who threw a spanner in the works. Wilful, uncontrollable little blighters that we were. The two dead boys had tried to arrange a rebellion. An escape. And they paid the ultimate price for that deceit.

After their deaths, two families escaped, stumbling away from that awful place at Sienna's urging. She knew that their sons were next, that this was all she could do to stop it. Though she still didn't find the strength herself.

They could have – *should* have – gone straight to the authorities. I've raged about the fact they didn't many times over the years. Thinking about it as I draw my left hand to my right arm, my fingers feeling out the twisted ridges of skin. My mind filled with the face of my dazed, drugged mother. Her eyes meeting mine and a moment of . . . what? Realisation? Remorse? *Sorry* . . .

I would never know, since I couldn't ask her.

There is a ringing and I jump at the sound. The telephone in my room.

Reception – I have a visitor – Brodie Dryden. I tell them to send him up.

CHAPTER FIFTY-FOUR

NATASHA

I always knew it would come down to me. When Brodie had told me, sobbing, about the boys from his dorm, I'd been mildly impressed by their big ideas, but unsurprised that they hadn't managed it. Hadn't pulled it off.

Men were weak; men were stupid.

Boys were just men waiting to happen, after all. You had to be smart. Clever. You had to be tough. I loved Brodie, but he wasn't tough. He almost jeopardised us all, going back for our mother. I thought about leaving him. Certainly Blue and Lisa were my focus.

I knew Nicholas would have run, taken Martin with him. Brodie probably could have caught up to him, would have been OK in the end. But it was Blue's face every time she looked at my brother that stopped me. He'd shown her kindness. I knew that.

It was – still is – important to me that Blue has respect for me. Even in the years we've been apart, I knew it wouldn't be forever. If I'd have harmed Brodie it would have made things difficult.

In the end, the fact we had Sienna with us worked out well enough. She was laughably deemed fit to look after me and Brodie. It was me who took care, though. Always me. I'd have taken him with me to London too, but he wouldn't leave her. Mummy dearest.

Men. Boys. They just aren't that tough, and nor are the women who fall for them . . .

CHAPTER FIFTY-FIVE

Annie is perturbed. She's just discovered that Blue has taken herself off on a trip to Wales. Whilst she obviously didn't need police authorisation, Annie feels the least she could have done is told her. Especially in light of Lyndsey Dunmore and Natasha now being missing – not even necessarily presumed dead. There is no body. They only have her word for it. The more Annie learns about Natasha, the more she understands that she is a woman deliberately shrouded in secrecy.

Does Annie trust Blue? Probably not one hundred per cent. But then her default setting is to mostly trust no one. She sort of trusts Isaac, though, and perhaps that's why it's his shop she finds herself standing outside of now. Debating whether to go in. He's not going to like what she has to say. But she needs to say it anyway. She smokes a cigarette, leaning to the side of the main glass window. She contemplates turning and walking away, but just as she's about to, he comes out holding out a mug of coffee.

She frowns, but takes it from his outstretched hand.

He says, 'I can see you from the counter.'

'Oh.'

He lights a cigarette, she lights another, and they stand out there in silence, sipping coffee and smoking. The sun beating down on the pavement and her face. Annie is a redhead but also has light olive skin eyes, which she thinks somehow saves her from burning to a crisp. She likes the sun and thinks she probably needs a holiday. The last one she'd had was with her soon-to-be ex-husband and had been a disaster. They'd come home early and she'd decided to start divorce proceedings that same month. She's somewhat shocked when she realises that was, in fact, over a year ago.

She puts the cigarette out. Isaac says, 'I'm stocktaking, come inside?'

They head in and she looks pointedly at the pile of records. 'Is this all you do all day?'

He shrugs. 'Pretty much.'

'Don't you get bored?'

He shakes his head. 'Nope.'

'From being a rock star to this – bit quiet, isn't it?'

He nods. 'Yes. But I think I've had enough excitement to last a lifetime.'

'You have a point.'

He grins his good-looking smile and she looks away. Nervous now for reasons she really ought not to be.

She says, 'It's about Blue.'

'Oh?'

'Going to Wales.'

'I'm looking after young Penelope, you know.'

'How is it?'

'Aside form a rather brutal introduction to various boy bands, rather nice.'

She laughs. 'Not your cup of tea?'

He frowns. 'I played her X-Ray Spex.'

'She's not even ten.'

'It's never too early for X-Ray Spex.'

He is writing down the name of each record onto a large unwieldy document on A3 paper.

Annie says, 'You'd be better doing that in Excel.'

'Oren said that. He's going to input it later.'

'So you really don't need to do it by hand first then.'

He shrugs. 'I find it soothing.'

She frowns.

He adds, 'And I dislike change. I'm sure Oren, and you, are right. But if he's not and it fucks up, I have it here.'

'Right.'

'Anyway, about Blue?'

'I'm not happy.'

'That's a big statement. Perhaps happiness should not be our ultimate aim in life.'

She rolls her eyes but is suppressing a grin. 'You know what I'm getting at.'

'You don't think she should have gone to Wales?'

'No, I don't. And David Belsham seems to know more about a lot of this stuff than we do, which can't be right.'

'Yet there it is.'

'I don't like him at all.'

Isaac says, 'Me neither.'

'Then why don't you tell Blue to steer clear?'

'I'm not her keeper.'

'You're the closest thing to a parent she has.'

He nods. 'And I love her as fiercely as I do my own children. I also enjoy a much better relationship with her than I do them. Part of the basis for that is not interfering when it's not appropriate.'

Annie says, 'She said you told her to take Pen in.'

'I recommended it, yes.'

'So interfering was appropriate then?'

'Felt right.'

'And that's how you do things, based on feelings?'

He grins at her. 'Annie, you sit in the same meetings I do. Even if you've not started any work yet, you've heard them say many times that we will intuitively know how to handle situations that used to baffle us.'

She glares at him. 'That has no bearing on real life.'

He laughs. 'Annie, pardon me for saying so, but this is why you go on the piss every few months.'

She opens her mouth. Can't think what to say. By the time she figures it out her voice is a hiss. 'I have it under control. I go to meetings to ensure that it's every few months. Which isn't doing anyone any harm.'

'Other than you.'

She stands. Getting her bag and sliding it onto her shoulder. 'If you could ask Blue to call me as soon as possible, I'd be grateful.'

He nods, then: 'Pen and I are going to Wales to meet her.'

'When?'

'Today, after school.'

She murmurs a swear word and is extra annoyed to see him grinning. 'I'm telling you first so you can't be mad.'

She leaves without saying goodbye, the door slamming behind her.

CHAPTER FIFTY-SIX

I've had sex a total of two times. Three, now. The first time was dreadful and I honestly thought I wouldn't bother again. The second time, with the same man, wasn't too bad, but the feelings that accompanied it had been overwhelming. I'd ended the relationship before it blossomed into anything more and though I'd been on a few casual dates since then, I'd pretty much given up on the lot of it.

Perhaps until now.

I've been awake since five. It's almost ten and Brodie is still lying in my crappy hotel bed, snoring softly.

I've showered, got dressed and been downstairs to buy pastries and still he sleeps.

I cannot believe what has happened and how I feel. Confused. Overwhelmed. But also . . . *alive*, somehow.

Suddenly I understand all the schmoozy, ridiculous crap you hear in songs and watch in movies. Is it because this man was my childhood crush? I don't know. In all the madness of the Black House. Those moments in the cave with Brodie, or where he'd catch my eye and smile. The little white pebble with the smiley face that I still have, though the face is so faint now it's barely there. Those tiny moments of peace and something else. Something better – understanding. I have it with Isaac to some degree and with the rattling junkies who come through the door. I'd felt a faint glimmer of it with David Belsham. Trauma changes you. The fabric of who you were going to be, who you were meant to be even, or so I used to think.

But this is all I can be. The girl running from a house on fire with the scalded arm and other scars – ones that sunk below the skin into every bit of me. I couldn't escape who I was, where I'd been, any more than Brodie could.

Not everyone got it. How could they? Some people grew up in homes filled with love and laughter. They went to school, had friends, first loves, and lives similar to the ones their parents had provided for them.

They didn't know that everything could go wrong; they didn't know who they were when faced with the worst possible circumstances.

But I did. Brodie did. Natasha did. Of course I have feelings for him. The boy who took my hand, led me through the woods to momentary sanctuary. Of course I conjure such feelings in him. We are connected. Together even after so many years apart. Like back then, last night with Brodie, I simply forgot about everything else going on, everything I've been through.

'Hey.' His eyes open; he blinks twice.

I smile, suddenly shy, which is ridiculous. Particularly as I'm dressed and he's naked . . .

I say, 'Hey you.'

He stands up and the covers drop. I blush, which he either doesn't notice or completely ignores. He steps past me to the tiny bathroom and pauses to press his lips against my hair, then he mumbles, 'Morning breath. Can I use your toothbrush?'

'Sure.'

He does so, and then comes out and sits completely unselfconscious on the edge of the bed, pulling his clothes on.

I ask, 'You in a hurry?' Trying to keep my voice light even though my heart is hammering in my chest, perturbed at his eagerness to leave.

He says, 'I have to nip back and check on Mum. Shall we meet later?'

I'm about to say yes when I remember it's Friday. Pen will be here tonight and David Belsham is due any minute.

His face falls when I shake my head. 'I mean, if you don't want to see me, like if this was a mistake . . .' He runs a hand through his hair. 'Shit, I just assumed . . .'

I move to kneel in front of him. He is in jeans and socks, no top. I press a hand to his chest, one resting on his knee. 'No. It's not that. Not at all.'

His eyes meet mine and we stay like that for seconds, him looking at me.

I say, 'This is weird.' And he nods.

'Good weird though, right?' And I hear the same desperate freaked-out edge that has entered my heart and my thoughts.

I nod. 'Definitely good.'

'So you're, ah, busy later?'

I decide I may as well just be honest. 'Pen's coming.'

His face breaks into a smile then, which I return. He looks much better when he smiles. 'Oh wow.'

I nod again. 'So I need to be here, to settle her in. We're moving across to an Airbnb.' I pull my phone out of my back pocket, find the address Isaac sent and forward it to Brodie.

'I've just sent you the address so call me Saturday and we'll arrange for you two to meet.'

He's properly grinning now. 'Really?'

I nod. 'Yes. She'll be pleased.'

'OK.' And then: 'How's she getting here?'

'My friend Isaac is bringing her.'

254

'Friend?'

I laugh. 'Yes. He's super old and also my boss.' I pause. 'It's a long story.'

He says, 'I can't wait to hear all of your long stories.'

I find I'm grinning now and can't stop. I say, 'I can't wait to hear yours.'

He kisses me at the door and then he's gone.

I allow myself five minutes of sitting on the edge of the bed, totally freaked out and for once, not in a bad way.

Brodie Dryden.

Isaac calls a few hours after Brodie leaves. I pick up the phone with a mixture of exhilaration and misplaced guilt. I wonder if this is how teenage girls feel after they've just had sex and spoken to a parent. I savour the normality of it for a second. Even if I am a woman of thirty and Isaac isn't my Dad, it's good to know that hidden in my depths I can do giggly and awkward. I didn't manage it during my adolescence and I'm glad I'm capable.

It's only one, but Isaac tells me they are on their way. Pen has taken a half-day, which Mrs Williams has reluctantly agreed to. Stressing, of course, that we ought not to make it a regular thing.

Isaac does a hilarious impression of her on the phone and I find myself giggling again. He tells me to go to the Airbnb and he'll meet me there. He also tells me Annie is on the warpath and not at all pleased with us being here. I promise to call her and hang up.

She picks up on the first ring. 'Having a nice trip?'

'Hardly.' Though that is not entirely true. 'Look, I probably should have told you I was coming.'

'You should, yes.'

'I'm sorry I didn't.'

Silence, which I take as surprised petulance.

She says, 'I'm actually trying to help you, though God knows why.'

I say, 'I mean, this case turned out to be more interesting than it seemed, I guess.'

She bursts out laughing and I grin into my phone. I'm on a roll of unexpected goodwill and I wonder if this is what the world is like when you're what? Happy, I suppose.

She says, 'OK, OK. Isaac says he's heading there with Pen?'

'Yes. I'm going to introduce her to her uncle.'

'Brodie Dryden?'

'Yes.'

'You're sure that's a good idea?'

I bristle at that. 'You and Dee were all for her connecting with relatives.'

'But in light of everything.'

'You think Brodie knows where Natasha is?'

'He might.'

'He doesn't,' I say quickly.

'Oh. How can you be sure?'

'She hated her mother, left as soon as she could. They are not who she would go back to right now.'

'Then the question is, who is?'

'Yup.' I pause. 'I'm meeting with Belsham again.' It's a reluctant admission but she'll find out anyway.

'Great.'

'He's already here, digging around.'

She sighs. 'I'm sure he is.'

I say, 'He's trying to help too, in his own way.' Though I don't know if that's entirely true. He's a ghost writer who hasn't had any work for a few years. His motives are largely financial. But still.

DI Grafton says, 'I'm going to come up there.'

'OK.'

'Not to spy or anything. I have to talk to Sienna and Brodie.'

'Of course.'

I hang up, text Isaac that everything seems fine and head to the Airbnb.

CHAPTER FIFTY-SEVEN

The Airbnb is, of course, nice. Isaac, by his own admission, has grown accustomed to luxury over the years and wherever he ends up in the world you can bet your bottom dollar it'll be rated five stars. Our 'home' whilst we're here is a huge apartment in a block of three. The others appear to be empty. I unpack my few bits for the second time in twenty-four hours and stand on the balcony looking out over the city. I can see the mountains in the background and know that the Black House, or what remains of it, is not too far away.

The buzzer goes and I jump out of my skin.

Stupid, of course. I knew David was coming. He's half the reason I'm here, treading carefully through the broken shards of the past, trying desperately not to cut myself on any of their awful fragments.

He comes inside and lets out a low whistle. 'This is nice.'

I nod. 'My friend Isaac has some cash.'

He waggles his eyebrows. 'Good friend to have, eh.' He emphases the word friend.

I realise then that I don't like him very much. It's not necessarily his fault; he has one of those irritating personalities. Like, he's pretty good-looking but there's something a bit annoying that stops him being devastatingly handsome. He's clever, but prone to saying inappropriate things. A lack of awareness maybe, or an inability to read other people. He had said he had a traumatic upbringing and my annoyance is replaced by a wave of sympathy. I of all people understand being awkward in your own skin. The damage that being given little, or the wrong, instruction can do to a person.

I say, 'Yes, David. Friend.' Firm but gentle. 'Can I get you a tea? Coffee?'

'Tea would be lovely.' He puts down a large laptop bag by my sofa and follows me into the kitchen.

We drink tea and I ask what his plans are.

He says, 'I'm going there today.'

'To the Black House?'

He nods. 'I've been before, but I want to get some photos you know.'

I nod like I do, but even the thought of that place brings with it a swell of nausea. How has Brodie stayed here for so long? The mountains alone give me the heebie-jeebies. I wonder if he's been back and I make a mental note to ask him next time we speak.

David's been talking.

I say, 'Sorry, David, I missed that.'

'Oh, just saying Sienna Dryden is back in the hospital again.' He says hospital with an eye roll. I look at him, sharp now. 'What do you mean?'

'She had some sort of episode from what I gather from my source.'

'Who is your source?'

He waves a hand. 'Noreen Fagin, a nurse who works there.' I am horrified at the number of so-called caring professionals willing to sell out clients and patients for cash. I'm also desperately going over the fragments of my conversation with Brodie. He'd said he was going home to check on his mum. I'm sure he had. Or had he just said checking on her? Even if he hadn't, why hadn't he told me Sienna was in bad shape? Should he have? I feel like I would have.

David finishes his tea and we stand around awkwardly while he does so. I'm so relieved when my phone rings that I almost jump for joy. I take the call, listening and then hanging up.

'My friend Isaac is on his way.'

David nods. 'With Pen?'

'Yup.'

'OK. Guess I'd better get out to see her whilst there's still some daylight.'

I think by *her* he means the Black House. Referring to that awful place as a she is off-key but I don't push it.

I smile and say, 'Great, keep me updated, yes?'

'Course.'

It isn't until an hour later as I'm tidying up that I realise he left his laptop bag with me. I put it in the hallway cupboard.

Pen and Isaac burst into the apartment in a wave of blissful chatter and brand new in-jokes. I feel a swell of happiness at their arrival and even manage to put the uneasy feeling I have about Brodie not telling me about Sienna to one side, though I will have to ask him about it. I've learnt from Isaac that without honesty relationships are meaningless.

Pen buzzes about the place, in and out of rooms, oohing and ahhing over the bath that sits on four legs and the walk-in rain shower.

I roll my eyes and tell her. 'Isaac has more money than sense.'

Pen retorts that her mummy says money can't buy you happiness, but poverty guarantees misery.

I have nothing to say to that since it's so obviously true.

My phone rings. DI Grafton.

'Hey.'

'Hello, Blue. Are they there yet?'

'Yup. We're in a proper fancy Airbnb courtesy of moneybags.'

'Sounds swell. I'll be in the crappy Travelodge, courtesy of the stingy police force.'

'Sorry.'

'It's OK. I'm hoping it'll only be a brief visit.'

'You're going to see Sienna?'

'Yes, she's staying at a place called the Georgian Group apparently.'

I write that down, grabbing a pen from a jar of them on the kitchen counter and scribbling it on my hand. I probably could have asked David, of course.

Annie says, 'I've been looking over the old files.'

'On the Black House?'

'Right.'

'OK.'

'Did you know it was thought, though couldn't be proven, that Sienna poisoned everyone, before the fire?'

I think on that. All we knew was that strong sedatives had been mixed into the pasta sauce served at the main house that evening. None of the kids had been dosed. But food was batch-cooked well in advance and we ate different meals to the adults, at different times.

I say, 'I don't know about that.'

'Me neither. It's just a theory.' Then: 'Maybe I shouldn't have told you that. I just wondered if you had maybe suspected?'

'No. I assumed it was Carillo.'

'Even if it wasn't him directly, I'm sure it led back to him.'

Though of course, part of Carillo's defence had been that the same sedative had been found in his system, too.

He was a big man though, and hadn't ingested enough to knock him out, which is how he escaped the fire. He wasn't, however, immune, and the drugs had caught up with him an hour later, ensuring his capture and the rescue of the two boys in his care. It was one of the many anomalies about the case. Nothing really made sense; nothing could be completely proven. Though it was widely believed Carillo set the fire himself, no definitive evidence was ever found.

I say, 'You're going to talk to Sienna about that, then?'

'I will. That's why I'm coming.'

'OK, call when you arrive. Isaac's threatening to cook and says you're welcome to join.'

'That bad?'

'You tried his coffee?'

CHAPTER FIFTY-EIGHT

Annie has probably crossed many professional lines during this case. Not least in her somewhat pathetic crush on Isaac. Or that she is inexplicably fond of Blue and Pen, even if Blue is a wilful bugger who causes her nothing but hassle. Perhaps because of it.

From one difficult woman to another!

Her phone rings. Ian, who she's already spoken to that morning. His hangdog face is an annoyance she is glad to be rid of and she's looking forward to divvying up the finances and finally being free. She'd gone into that marriage half drunk, high on cocaine and hoping it would be third time lucky. She really should have learned by now that relationships just weren't her thing. On the upside she's heading towards four months clean and sober, her longest stretch yet.

She knows it's the case that's keeping her straight. The adrenaline she gets from her job can be just as good as a chemical high, a stiff drink or the fantastic feeling of a new relationship. She knows too that she'll feel deflated when it's solved, and it would be then she'd need to watch herself.

Right now though, she's starting to feel concerned that the puzzle may never be solved at all. The whole thing is a tangled mess. There are too many unanswered questions. The main one being where the hell is Natasha Dryden? Annie is quite certain that the answer lies somewhere in

Wales, hidden in those hills – if not the woman herself, at least an idea of where she might be hiding out. That's what Annie thinks, that Natasha is hiding somewhere. And if she is, what about poor Lyndsey? Was she simply a substitute body?

Was Natasha Dryden not a victim, at all but a murderer?

CHAPTER FIFTY-NINE

Isaac takes Pen out to 'see the sights' after I tell them I need to do something. Pen looks put out about it until I kneel down and tell her, 'Tomorrow, we'll meet your uncle.'

Her face lights up. 'Brodie?'

She looks from me to Isaac. Isaac looks at me with million questions in his eyes. I mouth 'later' to him and he nods. As soon as they leave, I google the address for the Georgian Group.

My phone pings and an image comes through from David. *'Your old room?'*

I drop the phone and double over, hands moving to clutch my sides as I involuntarily heave. The phone pings several more times from the floor, but I am busy trying to push my feet down into the ground, to control my breathing and not throw up.

Jesus Christ.

It's just an image on a tiny screen of somewhere I haven't been for so long, and it has ruined me. I focus on breathing and sink down to the carpet. Picking up the handset, I scroll through the images. The place is dilapidated, that's for sure, some bits outside are just crumbled ruins. It also looks a lot smaller than I remembered it. The dorms, the barn. The next image is of large, dug-out holes. That was where they found Amy and the boys. I feel my rage swell. Why had no one filled them in? What a dreadful, macabre thing to leave behind. Though I suppose no one went there anymore. Aside from the ghouls who visited and posted pictures on creepy online forums. I'd seen such things but never paused to look properly. Never allowed my eyes to focus.

I shut them now. My phone pings again, breaking into my unsettling meditation. *'I have some questions. Would you come out here tomorrow to walk around the place with me?'*

I turn my phone to silent, slide it into my bag and move into the extravagant bathroom, splashing cold water on my face.

When I finally feel OK, I dial for an Uber and head downstairs to meet it. DI Grafton is going to be super pissed at me, but I'll deal with that as and when. I can't bring myself to explain to her, or even to Isaac yet, that I need answers. Mainly as to whether or not I can trust Brodie.

The Georgian Group isn't dissimilar to the place I found myself in after Lisa's death and my breakdown. I stroll with confidence to the front desk. I ask if I can see Noreen Fagin, praying that she's on shift and that I give off enough air of authority not to be questioned. Luckily for me she is and comes out to meet me. The receptionist goes back into the back office and I say to the nurse, 'I'd like to speak to Sienna Dryden, please.'

She shakes her head, 'Only her son's allowed in to see her, I'm afraid.'

I smile, wishing I didn't have to do this and say, 'And David Belsham, of course.' Her face visibly pales and I feel equal parts guilt and fascination.

She stutters, 'I was desperate. My mother . . .' But I don't want her sob story. I can't afford to feel sympathy.

I say, 'So am I. Take me to her.'

I follow Noreen, remaining a few steps behind her, feeling like a colossal arsehole. We get to a large room with high ceilings and there she is.

My knees seem to liquefy and I feel a tremor in my steps. I push my feet down into the floor, sweat breaks out on my top lip and I throw my hand out, pressing my fingers to the wall to steady myself.

The nurse – Noreen, who can't meet my eye – snaps, 'Five minutes,' and turns to go.

Now it is just Sienna and I.

She is sitting quietly, staring out of the window at yet another mountain view. I wonder if they disturb her as much as they do me. I feel a deep longing for London as I stand there watching her. For the busy streets and tall buildings.

I only have five minutes. I force myself to go and sit opposite her and her eyes turn to find me. They seem to drink me in, looking at me with the same fierce intensity as her son had just last night. I am so linked to this woman. Not by my own design, but somehow by destiny, as our paths are meshed together.

When she speaks her voice is soft, her accent strong, and I am taken back to that place. 'You look very like her.'

My mother. I do. I look very similar to the face grinning back at me from my single photo. But I never hear it. Who would say it after all?

'You know who I am?'

'I wouldn't have. But Brodie said you'd been.'

I feel . . . relief?

I ask her, 'He came to check on you?'

She nods. 'Yes.' Frowning, she says, 'He said he'd told you that?'

I swallow thickly. Oh thank God. He wasn't lying. He wasn't specific, but it wasn't an outright lie. My heart is still racing and my palms are damp. I wipe them on the tops of my legs.

Sienna says, 'You're frightened of me.' It's a statement, not a question.

I look away from her, out of the window.

'Did you poison them, that night? Were you cooking?'

I look back at her. Her pale, thin face is startled now. 'No, why would I . . .'

She pauses; takes a deep breath. As she does so, her shoulders rattle. They are like sharp sticks pointing upwards from the thin cotton of her top. She is dressed, but in the type of clothes that show she has nowhere important to go. A shirt. Wide trousers. Everything too big for her brittle frame. This place is for people with eating disorders. I refuse to feel sympathy for her.

I hiss sarcastically, 'Oh right, because you wouldn't have hurt your friends.'

'I didn't want to hurt anybody.'

'And yet, by doing nothing, you did.' Adding, 'Your own children, for example.'

She flinches. I don't feel sorry. 'Yes.'

I meet her eyes properly. They are damp, like my own. 'Why?'

'I didn't know what else to do.'

'That's pathetic.'

She nods. 'I know.'

The fight goes out of me then. I feel an internal deflation and my body contracts, my arms wrapping around myself.

She says, 'I tried to help.'

'It wasn't enough.'

She nods agreement. 'I know.'

'But it was something.' The words are out before I realise I even think them. Before I have chance to know if

I mean them. Years of Isaac bleating on about forgiveness, words I humoured but essentially rolled my eyes at make sense. Just a little bit as I look at this shell of a person.

She leans forward as if she might take my hand then thinks better of it.

'You were next, you know.'

'Sorry?'

'You and your mother.'

'Next for what?' My voice is barely a whisper.

'To go. She and I had been trying to plan for weeks.'

I think of her. My mother, pressing that photo into my hand. So unexpected.

Sienna is nodding. 'She was ready to act and in time for you, too. Not like me. I'd left it way too late.'

I shake my head. As if the movement will take away the words. Words that I am unsure whether to use as a salve or a terrible, punishing truth. She was going to take me and leave. We were going to go.

I press my fingers to my mouth.

Sienna says, 'Natasha was going to help me to get you both out.' She shrugs. 'Your mother would go to the police. She promised. We'd have all been free.'

I know then with certainty that she hadn't poisoned everyone that night.

I say to her, 'Who knew?'

'What?'

'About this plan?'

'Your mother, Natasha. Nicholas, one of the older boys. He was supposed to be Natasha's husband. Did you know that?'

I frown. I could remember Nicholas – Nick we called him. He was just another kid, but not in my dorm. Not in my tiny, claustrophobic world of four. Until there were three.

Sienna nods. 'Not a bad boy. He would have done anything for her.'

'He was the same age as Natasha?'

Sienna nods, then looks at me, wide-eyed, 'It wasn't all for nothing, was it? Some got out. But I don't know about the poison, or the fire.'

'You weren't poisoned.'

She laughs then, though I can't see what's funny, and it's a sound devoid of humour anyway.

I frown and this time she does take my hand, quickly, before I have chance to snatch it away. In her touch are too many memories. Her hand representing all of the Aunts with their quick, cruel slaps, indifferent faces and measured punishments. She is Amy's mother beating her, my mother telling me to call her 'Aunt' in a room full of other children.

I stand abruptly, the chair sliding back. I am shaking but we are no longer touching. Thank goodness we are no longer touching. Her face has fallen, sad now. Real sadness.

She shakes her head. 'I forget the damage we did. Brodie is so . . . normal. So wonderful. It's easy for me to forget, to pretend. I didn't ingest poison because even then, I didn't eat. We all have our own things going on, but Joseph controlled *everything* I did, everything I thought. What I wore, when I went to the bathroom. He couldn't make me eat, though.' She smiles but it disappears quickly. 'I am sorry. About everything. You might not believe me and I don't blame you, but for what it's worth, I am. And your mother was too. She knew she was damaging you and she had plans to go. Please believe that. Hopefully you can find some solace in it.'

Her eyes are looking at mine, begging. But she misunderstands. I don't feel vengeful; I feel horribly, frighteningly disjointed.

I say, 'If Brodie is a good son, if you are free, why are you here?'

She shrugs. 'Guilt is a funny thing. I've earned mine, haven't I?'

I can't disagree with that. She wipes her delicate hand across her brow, looking suddenly very tired.

'The last thing Natasha said to me when she left was that being me was punishment enough.'

I am saved from having to respond by Noreen, who hisses, 'You need to go.' I follow her out and she looks at me, flustered. 'There's a policewoman coming to see her.'

I don't say anything and her eyes widen. 'You knew?'

I shrug.

She says, 'I'll get into a world of trouble.'

I don't say anything. Cannot find the words in my heart. My phone rings. David Belsham. I'm tempted not to answer.

'Hi.'

'Blue, hey. Look, I know you probably don't want to, but can you come out here?'

'To the Black House?'

'Yes. Uber it. I'll drive you back?'

My heart has started its crazy dance again. I feel everything and nothing. That overwhelming sensation of overload that led to me numbing out for years. I slunk through my adolescence doing things on autopilot. Stepping through each day as blank as the Aunts I'd left behind. The only thing that punctuated my malaise had been anger.

The sound that fear makes.

I'm scared now, terrified. Tempted to just pack Pen and Isaac up. Send Brodie a message – thanks, but no thanks. Try and put Natasha out of my mind.

Try and ignore it all. But I've done that for so long and here it all is, anyway. You can run, but you can't hide. Not forever.

Besides, how much more fucked up can one day get? May as well get the whole awful thing over with.

CHAPTER SIXTY

I have imagined this moment for so long and it is every bit as bad as I had thought it would be.

I can hardly breathe by the time I pull up. The familiarity of the long dirt road, everything we pass, aged by the years and the neglect. Brambles grow tall and the grass is higher than my waist now. The taxi driver asks if I'm OK. I assure him I am, a lie through gritted teeth. I step out and stand, waiting for him to turn and drive away, and then I head towards the place that's haunted my dreams slowly. Like a cat sneaking up on its prey, or maybe more like a lamb to slaughter.

The barn is smaller than I remember it in real life, but still big enough to scare the absolute shit out of me. I take the steps to the main door, which is now just a few tattered boards hanging down and not covering the entrance at all. I nearly jump out of my skin when one of the steps creaks beneath my foot. I stop pressing my feet down onto it, into it.

The building has been abandoned. No repairs were undertaken after the fire. Everything inside was cleared out. The bean bags and yoga mats. The awful futon mattresses. The desk and the chairs.

The bodies.

I step inside, aware of a damp smell and the fact that puddles of water pool in little dips in the floor. It's a mess in here. I suppose once it was a nice enough building. Certainly it was kitted out like every juicing yogi's dream. It had never felt calm to me, though, and I still steered clear of those kinds of places now. Never trusting anyone less than I do a benevolent hippy.

Carillo had seemed to be a man of principle, seemed to be a man of love and light and all that jazz. He must have been at least vaguely credible to have managed to cobble together his band of followers. But all he was really was a narcissistic maniac.

I walk around the shell of the barn. It is empty. I call for David a few times, but to no response.

I go to the dorms: the boys' first, which isn't too bad. The layout is different to the girls' ones and as such bring with them no real foreboding.

Still no sign of David. I move outside, my foot landing immediately in a murky puddle. It had rained during the night. I remember hearing it whilst I lay next to Brodie, listening to the soft sounds of his sleep.

I pull my foot up. Some water has got into the opening where the tongue meets the top of my boot and it is trickling inside, splurging onto my sock and spreading.

Being here is no good for me, no good at all. I need to get David and go.

Out of the corner of my eye, I catch sight of the girls' dorms and now I am overcome. Flooded by images of four little girls: sometimes happy, sometimes sad. Always frightened.

I think of Pen. She is so small, so delicate and unformed. Full of bright, curious intelligence, but just a child. I had been five years younger than she is now when I was bought here. Shoved in this awful room with three other children I didn't know. Left to cry out during the night for a mother who never came.

The sadness hits me in waves. Moving into the dorms, I press my back flat against the wall of the room I used to sleep in. It is just brick, no paint, and I know if I press my hand to it, my skin will recognise the grooves in between the bricks where cement holds each one pressed against the next.

How many nights had I fallen asleep running my fingers between them, over them? How many days had I woken here at five a.m., a siren blaring? Usually still exhausted. Eyes snapping open to the terror almost as if it was new and fresh every day. Morning. This is your life.

This is hell.

I had thought David's pictures had at least in part prepared me to be here, but I'm in no fit shape for this. For everything . . .

The picture.

Your old room . . .

My mind spins. My stomach churns.

I had never told David where I slept, which dorm I was in. And that information does not exist anywhere. No one had ever specifically asked which room had been ours.

Oh my God.

I stumble outside, my legs like cotton wool, my heart thumping, my palms damp. I scramble in my pocket for my phone and almost laugh when I see that I have no signal, except that I choke instead.

No fucking signal.

I have to get out of here. Something is not right.

I know the way roughly to town. I could maybe trace back the way the taxi drove, or at least walk until I can get signal. I turn around and stare behind the dorms at the woods, wondering at the possibility.

But no.

I can't do it. I can't go in there. It was bad enough twenty years ago, stumbling through that place, my arm scalded and burning, my heart smashed to pieces and my mother's face mouthing *sorry* on a loop. Forever imprinted in my brain, my clearest memory of her.

I will walk all day long roadside if I need to, but I will not go into those woods.

CHAPTER SIXTY-ONE

NATASHA

Everything was fine.

Until Lisa.

Pen was my secret. My baby. My child.

I had left the space for 'father' on the certificate blank on purpose. That should have been enough. I shouldn't have needed to defend myself, after all.

He came to Lisa's funeral. God knows how he'd found out about it, though of course he had. So interested was he still. So unable to ever let anything go. He did the maths when he saw Pen with me. Was she his? Ours? The thought made me feel sick from the inside out.

Ours.

She was *mine*.

He was irrelevant, as he always had been.

The problem was, of course, that he knew so much. In order for my plan to work, I'd needed assistance, that night at the Black House. From him and Lisa. I never doubted her, and I figured he was someone I could control. Mostly I'd been right.

Over the years he's had his meltdowns, his urgent sudden need to 'talk', to 'tell all'. He'd stopped being fun a long time ago. I'd thrown him the odd mercy fuck, then I'd done it to keep him quiet. But I'll admit, he has been a thorn in my side. A single problem in an otherwise tranquil sea that needed sorting out.

'We could be a family,' he'd said.

Even the word makes my skin itch. The inside of my head roar.

Family.

We are all as one.

The greater good.

The Black House.

A mad man taking me from my bed, putting me in his and then passing me around to all of his friends.

My mother looking the other way.

A family.

Family was me, and Amy and Lisa, until they couldn't cope.

Until they forgot how to be tough.

It is Blue and Pen.

Not me and him.

'Let's have it, just you and me, for now. Some alone time, first. We'll come back for Pen.' Soft words I'd whispered. My brain buzzing. Thinking it all over.

'OK,' he'd said. Mollified, but for how long?

So I'd gone. Leaving in the dead of night.

Telling him what I'd done in a desperate voice through a rainfall of tears.

He'd been horrified. Terrified.

I'd pointed out that it was all his fault.

My life.

Pen's.

He had to acknowledge it. Had to do what I said now.

I told him, 'Baby, we've got to run.'

CHAPTER SIXTY-TWO

I've been half-walking, half-running for ten minutes. There is nothing here. Just a long, widening stretch of road where the grass alongside is flattened, worn by feet into the side of the mountain. But every step I get away from that place feels like a victory, albeit a tiny one.

I shouldn't be here. I shouldn't have come. I have no idea what is happening. Did David kill Natasha? And Lyndsey? Did he kill Lyndsey and take Natasha? And what does he want with me? To mess with me? To kill me, too?

DI Grafton was right. All I needed to do was pass information on to her, be passive, in the background. Let her do her job. Brodie could have come to London to see Pen. If we were meant to be, it could have happened that way. It still can . . . right?

I cling to that thought my tentative belief that good things can happen. The healing that began for me when I got away from here. From this place. That happened behind the till at Planet Pop, over endless cups of tea with Isaac, and Oren, bent over a sketch pad, pencil running across the page.

I'm crying now, little hiccuppy sobs. And it's not a very hot day but I'm sweating through my thin jumper, terrified to turn around to see if I'm really alone.

I look again at my phone and see one blessed bar of signal. I dial Isaac but it goes straight to his voicemail. I don't know the number for the Airbnb.

I try Brodie, no answer.

Now I'm finding it difficult to think straight.

DI Grafton.

She picks up on the first ring.

'Yes.'

And for a few stupid seconds I simply whimper down the phone.

'Blue? Blue?'

I am still running, somehow managing to put one foot in front of the other at a definitely faster-than-walking pace. My lungs hurt. My arm aches, as though the wounds are fresh. I half imagine that when I take my jumper off it will take with it the top layer of skin, gloppy and warm, like boiled glue.

DI Grafton says, 'Blue can you stop and stand still?'

I can do that.

'Blue.'

'I'm here.' My voice is a whisper, nothing more. A sound behind me and my heart leaps. I drop my phone. Leaning down, scrambling for it. Then I turn look around blindly, the mountain in the distance. I'd stayed to the roads. Stuck by them.

But does that mean he has seen me? I am sobbing now. Snot crusting fast on my upper lip. I can hardly breathe and I fumble, jabbing at my phone, unable even to unlock it.

It rings again. DI Grafton.

Telling me to breathe. Calm down. I try between sobs, between whimpers, looking in every direction. The sounds of the woodland small but plentiful. Wind whistling. Trees bending in the breeze.

I stumble my way through a conversation full of practicalities and information that DI Grafton has to pick out of me.

She takes twenty minutes to arrive. I watch each minute tick by on my phone in between jumping at every single noise. Real and imagined. I am a nervous wreck. Every single horror movie I've ever watched plays out in my mind, with David as the big bad monster, jumping out from thick woodland, careening onto the road, grabbing me from behind. I hate this place. An area of intense natural beauty holds nothing but fear for me. I feel as though the trees, the mountain, the wilderness itself is reaching out for me. Trying to draw me back. I swipe tears from my face, focus on breathing in and out. Watch the minutes tick by. DI Grafton is frowning as she steps out, but she takes one look at me and her face immediately softens.

She kind of hugs me – an awkward gesture, but I'm glad for it even if she isn't, and I throw myself into her, letting my arms circle her body. 'Thank you. Thank you for coming.'

Her eyes are wide. Freaked out by . . . me? I must look a bloody mess.

She says, 'The Black House.' Finger pointing to where I just came from. Where I have run from a second time.

I nod.

She sighs. 'Let's get you back to Isaac and Pen.'

CHAPTER SIXTY-THREE

By the time we pull up outside the Airbnb, my heart rate has slowed almost to normal. I garble out to her what has happened in a rush of words. I see her face frown and pucker. Realising what this means.

I add, 'You were right about him.'

She shrugs. 'Copper's instinct.'

I realise my own instincts towards him were mixed. I hadn't warmed to him, but I'd also felt sorry for him.

DI Grafton, to her credit, does not assault me with more questions. Perhaps realising that I don't have the answers. Nothing to say that would make any sense. David knew where my bedroom was. No one should know that. The only people who would are people who lived there, or officers and officials who came in later.

But David is my age or thereabouts.

So who the hell is he?

When she offers to come in with me, I accept gratefully. We make our way up the stairs and when I see the door ajar and am met with silence when I call out, the panic returns, only worse. I rush forwards, but DI Grafton stops me, shakes her head and presses a finger to her lips. I smash my own hand over my mouth, the only way I can think of to stop myself screaming.

Please let them be OK, please let them be OK.

Annie stalks in carefully and slowly. I follow directly

where she's just walked, but then I see him and I'm pushing past Grafton to run to his side, nausea rising in my throat.

I kneel down and take Isaac's hand, reaching out to move his face towards me. His head is in a pool of widening blood.

A hand on my arm. 'You might hurt him.'

Hurt him.

Grafton kneels, pressing fingers to his neck, phone held between her ear and shoulder. I don't hear what she's saying for the blood rushing in my ears, but I do hear the words *ambulance* and *back-up*.

She turns to me. 'He's alive.'

But when I bend down, reaching for him again, she pushes me back gently. 'But not conscious.'

I say, 'Pen.'

I'm up and running around the 'fancy' little place yelling her name. But knowing. Already knowing that she's gone.

I stare at the detective and her face mirrors the same horror pulsing through my veins.

She is gone.

I don't know how I survive the wait, but eventually I hear a siren and Grafton is at the door, letting people in, speaking in an official tone about official things. Isaac is moved gently and carefully onto a stretcher. Carried down the stairs. He is a big man, over six feet tall, but he looks small and diminished between the two paramedics. I find I am crying again.

As I go to get in the ambulance with him, I feel a hand on my arm. I look up at Grafton fiercely. 'I have to go with him.'

'Give me five minutes and I'll drive you.'

I pause.

She says, 'We also need to find Pen.'

I say to Isaac, 'I'll be there soon.' Stupid, really.

She says, 'Let's go inside just for a second. You need to change anyway.'

I frown, but when I look down I see blood on my jumper. He'd been lying in it, a pool of it.

I stink as well.

I murmur, 'David Belsham?'

She nods. 'I suspected he was somehow linked and when we started looking into him, two names came up.'

'Oh?'

'Change, wash up come back out. I'll call the station.'

I think about a shower, but it would take too long. I use some of my face wipes to clean the skin where the patch of blood was. I throw the jumper in the bin, unable to drag my eyes away from the stain. It makes me think of Amy's thin blue pyjamas and again I feel like screaming. I clamp my hand across my mouth and turn away from the bin, only to catch sight of myself in my fancy bra that I'd worn to meet Brodie, just in case. My eyes are drawn to my arm and my left hand brushes over it.

I spray deodorant on, looking only at the floor, then pull on a long-sleeved grey T-shirt.

When I get out, Grafton is on the phone.

I say, 'Thank you.'

She waves a hand.

'What are the names?'

She sighs and hesitates. 'We think his real name is either Martin Shaw or . . . Nicholas Carillo.'

Carillo.

The word punches my gut so viscerally I almost double over.

Nicholas.

A tall thinboy with shaggy hair. Cried the night Amy jumped. Silent tears that made his small shoulders shudder.

I look at her open-mouthed. 'Why? Why do you think that?'

She says, 'They are the boys who escaped from the Black House.'

My shoulders drop. Her phone rings. But I already know. It's not Martin. I can hardly remember Martin. But Nicholas, I recall, followed Natasha around like a lovesick puppy. He was supposed to be Natasha's husband. That's what Sienna had said wasn't it.

I shake my head, trying to push sense into it.

Annie hangs up. 'We've found Martin. Married with two children.'

I smile faintly. 'That's nice.' And somehow, I mean it.

She says, 'He was younger than you, I think?'

I nod.

She says, 'He was adopted. Happily.'

'And Nicholas?'

'Just had confirmation that he changed his name at eighteen to David Belsham.'

I say, 'God.'

She nods. 'He was in care in Cardiff. Had a juvenile sentence. Underwent a program for young offenders and then asked the powers that be if he could change his name. Said it was like being branded. Blamed his identity for why he kept getting into trouble, like he might as well be bad with a past like that.'

'Carillo gave him his name to begin with?'

Annie nods again. 'His mother gave Joseph sole custody.'

'And since taking this program?'

'Since then he's been writing, just as he told you. Managed to get work experience at a true crime magazine, landed a few ghost writing jobs. Then this latest project.'

I laugh. 'Project.'

'Sorry. This is an awful situation. I wish we'd found this out sooner.'

'It really is. But it's me who trusted him. Let him in here.' I swipe a hand over my face.

She says, 'You weren't to know. How could you?'

I nod. But it's my fault. Whichever way she dresses it up. Nicholas. Was he still in love with Natasha? Had he threatened Pen? Would he hurt her now?

I slump down, because I don't think I can stand for much longer. 'Where the hell is Pen? What does he want with her?'

She shakes her head. 'I honestly don't know, but we're trying to find out if David or Natasha have property here.'

'Natasha?' I startle. 'They must have something to do with Lyndsey's death.'

Annie nods. Which doesn't make me feel any better.

I say, 'Natasha loves Pen. I'm sure of it.'

Annie's lips are set in a grim line. 'I hope you're right.'

I know I am. 'Great, a killer has Pen.' I moan, sinking into myself.

I feel untethered, like the last tiny bit of me is clinging on to the world and losing.

'Did he mention anything about where he was staying?'

I shake my stupid head. My silly, trusting head. I'd been spoiled with love from Isaac and surrounded by good people for too long. I'd forgotten about the badness. It had been a long time since it was my reality.

But as I'm spiralling into despair, I remember something and jump up, run to the hallway, wrench open the cupboard and sag with relief when I see the laptop bag is still there.

'He left his laptop . . .' I say, holding it out like the last beacon of hope.

CHAPTER SIXTY-FOUR

NATASHA

Silly Nicholas. Couldn't let the past go. Couldn't let me go. Couldn't assuage his guilt.

He'd always done as I'd said. Joseph used to mock him for it. Made a show of his dominance over me. I was to be Nicholas's wife, but we all knew Joseph would still take me whenever he wanted.

Stepdaughter, daughter-in-law, lover. What did it matter? One love. One people. One life.

Sick.

Joseph was really, truly, sick. He passed the sickness on, spread it about until we were all infected with it one way or another. That sickness has chased me my whole life. My past biting at my heels. Every time I felt I was free, or close to it.

I made plans. People got in the way.

Amy, with her desire to leave too soon. The problems it would have caused to my plan. I'd seen her whispering with Sienna. Plotting with the woman who handed me over to a madman.

Lisa falling in love, desperate to tell someone the whole truth, nothing but the fucking truth.

She was so sure he'd understand. So sure he wouldn't say anything. But you *can't* understand what it was like unless you were there. You've no way of knowing what you're capable of until you are pushed.

Problems, both of them. Only causing me problems.

Lisa and I were cooking that night, but it was Nicholas who broke into Joseph's stash. Nicholas who brought what we needed.

'Just enough.' I'd assured them both, 'To put them to all to sleep. To buy us enough time to get out.'

They didn't know I'd stored tubs of accelerant, that I was more than liberal in my dosing. They were mad to think those people had a right to live. They had stolen from us things we could never get back.

They had almost . . . almost made me a victim.

I'd never felt sorry. I didn't feel sorry now. Maybe about Lyndsey. She hadn't deserved that, of course. But if you have to choose between your child and a colleague, who would you pick? Lyndsey was unfortunate collateral damage. I needed enough time. Enough confusion. Enough moving parts in place to get everyone where they needed to be.

To bring Blue home.

That is my goal.

She is the missing piece and Nicholas bizarrely, unwittingly, has given me a path back to her, convoluted though it is, and he will not be part of our life in the end.

Now I have to hope everything else will run smoothly . . .

I cradle my daughter to me, her ashen face blinking up at me, in love and wonder. My heart tremors in my chest.

Worth it. It's all been worth it, and soon it will be over.

I will have the only people I need around me. Only the strong ones. Only the ones I can trust.

CHAPTER SIXTY-FIVE

The laptop is of course password-protected. Only an idiot wouldn't do that these days. And whilst David Belsham – or Nicholas Carillo – may be unhinged, he isn't stupid.

Though the fact he left the laptop and slipped up in mentioning 'my room' does show he's getting careless. I wonder why he's not freaking out that his precious laptop is missing. Why he hasn't come back for it.

Annie drops me at the hospital on her way to the police station. She says they will have to remove the hard drive, download everything elsewhere and then sift through. That sounds to me like it's going to take a worryingly long time but she tells me, 'Trust these guys, they know what they're doing, and they know we are looking for a location. Go see to Isaac and keep your phone on.'

I nod and it takes me two goes with my fumbling, quaking hand to open the car door.

Annie leans over, rests a gentle hand on my arm. 'We'll find her.'

I stare at her, wide-eyed.

She says, 'The laptop was a good call, OK?'

I nod. 'Thanks.'

I'm in a daze the entire way to the hospital and I climb out onto Bambi legs to make my way inside. It is too bright and too warm. There is a sharp smell of antiseptic and people only talk in soft murmurs. A&E.

I find where I'm meant to be and give his name to the person on the desk, adding that DI Grafton dropped me off.

She nods and takes me to a private room with a uniformed officer outside. I note that his clothes and insignia are different to English police, thinking that the officers who rescued us must have been wearing the same uniforms and that I'd never noticed.

I still avoid the police. I know deep down that they are not my enemy any more than bus drivers, teachers, university professors or ticket inspectors. All people we were taught to fear. Logically I understand conditioning, but the things we were taught are incredibly deep-rooted and that feeling of having to walk quietly under the radar so as not to be seen still follows me. It has never truly left. Though it has been salved over the years. Mainly by the man I see lying unconscious now in a standard-issue hospital gown.

Isaac's thin but muscular arms are resting on top of the covers. Every spare bit of skin is covered in tattoos from the neck down. They meet and match and combine. His body is a work of art that he adds to constantly. He still has a tattoo of a ring on his left finger from his marriage and is currently deciding what to get to cover it up. Tears spring into my eyes. He is in the middle of so many things. People need him.

I need him.

The officer says, 'Can I help you, Miss?'

'I'm Blue Sillitoe.'

He frowns. 'Are you family?'

'Yes. Well . . . no. Not officially.'

He says, 'Ah.'

I resist the urge to punch him, instead finding myself saying, 'Please call your superior, DI Grafton, if there's a problem with me being here. She phoned this in; she'll vouch for me.'

He's still frowning, but he takes out a mobile and calls the station, I suspect.

He steps away from me, but I can still hear the outline of the conversation well enough to deduce that he's on hold while someone calls Annie.

He comes back with a nod. 'Sorry. Had to check.'

I say, 'Of course.'

'Your DI is on her way in to the station, apparently.'

'Yes, she just dropped me.' Then I ask, 'Is he sleeping?'

'Out cold, so I'm told. I'm here to keep him safe but also to ask him a few questions when he wakes up. As I understand it a little girl is missing.'

I nod, pressing a hand to lips and trying not to cry.

He says, 'Go on in, pet, a familiar voice might be just the thing, eh.'

'Is he . . . will he . . .?'

'Oh, I see. I'll get the doctor. OK?'

The doctor comes, nodding at the officer, at me. Introductions are made. My patience wears thin. He tells me, 'He'll be right as rain, sore head for a few days, and we've had to stitch up the back so he'll have a bit of a bald patch. But other than that . . .'

'Thank you.' The doctor and the officer both smile. The doctor heading off on his way.

Isaac looks slightly pale but other than that, just like he's sleeping. If it wasn't for the gown and the odd set of complicated blankets they always have in hospitals, he could be at home above the shop catching a cheeky forty winks during his lunch hour. Sleep is one of Isaac's favourite things. He said he spent so many years too high to get more than a few hours strung together at a time that he absolutely revels in any kind of real rest now.

He's not sleeping though; he's unconscious in a hospital

bed. Caught up unwittingly in trouble from my past. A past that is reaching out still for my life. Twenty years later. I sit next to the bed and take his hand in mine. There is a cannula in his vein and a bag of some sort of fluid keeping him hydrated.

I say, 'You're going to have a terrible headache.'

He stirs, makes a sort of murmuring sound, but doesn't wake.

My phone rings, making me jump. I expect to see Grafton's name, but it's Brodie. I tell him what's happened in a voice that sounds much calmer than I feel.

He swears then says, 'I'm on my way.'

Before I have a chance to protest, he has hung up. I think about calling him back, telling him not to bother, but the truth is, I could use some company for this agonising wait.

I keep hold of Isaac's hand. The only sound in the little room is the tick tick of the clock. I hate ticking clocks, have never understood why anyone would choose to have such an irritating sound in their home. But now I find it sort of soothing, and I must drift off, because I wake up, head resting by Isaac's legs and my phone ringing shrilly beside me.

Grafton. I scramble, dropping it before I can pick it up properly, and have to call her back.

She starts speaking as soon as she picks up. 'We have an address. A rental near here. We're on our way.'

'Oh thank God.'

'There are emails, between him and Natasha.'

'Oh?'

'Yes, he was after meeting. She tried to put him off. Politely at first but then they get more . . . I don't know. Desperate-sounding.'

'God.'

'He thinks Pen is his.'

'Jesus.'

'I know, and there were obviously phone calls, meetings. Bits of the conversation are missing.'

'He was . . . what, obsessed with her?'

'Could be, stalking run to kidnapping.'

'Why not take Pen at the time, too?'

'The million-dollar question. I've got to go, but I'll call you.'

And she's gone.

Isaac is still out of it.

I hear a tapping sound and turn, startled. The officer. I squeeze Isaac's hand and go out to see what he wants.

He says, 'Chap at reception asking after you rather than him.' He nods his head at the room. 'Brodie, he says.'

I nod. 'Will you be here?'

'Yes, get a coffee with your friend. I'll have you paged if anything changes.'

'Thank you.'

CHAPTER SIXTY-SIX

Brodie is in reception and the first thing I feel is a swell of relief that he is here. I run to him and almost immediately throw my arms around his bulk, stopping just before I do and standing awkward and defeated in front of him.

He looks at me levelly. 'No sign of her?'

'The police have an address.'

He nods. 'That's good. That's got to be good, right?'

I nod, not even able to contemplate any alternative to Pen being absolutely fine.

He takes a step forward, folds me in his arms and I can feel his breath on the top of my head when he says, 'How's your friend?'

'He'll be OK I think. He's still out cold, though.'

'OK, so he can't tell us anything.'

Us.

I shake my head. 'The officer said we could grab a coffee. He'll call if there's any change and so will Grafton.'

'The policewoman?'

I nod again.

'OK. Coffee it is then, come on.'

The café is only one floor up and yet it feels way too far from Isaac. I am a nervous wreck, hands shaking as I try and open the sugar or pour in milk. In the end, Brodie takes the sugar packet gently from me, opens it, tips it in and stirs.

It tastes like shit. Way too strong and not enough milk. I think about taking it back and asking for more. But the urgent need is for caffeine rather than taste.

Brodie says, 'So tell me again.'

I go over my day once more, sharing once more my disbelief that David Belsham had been Nicholas Carillo. Brodie shakes his head. He looks almost sad.

I say, 'What?'

Brodie shakes his head, 'He was . . . my friend.'

'I know. I'm sorry.'

'No, I mean. God. I don't know what I mean. I just can't imagine . . .'

Yet here we are.

I ask, 'What was he like?'

'Soft, you know. I mean, me and the others toughened up; we had to. Nicholas was older than me, but more sensitive. Took everything to heart.' He adds, 'Had a killer crush on my sister.' Then he winces, realising the choice of his words. 'Sorry.'

I take his hand across the table. 'No need to be. This is all pretty hard to make sense of.'

He nods. 'So, Natasha?'

'With him, they reckon, I think maybe Grafton thought Natasha was part of it, complicit. But there are emails that suggest he was hassling her.' I shrug. 'They don't know.'

Brodie's eyes widen. 'What did Natasha say to him?'

'Not a lot. But there is mention of phone calls. He told me he'd contacted her when he decided to write the book.'

'So he's not Penelope's dad?'

'We're not sure. If he is, Natasha must have been in contact with him. He was in Wales until 2015. Came down to London then. We know he attended Lisa's funeral four years ago and that he approached Natasha there, but they could have been in contact before that. Who knows?'

'Just them, I guess.'

My phone rings and I jump.

I answer it and then hang up, scrambling to my feet. 'Isaac's awake.' I go to him, taking his hand.

He looks at me through glassy eyes and mumbles, 'They've given me the hard stuff.'

I frown. 'Don't enjoy it, old man.'

He smiles but it's weak. 'Pen?'

I shake my head.

Tears spring into his eyes. 'I'm so sorry.'

'It's not your fault.'

'Someone hit me, from behind.'

'Pretty hard too, I'd say.'

He nods, winces. Then says, 'But whoever it was, Pen saw them coming. And she looked happy about it.'

CHAPTER SIXTY-SEVEN

Annie Grafton is trying to rush three officers through what they know whilst persuading the man in charge to let her take at least one armed man with her. He is understandably reluctant and grumbles more than once about that cult being the root cause of any and all trouble he'd ever had here.

She sympathises; she really does. She is a metropolitan police officer. A conscious decision because she knows she'd die of boredom elsewhere. Cops out in these sleepy posts have made their own decisions and she isn't going to judge the rights and wrongs of it.

This man had wanted a quiet life. Instead, he'd had a mass murder and now, as he edged very close to retirement, the same crew were back and causing trouble.

She says to him, 'There is a child in danger. Our sole aim is to get her out safely.' Adding, 'Then it'll all be over.'

He sighs. 'Fine. Fine.'

Calls are made, a small team is assembled. Annie's mind is one hundred per cent focused on the task ahead. They drive as far as they can without detection, then they get out of the cars and make their way on foot. She feels her phone vibrate. It's Blue.

'Isaac awake and OK. He says Pen knew the person who took her and was pleased to see them. I mean she might have met David . . . Nicholas, whatever . . . at the funeral, but I don't know if that would mean she'd be pleased to see him, exactly.'

Annie's mind races. Pen would be pleased of course to see her mother. She doesn't say this to Blue, just: 'OK.'

Blue adds, 'I just got a text with an address from Belsham's phone. I'm assuming from Natasha?'

She reels off the address and Annie confirms it's where they're headed now. She is pleased Isaac is OK, but aware that time is running out, and fast. She's also mulling over the implications of who hit Isaac, and what that means about the wider case. So much history, so much at stake and the waters are still muddy.

She says to the armed officer, 'I want you to shoot to wound, not kill.'

Ideally, she wants them all out alive.

Annie is very keen to hear Nicholas Carillo's version of events.

They surround the little cottage, ready to burst in. But there is a people carrier sitting outside, and a sudden movement catches Annie's eye. A figure in the back. Small and familiar. If Annie isn't mistaken, it's Penelope Dryden.

No one in the front.

She whispers urgently to the other officers, who spread out in a protective circle and then she half crouches, half runs to the car, moving to the side hidden from view of the house.

She is so close, she could reach out and touch the door handle. Pen sees her, eyes widening. Annie shakes her head slightly, pressing a finger to her lips.

Through the car windows, Annie sees the door to the cottage open and David Belsham appears, followed closely by a woman she's seen only in pictures. Natasha Dryden, alive.

Shit.

Annie makes frantic hand signals for the armed officer to get into position, then she steps out from behind the car, arms raised above her head.

David reacts like a deer caught in headlights. Annie wills Natasha Dryden to run, but she doesn't move. Seeming to almost hesitate first, looking at Annie with wide eyes, David grabs Natasha, arm across her neck, the other hand fumbling in a bag slung over his shoulder.

He pulls out a knife, blade flashing and glinting in the sunlight.

Annie yells out, 'Come on, David, you don't want to hurt her.'

He nods. 'I don't. I really don't.' Then, after a pause where he looks like he's struggling to think what to say next: 'So don't make me.'

Natasha is beautiful, almost as tall as David, but she looks absolutely petrified. Her eyes fix on the people carrier with its precious cargo. Annie is more than aware of the kid, but refuses to look, keeping her gaze firmly on Belsham, her hands laid flat before her.

'Everything is going to be fine, David. Just step out and let Natasha go, and we can get everything sorted out. We just want you all to be safe. Especially Penelope.'

He says, 'I'm looking after her. Them. It's all I've ever wanted.'

Annie can see his arms starting to relax. 'I totally get that. Let's talk it out, OK?'

In a split second Natasha springs forward out of his clutches. He makes a lunge towards her, knife held out in front of him. The armed officer steps forward. Annie can see him trying to line up a clear shot, but now Natasha and David are mingled in a thrashing fight, arms and legs beating, struggling on the ground. Natasha manages to get on top of David and before she can call out, Annie sees the glint of a knife in Natasha's hand as her arm smashes down, once, twice, into the man's throat. Then Natasha is crying and up, running towards the car.

Annie rushes over to where David is lying in a heap on the ground, a gurgling sound coming from him. She tries to stem the bleeding but there is too much blood lost and she can see the frayed vital arteries. He's not going to make it.

His death will almost definitely go down as self-defence in favour of Natasha. He says something. Annie leans closer, hears the word: 'Sorry.' Liquid and garbled.

Behind Annie, Natasha is yanking open the door of the people carrier, dragging her daughter out and into her arms, sobbing. Pen, pale as a ghost and floppy, lets her mother hold her.

Annie's yelling, 'Call for an ambulance. Now!'

CHAPTER SIXTY-EIGHT

One month later

I try and see Pen at least once a week, and with Brodie visiting more and more often, sometimes we take her out together. Natasha and Brodie are still wary of each other and she's flat-out refused to have anything to do with Sienna. I often think that she is much the same as she was then: a strong, forceful personality and also a bit of an enigma. I never know what she's thinking, and strangely I find I don't actually enjoy her company. She can be oppressive. Too loud, too opinionated. Too much. But I accept she is a part of my life again because I don't think I can ever be without Pen.

Pen is different around her mother too, as though Natasha's personality clouds out her sense of self. But her grades remain good and she spends Saturday afternoons hanging out at Planet Pop. Isaac is on the mend. Joking that he's used up his last life and whilst I laugh along, I hope that's not true.

This morning I am heading over to Natasha's house on my bike. One thing that is still niggling at me is what Isaac told me about his attack. About how Pen's face lit up as though she'd seen someone familiar over his shoulder at the Airbnb. Just before he was knocked into unconsciousness. She might have recognised Belsham from Lisa's funeral of course, but I don't think she'd have been exactly happy to see him. Besides, Natasha said he'd watched the service from afar and spoken to her privately outside. She'd asked him to leave and felt worried even then for her safety.

He'd threatened Pen the night he showed up at Natasha's door, pressing a knife to Natasha's throat, full of instructions. Write a letter. Post it. He had insisted she leave and come to him. She'd done so on the understanding that he'd leave her daughter alone. She'd had no idea until they were in Wales that he'd killed Lyndsey in her place.

Her will, she said, had always named me and she was pleased I had been there for Pen. When I asked *why me*, she shrugged. 'I knew you'd never let me down.' With her dazzling, cheery grin.

Light. Breezy. That's how her attitude towards everything feels. Now as I slide my bike down the side of her house, I marvel at the fact we seem to have slipped straight back to where we were and how easy, and yet uncomfortable, it all feels.

I go in through the back. The house is beautiful and grand. Natasha's on the phone and waves at me to sit at the table. She makes a mug of tea, putting it down in front of me. Leaning over to touch my shoulder as she hangs up the call.

'Hey, lovely.'

I ask, 'Work?'

She grins. 'Yup. I just made a fortune.' Her laugh tinkles and I smile back. She frowns. 'Sure you don't want a job?'

I roll my eyes. 'No thanks.'

She sighs with a shrug. 'And my brother has turned me down too.' She raises an eyebrow.

I say, 'He won't leave Sienna.' Which is true and proving to be the first bump in the road our relationship has hit so far.

She makes a derisive sound. 'Always was his problem, his devotion to that woman.'

There is a silence that stretches and the question I want to ask burns on the tip of my tongue.

I say, 'Natasha. That night, at the Black House . . .'

She smiles, and I wonder if she knows what I'm going to say. Everything I've learned runs through my mind. She knew my mother wanted to leave. She knew things were coming to an end.

I say, 'You made them dinner . . .'

'The Aunts and the arseholes?' She giggles at our old nickname.

I nod. 'Sienna served, but you were in the kitchen.'

She's still smiling and her eyes seem to sparkle and glitter malevolently. She is so pretty and so clever. I think of Amy the night she died, me waking in the early hours, hearing Natasha whispering furiously in her ear. She must have been dead less than an hour later.

'I was in the kitchen, Blue. Someone had to be. Someone needed to take control.'

I say, 'But my mum . . .'

She laughs. 'Your mum, my mum. A load of talk and no doing. That's the problem. People like to talk about things, *plan* things, but taking action isn't for women like them. They weren't strong. They weren't tough enough.'

I don't say anything. My heart is racing at her calm.

She picks up her cup, takes a sip and says, 'Try your tea, it's chamomile. Pen's hooked on it. She said this is the brand you buy.' I do try, but my hand is shaking and some of it spills. I put the cup down.

'Natasha, David . . . Nicholas . . .?'

She grins. 'He was always such a soft boy, just like Amy and Lisa.' She shrugs. 'For a while, I thought maybe he'd be fun. He wasn't totally useless. Gave me the best thing in my life, I suppose. But he was so needy, Blue. Wanted things I didn't, and threatening to make a right old fuss out of it all.'

I look at her, stricken. Up until now she'd flat-out denied that he was Pen's father, though Grafton had dug up more emails of David's that claimed otherwise. Natasha had dismissed them as the ramblings of an insane person.

She sighs. 'That night, in the kitchen, it wasn't just me on duty. You hadn't made that level yet, lucky you, but Lisa had, and Nicholas was to be my husband, so by then he had some freedom around Joseph's things. Certainly, he knew where the drugs were kept.' She laughs. 'Everything was all decided by then.' She shrugs, her face dropping, revealing a steel that I knew was there but hadn't seen since we were children. 'I needed some help with it all.'

I press my fingers to my mouth, knocking the mug with my speed, which topples slightly, a splash of hot tea sloshing out onto my arm.

It hurts to be burned.

It hurts to be burned.

Natasha calm and collected. Brodie and Sienna turning up and Natasha frowning, rolling her eyes, but resigning herself to their presence.

I say, 'He knew? Nicholas?'

She grins. 'We were a team then, just for a minute.' Her face falls. 'He couldn't let it go, though. Then he started researching everything. The cult, Carillo, what was reported about the fire, and more. Said we needed to talk, to get help. To atone for what we did.' She shrugs. 'He said we'd be forgiven and maybe we would. But forgiven for what, exactly? I didn't do anything wrong, Blue.'

She leans over the table, takes my hand squeezes it.

304

'I was protecting us. Protecting you. You were good and strong I always knew it, not like the others. Amy was ridiculous, bordering on hysteria most of the time, and Lisa was the same in the end. Disappointing. She fell in love, just like the Aunts. Then she started wanting to be "honest", at least with him. Mark.' She spits the word out. I think of the nice man I'd met who so clearly loved Lisa.

Natasha shrugs.

I say, 'What did he want from you?'

'Nicholas? He wanted happy families.' She laughs. 'For me to "get help". Whatever the hell that meant.'

I say, 'It was you who Pen saw at the Airbnb. You hit Isaac.'

Her face drops. 'Isaac means a lot to you. I'd never hurt him. Not seriously. David and I both went to collect Pen. I'd told him we'd get her and go. But figured she'd be more likely to leave with me.'

Her phone rings on the side and she says, ''Scuse me.' In a tone so casual I feel disjointed from reality. She picks up – her voice high and light and breezy.

My insides feel as cold as ice. My eyes fall onto the photo that has pride of place in her big, designer kitchen. Four little girls, arms wrapped around each other, grinning at the camera. I nearly jump out of my skin when the doorbell sounds. Natasha comes back in with Pen tucked under her arm. She turned eleven last week. We had a big party for her and for the past few days she's been allowed to walk home with a friend. She comes to me and hugs me close. I pull her to me, breathing in the soft scent of her hair.

I watch her sit at the big table, pulling out her books and asking Natasha, 'What's for dinner?'

Natasha frowns. 'God I haven't been to the supermarket for days. Shall we just get pizza?' Pen cheers at that and

Natasha says to me, 'You'll stay, won't you, Blue? We can make an evening of it.'

I'm about to say no, to stand up, to get out of there. Away from her.

But then Pen is grinning madly at me and saying, 'Yay – girls' night.'

And I find myself nodding, wondering if, really, I should go straight to Annie.

But what would I say? What proof would I have? What difference would it make?

Amy.

Lisa.

Nicholas.

Everyone in the fire, all the lives she has destroyed.

All I can do is be here now. To look after Pen, like Amy once looked after me . . .

Acknowledgements

Thank you to the Orion Crime team, in particular my editor Lucy Frederick, also to Helena Newton for copyedits and Rachael Lancaster for a fantastic cover – I'm blessed to have had great covers for all of my books but this is one of my favourites so far. Thank you to my agent Hattie Grünewald and all at The Blair Partnership. Thank you to Elle Croft and Victoria Selman (my very own #CrimeGirlGang), and all of the Criminal Minds for all the lols even in less than amusing times!

I have wonderful friends whom I've appreciated more this year (I'm writing this in 2020) than ever before. So for all the phone calls, the Zooms, and the cards that have popped through my door and kept me going – thank you! I really do know the best people and I can't wait to see you IRL again soon.

Thanks to my Ma and Da and Brenda and to my sons for keeping me grounded in reality (at least some of the time).

And last but never ever least, Andrew, my best friend, most critical editor and biggest champion.

Lightning Source UK Ltd.
Milton Keynes UK
UKHW040116210721
387499UK00002B/231